To Yeri and Yenny,

With warmest congratulations on the arrival of Dan.

Tom Faulkner.

28/2/ '94.

THE MACHIAVELLIAN LEGACY

THE MACHIAVELLIAN LEGACY

Tom Faulkner

The Book Guild Ltd
Sussex, England

The Book Guild Ltd.
25 High Street,
Lewes, Sussex

First published 1994
© Tom Faulkner 1994
Set in Baskerville
Typesetting by Southern Reproductions (Sussex)
East Grinstead, Sussex
Printed in Great Britain by
Antony Rowe, Ltd.
Chippenham, Wiltshire.

A catalogue record for this book is
available from the British Library

ISBN 0 86332 889 X

For Hannah and my parents

PREFACE

Unless you establish settlements you will have
to garrison large numbers of mounted troops
and infantry. Settlements do not cost much,
and the prince can found them and maintain
them at little or no personal expense. He
injures only those from whom he takes land
and houses to give to the new inhabitants, and
these victims form a tiny minority, and can
never do any harm since they remain poor and
scattered.

Machiavelli – *The Prince*

For centuries, Ulster was looked upon by the English as
the most barbarous of the provinces of Ireland. The
defeat of the Great O'Neill, and his flight to the
Continent in 1607, broke forever the power of the Gaelic
chieftains and laid open the territory for conquest.
Seizing the opportunity, James I declared the lands
forfeit to the Crown, had many of the natives driven from
their holdings, and encouraged a large-scale settlement
of loyal English and Scots. This, it was hoped, would
make the area more amenable to rule from London.
It was Protestants who came; the native Irish were

Catholic. To complicate matters further the Scots, who proved to be the most effective settlers, were Presbyterian and hostile, not only to Catholicism, but to their Church of England neighbours as well. There was a general change in land ownership and towns were built, but for various reasons the planned removal of the native population never took place. The resentment of the Irish at being deprived of their land at times erupted in great violence, as in 1641, resulting in the deaths of many Protestants and deepening the gulf of hatred and suspicion which has divided the two communities ever since. The behaviour of a number of English officials towards the Scots, or Dissenters, was also to give them a good reason to be wary of their political masters in London.

While remaining, politically, in the seventeenth century Ulster was to make great strides on the industrial front. Cotton was responsible for transforming Belfast into the island's first industrial city, and in a later century manufacturers could justly claim that there were more linen spindles operating in the city than in any other country on earth. To the east, on Queen's Island, the shipyard of Harland and Wolff was built, which, in the early twentieth century, turned out some of the largest ships in the world, among them the *Titanic*. All of this was to contrast greatly with developments in the rest of Ireland, where the industrial revolution had little impact and the people remained dependent on agriculture.

Therefore, when in the 1920s the Nationalists in the south struggled to win independence from the British Empire there were both religious and economic reasons why the descendants of the original planters should fight to maintain the Union. They succeeded in keeping six Ulster counties within the United Kingdom and have since then declared their undying opposition to the idea of a united Ireland; a desired objective, at least in theory, of the Dublin government. The Catholics who were trapped within this Protestant enclave always resented their separation from the rest of the country, and from the beginning rejected the institutions over which they had no control. They too want a united Ireland. Most are prepared to work towards this by constitutional means, but a significant number are prepared to condone the use of violence and support the IRA.

The legacy is one of mistrust. There is a majority who suspect a conspiracy to drag them into a state they detest, and a minority that, because of centuries of discrimination, will never accept the legitimacy of those who claim the right to govern. The Protestants look towards London for support but are forever wary, as they have been disappointed many times in the past. The Catholics appeal to Dublin but have long distrusted the commitment they find there. It has imprisoned in its web of hatred and suspicion, not only those who belong to the two main traditions on the island, but also the men and women who make up the armed forces of the original imperial power.

Those in search of a solution thread through a political minefield; a minefield in which a miscalculation can result in the loss of innocent lives.

1

The flashing neon sign highlighted the hawk-like features of the newcomer. He was tall, well over six foot, with a hooked nose which was slightly too long for his oval-shaped face. The jet black hair was combed well back adding emphasis to a pair of deeply set eyes. After pausing to allow time to adjust to the dimly lit interior, he moved to the bar where the Irishman was sitting, and ordered a drink.

Philip Weston glanced towards the entrance before letting his eyes drift slowly back to the magazine. It was a natural reaction to the sound of swinging doors and would have gone unnoticed. The brightness coming from the pool room directly behind him was strong enough to read by, but there was too much on his mind for that. Surrounded by deserted tables he was feeling isolated and vulnerable. The young couple who had been sitting opposite when he came in had finished their drinks and left, and now the only customer in his section was an old black woman who occupied the corner nearest the door; the hopelessness on her wrinkled face illuminated by the sharp red light which bathed the room at regular intervals. Weston lifted the glass from the table in front of him and forced himself to drink. He disliked American beer, not enough body, but to leave it untouched any longer could arouse suspicion.

11

Contact was made without ceremony. The signal was probably contained in the title of the newspaper the tall man placed on the bar, or the way in which he ordered his drink: something that was invisible even to the interested onlooker. After the barman pushed a second beer towards the Irishman to replace the one he had hurriedly finished, both men moved slowly through the tables towards one of the alcoves which were situated along the opposite wall. Weston knew, from the beginning, there was something wrong about the tall man's clothes. The light cotton shirt and trousers were what you would expect in the humid mid-summer heat which enveloped the capital. But the jacket, with its zipper pulled up half-way, was too heavy, out of place. He cursed silently when he noticed the bulge indicating the shoulder holster, the tightly fitting jacket intended to emphasise rather than disguise its presence. The contempt he usually felt for the over-cautious Skeffington turned to a cold fury as he realised he was now defenceless in hostile territory.

As he sat down, the Irishman placed the newspaper he had taken from the bar on the table in front of him. Then, after removing a blank sheet of paper and pen from his pocket, he laid them carefully on top of it. The casual clothes still gave him the look of a tourist but the face was harder, more determined then before, for the first time betraying the iron will which lurked beneath the surface. As they spoke, both men placed their elbows on the table and leaned towards each other, every effort being made to make their conversation inaudible to unwelcome eavesdroppers.

Without looking towards them Weston reached down and lifted up a black sports bag which was at his feet. Having opened it he put the magazine inside and then, after searching roughly through its contents, he pushed it

12

carelessly from him towards the centre of the vinyl covered table to his left. Lifting his glass again he forced down some more beer, before turning his attention to the large television set which was placed in a prominent position above the bar. His bad humour deteriorated even further when any attempt to concentrate on the programme was made impossible by the noise coming from the youths playing pool.

'To date, our subject has proved to be a model member of his party.'

Skeffington glanced from time to time at the file in his hand as he spoke.

'He's with a group of teachers who are over to study the American school system, and so far the most demanding educationalist would have no reason to complain. A regular at the lectures which take place on the campus of the University of Delaware, a keen attender at all functions arranged for the visitors and what with spending his weekends swimming in the Atlantic or walking along the boardwalk at Rathobath one could hardly ask for anything more.'

'We are expecting something to happen?' Weston interjected abruptly. He was in no humour to indulge the chief in his irritating habit of skating around a subject before getting to the point.

'Oh, we are expecting developments.' Skeffington, a slight look of annoyance appearing on his face, closed the file and placed it on his desk. 'Our information now is that, despite appearances to the contrary, this man is one of the main movers in Belfast. He keeps a very low profile, preferring to let others bask in the limelight, but the source is reliable. All of this leads us to conclude that he has crossed the ocean with something more in mind than the improvement of his teaching skills.'

'I thought it was policy to request the Americans to refuse visas to anybody known to be involved in violence.'

'Yes. Just coming to that old boy.' Skeffington was now glaring at Weston, no longer able to disguise his anger at the younger man's interruptions. 'We did consider such a move and decided against it on two counts. First, we don't want him to know that we know, so to speak. We have been careful to make sure that any surveillance carried out to date would be low key so that he would be unaware of our suspicions. If we were to move on the visa he would immediately be warned off and this would put a very valuable source in danger.'

Skeffington paused while he swung his swivel chair around towards the window which gave him a view of the well manicured embassy lawns below. 'Second, we have given him enough rope to hang himself. If he makes contacts, and we are certain that he will, it can only improve our knowledge of relevant happenings on this side of the Atlantic.' Skeffington swung back to his desk. 'By the way, what do you know about chicken-necking?'

'Chicken-necking?' The question caught Weston unawares.

'Well, for your information chicken-necking is a form of fishing carried out in the lakes of Maryland. It is so called because pieces of chicken are used as bait.' A look of satisfaction appeared on the older man's face as if this small piece of knowledge had enabled him to gain some kind of revenge for Weston's earlier impertinence. 'You will need to know something about this because I want you to keep O'Donaghue under observation from now until he leaves Washington early next week. Every weekend the members of the project group are packed off to a host family, who keep them out of harm's way until it's time to return to campus. We have learned that the Irishman's family intend taking him on a fishing trip to Maryland and it is there that I want you to start watching him.'

'Do we know anything about the family?' Weston picked up the file Skeffington had pushed across the desk in his direction.

'Normally, members of the group are assigned to their hosts on a random basis but on this occasion we know that a special request had been made to have O'Donaghue. No more details as yet but that's enough to make us suspicious.'

'Any back up?'

'We have somebody in the group itself but there is no need for you to know anything about that. You're job is to watch him when he moves out on his own. The bulk of your work will be completed when he returns to the city, but keep an eye out just in case he breaks away from the group again after that. In truth, this is only a matter of form. We are not expecting much to happen until he visits the cities with the large Irish populations such as New York or Boston.'

'Equipment?' Weston ignored the put down contained in Skeffington's last sentence.

'The usual, you can pick it up on your way out. Oh, and one more thing – no firearms. We have had a few cock-ups lately and you know how I dislike having misunderstandings with our American cousins over the use of hand-guns.'

The hollow, insincere smile on Skeffington's face remained with Weston as he drove through the crowded streets. The drive was relaxing and uneventful and darkness had already fallen when he finally pulled up about a hundred yards from the small wooden house which was surrounded by shrubs, and situated a short distance from the lakeside. The large stationwagon parked outside told him that the Irishman and his hosts had arrived; the darkened windows indicated that they had already retired for the night.

The man who emerged onto the porch with O'Donaghue the following morning was small, little more than five foot in height, his wrinkled features partially hidden by a tattered, discoloured, straw hat. Weston, after allowing them time to row to the centre of the lake, took the fishing tackle from the boot of his car before taking up position on the shore. He used the concealed camera to get a few shots and then, although they were out of range, went through the motions of positioning the directional microphone concealed inside the large wicker basket. His humour deteriorated with the changing temperature; the comfortable coolness of the morning gradually gave way to a sweltering heat which brought with it a horde of marauding insects.

When, just before noon, the small craft was finally pulled ashore the pattern was set for a frustrating weekend. The evening was passed sitting in his car observing the entrance to a small Chinese restaurant where the two, now accompanied by the small man's wife, had dinner; and on Sunday morning, after all three had attended Mass in a nearby church, the boat was again pushed out forcing Weston to expose himself once more to the cruel sun. After the two days he returned to the capital with nothing more than a few photographs, tapes of irrelevant conversations, and a badly burned nose.

Back in the city he felt more relaxed. Now it was up to the plant inside the group to keep tabs on the target, and all he had to do was watch at a distance in case there were any unexpected moves. The first day brought with it the ritual visit to the White House, which included a short meeting with the Vice President, and was followed by a guided tour of Congress. After spending some time in the offices of a senator, whose staff apologised profusely for the absence of the great man himself, the tired travellers spent the rest of the afternoon relaxing on the steps of the Lincoln Memorial. It was not until the afternoon of the second day that O'Donaghue failed to appear.

The long air-conditioned coach had already been swallowed by the city traffic before the Irishman's stockily built frame emerged from the revolving doors onto the sweltering sidewalk. Weston, his gaze still fixed to the large store window in which he first spotted O'Donaghue's reflection, waited until he was well away from the hotel entrance before making his move. Within minutes they had left behind the large imperial buildings which dominate the capital's centre and moved into one of the black ghettos where the majority of the city's inhabitants live. When O'Donaghue got lost Weston found himself having to struggle to control the urge to cut and run. His pale skin was already attracting curious, if not hostile, looks from the local residents and when he saw the Irishman, after examining a piece of paper he had removed from his pocket, suddenly double back, he was convinced he was rumbled. Now his white face would be like a beacon. The sigh of relief was audible when his quarry turned down a side street without betraying the least sign of suspicion. The Irishman was travelling in unfamiliar territory and where all is strange nothing stands out.

O'Donaghue checked the name above the bar more than once before going inside. Weston, after deciding to play the naive tourist routine, waited for five minutes and then followed.

A sharp cry of pain from the pool room shattered the peaceful atmosphere which had settled over the dimly lit bar. Weston's reflex response turned him just in time to see the fear flash across the black youth's eyes as he fled past a brightly lit table into the relative darkness. Without warning, the youth grabbed Weston's sports bag from the table, pulling it towards him as if hoping to use it as a shield against an oncoming attack. A knife was hurled from the pool room into the bar, accompanied by a faint whistling sound which ended in a dull thud as it ripped into the bag's heavy material. What was revealed changed everything, the fear on the tall gangly youth's face disappearing to be replaced by curiosity and hope.

'Hey man, this guy's got some gear in here. Looks like a fancy camera and some sound equipment.' The large round eyes appeared to widen as he used his free hand to pull the tear open, allowing for a closer examination of what was inside.

'He's gotta be a cop. You got any sense, man, you'll split and quick.' The second youth, the reason for the knife throwing now apparently forgotten in the face of what appeared to be a greater danger, had already made his way from the pool room and was moving quickly towards the exit and the safety of the street outside. His companion, after dropping the bag as if it had suddenly become a dangerous substance, turned on his heel and followed swiftly.

'We got some talkin' to do, mister.' Weston's panic-filled attempt to recover the bag had blinded him to the reaction of the big man and now he found himself caught off guard and looking down the wrong end of a Browning automatic.

'You got a place I can talk to a friend?' The question was directed towards the barman, but the hawk-like eyes

18

never moved from Weston.

'Store room just there at the back.' There was indifference in the barman's voice. You stayed alive by not getting involved, and the barman obviously intended to stay alive. The old woman in the corner continued to sip her drink.

'OK. Let's go, and take your bag of tricks with you.' The tall man kept the gun firmly trained on Weston as he pulled open the heavy door. The naked bulb hanging from the ceiling was not powerful enough to light the room and all four corners were hidden in darkness. Crates of empty bottles were stacked on either side of the entrance, and the small windows in the wall opposite were well secured offering no possibility of escape.

The heavy blow from behind caught Weston by surprise, sending him sprawling over a number of beer barrels, which were thrown carelessly in the centre of the room. As he landed heavily on the dust-covered floor he lost his grip on the bag and it slid towards one of the darkened corners.

'Up against the wall and spread out!' The search was swift but expertly executed. The tall man then moved to recover the bag. He used his right foot to guide it to where Weston was spread-eagled against the wall and then, without once taking his eyes from his prisoner, went down on one knee and used his free hand to search for the zipper. His first attempt to open it failed. It was when the second tug also failed to wrench it free that he became irritated, let his concentration slip, and allowed his gaze to move from Weston towards the bag. It was only for a split second, but it was long enough.

Summoning up all his reserves of strength Weston hurled his closed fist towards the tall man's head. The blow struck home as the gunman was starting to rise, catching him off balance and knocking him backwards towards the floor. Weston wasted no time, moving in on his victim he aimed a kick at the hand which held the automatic. He was off target, but a glancing blow to the elbow was sufficient to send the weapon flying across the room.

The tall man recovered quickly. A flying tackle to the knees halted Weston's advance towards the gun. As the Englishman struggled to his feet for a second time he was suddenly caught in a vice like grip which squeezed the breath from his body. The fear of losing consciousness bestowed on him an almost manic power. Every muscle strained to the limit as he struggled to push the upper part of his body as far as possible from the cruel face in front of him. The big man closed his eyes with effort, and Weston's head butt, which struck just below the bridge of the nose, caught him totally umprepared. The sudden pain forced the powerful arms to loosen their grip, allowing Weston to stagger back against the crates, gasping for breath.

The single bulb, knocked about during the struggle, now swung wildly as if trying to further confuse the two combatants as they sized each other up before the next round. Weston spotted the Browning first, while the tall man examined his badly shattered nose. The swinging light illuminated the gun briefly, in the corner furthest from him, within inches of his opponent's foot. Weston shuddered involuntarily, which was enough to alert the tall man, and as his cold, deep-set eyes began to scan the floor Weston decided to make a break for it. He dived suddenly for the door and he had already pushed it open before there was any time for reaction.

Out in the bar he grabbed the nearest table and pulled it up against the door in an attempt to slow down any pursuit. The Irishman had already left, and it was instinct, force of habit, that caused him to reach out and

20

pick up the newspaper which still lay on the table where the two men had sat earlier. Weston could hear a loud thumping coming from the storeroom as he weaved his way through the tables and fled towards the exit.

Outside, he slumped back against the wall and glanced swiftly up and down the street as he slipped the paper into the deep pocket of his jacket. He decided against making any attempt to wave down a passing motorist. They were moving too fast and anyway, few were likely to stop in that part of the city for a complete stranger. About fifty yards from where he stood a car signalled and moved down a side street.

Deciding this was his nearest avenue of escape, Weston started to run to his left. He moved close to the wall hoping that the shadows and rapidly fading light would prevent him from becoming an easy target. Glancing back over his shoulder as he rounded the corner, he saw the silhouette of the tall man as he suddenly emerged from the bar. The table had not held him for long.

The distraction was enough to break his concentration and he did not notice the garbage cans until he crashed into them, before falling heavily onto the cement sidewalk. He struggled to regain his feet, cursing his stupidity at making such a basic mistake. The noise was deafening, one lid rolling noisily before coming to a clamouring halt in the middle of the street. A scavenging cat screeched in protest as it ran for cover in one of the surrounding buildings. A sudden shot of pain in his knee and the clammy heat which sapped away energy, slowed him to little more than walking pace.

Suddenly, red and blue flashing lights appeared at the far end of the street. He stared in disbelief at first, as a man in the desert might fear being fooled by a mirage. It was only as they moved closer and he could make out the clear outline of the patrol car that he allowed himself to

21

relax and his guard to drop. Moving from cover he stumbled into the glare of the oncoming headlights, waving his hands in the air.

'Stop! Emergency, police . . . . Help!'

The bullet ripped into his left shoulder from behind and he could feel his collar bone snap. The impact did not push him to the ground but hurled him around so that he could see the outline of the tall man as he readied himself to fire for the second time. He was standing in the weaver position, the right hand holding the automatic and pushing forward, the left pulling back.

Crack! His stomach was torn open. It was impossible to move and inside a fire was burning him up. As the tall man disappeared into the darkness, a siren roared into life, its wailing sound adding to the already intolerable pain. The two cops moved cautiously from the car, their guns already drawn. The doors were left open to protect against possible attack. When they felt safe one of them moved towards Weston and after a quick examination started to administer basic first aid in an attempt to stop the bleeding.

'Can you do anything for him?' The second cop was standing looking down at Weston as he spoke.

'Not a lot. Call an ambulance?'

'Yep. There's one on its way.'

Through his partially closed eyes Weston watched as a group of onlookers gathered around, their curious faces under the street lights reminding him of vultures waiting for their prey to die. Gradually the cops' voices faded into the distance and his eyes closed. Then, everything went black.

2

James Henry Skeffington allowed a slight feeling of satisfaction to momentarily break through the all pervading gloom as he slipped the pen into the inside pocket of his tailor-made jacket. At least the notes were complete, the groundwork prepared for what he knew would be an unpleasant confrontation. The feeling of depression rapidly reasserted itself as he struggled to concentrate on the key points neatly listed in his ever efficient style on the piece of paper before him. After removing his gold-rimmed spectacles, he stood up from the chair and looked again at the patient lying on the bed in the small private hospital room. As there was still no sign of him awakening, he moved towards the window and, having pulled open the venetian blind, looked down on the activity in the car park below.

The argument before leaving home had made his already dark humour even blacker. Disagreements between his wife and himself were now less frequent than they used to be, not because of a growing understanding but more due to a mutual indifference. They had for many years presented the facade of being the ideal diplomatic couple in public, only to drift further and further apart in private. The one area where they still battled with one another, where the conflict was still very real, was when it came to the boys. Their sons had come to spend a fortnight of their vacation from public school, as they always did, no matter where he was posted. Today was to be his last day with them before they returned to spend the rest of their holidays with their friends in Europe – and this damned mess had caused him to be called away. Emma had feigned shock and anger but in reality he knew she was delighted. How she would use this to undermine him even further. 'Your father is too busy, he has no time for anything but his work.' He could almost hear her as he looked down at the moving figures below. The battle was being lost for his boys' affection and there was nothing he could do about it.

'Weston, are you awake?' As he moved back from the window, Skeffington called out in a voice that was much louder than necessary. A feeling of anger now mingled with the frustration and he was tempted to disregard the doctor's orders and shake the patient until he was fully alert. He hated these amateurs, many of whom were just meddlers who had joined by accident, or know-it-all intellectuals, who even showed sympathy with those who questioned the need for a secret service. He was concerned about their lack of conviction, their cynical attitude towards the work they were involved in, and was convinced that they were easy prey for the propaganda of the very forces they were supposed to fight. Looking down at Weston, he could feel his temperature rise as he recalled what had happened. To make a mess of things was bad enough, but to blow an operation in Washington DC was unforgiveable.

Skeffington had inherited a rigid bitterness towards Americans from his father. Night after night in the years after the war, when still in his early teens, he had sat at the dinner table listening to the parent he idolised lecture guests on the treachery of their former allies. The country which had suffered least and profited most from the conflict, they were told, was not now prepared to provide Britain with the economic help she needed to avert disaster. When, just eight days after the war the Yanks had suspended Lend Lease, leaving no credit even to buy food, his father's great anger made an impression which would last forever. Later, as a young civil servant, Skeffington could only watch helplessly as the British army was forced into a humiliating withdrawal from Suez. Again Washington had pulled the rug from under them at a crucial moment.

A slight movement in Weston's eyes was enough to draw his attention back to the bed. 'How are you feeling?'

'As well as can be expected under the circumstances.' Weston, sensing the lack of sincerity in the question, decided against going into medical details. He had a vague recollection of Skeffington's first visit, but he had lost all sense of time, and had no idea when it was or what had happened.

'The last time I was here, four days ago, you only regained consciousness for a few minutes and even then nothing you had to say made much sense. I'm back now because your doctor feels you are ready to talk, and the quicker we can act on any information you have the more effective it's likely to be.' All pretence of concern had disappeared from Skeffington's voice as the professional intelligence man took over.

'Maybe you had better bring me up to date.'

'We have managed to keep the whole affair out of the newspapers through the good offices of our friends at the FBI.' The sarcastic tone was enough to reveal his anger at being left dependent on the hated allies.

'Anything on the newspaper I picked up?' Weston moved the conversation in another direction.

'Yes, at least it did yield something.' As Skeffington

settled back in his chair Weston sighed imwardly. The tone alone was enough to prepare him for a long-winded account which might eventually get to the point. 'In the lab they have a device known as a scanning electron microscope. It uses electron beams rather than light and this enables the boffins to identify fingerprints on both newsprint and photographs. What they do is paint the newspaper with a liquid which contains an amount of silver. When it comes in contact with any fingerprints on the page, the silver spreads out allowing it to be picked up by the scan. As luck would have it, they managed to isolate a print that we take to be that of your assailant.'

'Were they able to match it?'

'Yes, but it took some time, though.' Skeffington paused as if taking satisfaction from keeping Weston in suspense. 'First they tried it against all their computer files here in Washington but to no avail. Then they widened their field of search. It took three full days, but in the end they found it belonged to one Henry Vogel.'

'Do we have anything on him?' Weston immediately regretted allowing his impatience to show.

'Very little on record.' Skeffington glanced towards the piece of paper before continuing. The agony would be drawn out to the limit. 'The only reason he appears at all is because he made an assault on a young peace protester who spat at him when he had just returned from service in Vietnam. His sentence of six months was suspended and he was let out on probation.'

'So what? Thousands of Vietnam vets got into trouble after coming home.'

'Agreed. However, it's what is known unofficially that proves to be of interest. He acts from time to time for a type of Irish mafia who operate in the working class areas of Boston. In the past, we have had good reason to suspect them of running guns for the IRA as a sideline. Their main activities are drug trafficking, extortion, loan sharking and the hijacking of any commercial cargoes they consider worthy of their attention. Vogel is good with explosives – one of the more useful skills he picked up in the army – and it is almost certain that a number of business men who failed to pay their protection money on time had their premises blown away by him. He is also suspected of having a hand in a few gangland killings.'

A sharpness suddenly entered the diplomat's voice. 'Did you do any checking on that family before you went to Maryland?'

'No. There was no time.' Weston regretted answering so quickly. He was aware of the criticism contained in the question and had not intended to sound defensive.

'No time to request back up on the night of the shooting either?' Skeffington moved on before Weston could respond. 'Well, we did make a check on the host couple who requested O'Donaghue, and found that although they keep a holiday home in Maryland, they are actually resident in Boston where the police report that they are known to have links with that Irish gangster lot. It's obviously through them that the Washington meeting was set up.'

Weston did not respond, his silence being the most effective way of displaying his resentment at what he now knew was happening. He was being hung out to dry; the establishment needed a scapegoat for a botched operation and they had chosen him to be the sacrificial lamb. Not for the first time, he felt very much the outsider.

'The words Fionn and Cuchulainn mean anything to you?' Skeffington was forced to speak if only to break the tension. 'The lab found the impression of both those words on the newspaper. It was as if somebody wrote them on a piece of paper which was placed on top of it.'

'They are both important characters in Irish legend, but then I'm sure you know that already.' There was a remoteness in Weston's voice. He knew he was being humoured and had no intention of playing along. 'During my stay in the Irish, or Gaelic-speaking areas of Donegal I came across a lot of stories about Cuchulainn. It seems that among other things he once single-handedly saved the province of Ulster from a powerful lady known as Queen Meave. The other, Fionn, I know nothing about.'

'Well, as you say we already know that much.' Skeffington was now preparing to leave. Opening the briefcase on the floor beside him he carefully placed the piece of paper inside before snapping it closed again. He remained silent until he was making his way to retrieve the light raincoat which hung on the stand in the corner of the room. 'Well, I hope you continue to make a rapid recovery.'

'Thanks. Another two months, all going well, and they tell me I could be out of here.'

'Good, good.' Skeffington's lack of attention caused him to miss the sarcasm in Weston's reply. 'Oh, there was just one other matter before I leave. Your former editor is on the look out for a foreign correspondent in Italy and, as you have a working knowledge of the language, we thought it might prove very suitable.'

Weston was stunned. He had known something was coming from the critical tone that Skeffington had introduced into the conversation, but not this, not the push. He felt angry but helpless. Inside was a desire to scream, to lash out like a cornered animal, and appeal to the world against the ingratitude of those he had served.

'So I am to be sidelined, put out to grass.' The first response when it came sounded weak and pathetic.

'Oh, I wouldn't say that old man. I'm sure when you have had time to consider the matter you will see that it makes sense.' The sickening insincerity had returned to Skeffington's voice causing the anger welling up inside Weston to become even more intense.

But the diplomat had judged the situation to perfection and the door of the room was already closed before the torrent of abuse finally poured forth from his hapless victim.

Minutes had passed before Weston allowed his head to fall back on the pillow. Despite everything, he could at least take some satisfaction from the fact that he had got up the pompous idiot's nose, really screwed things up for him. 'Kuklinski', they called Skeffington behind his back; the name coming from the Polish colonel who kept the Americans informed of what his government was planning during the early days of Solidarity. A man or woman on the spot, Skeffington would argue –somebody who could watch the expressions on the faces, listen to the office gossip and get to know the personalities involved – was worth any number of infernal machines. Now, however, after the cock-up of yet another one of his undercover operations, it was possible to imagine the pained expression on Skeffington's round face as he again had to listen to the advocates of technology point out that the real action was in their area, and that the days of the undercover agent were gone forever.

There was another reason for the animosity between them, one that Skeffington would probably be slow to admit even to himself. An Oxford degree was not enough. You had to get there by the correct route. Over the years it had become clear that a scholarship from a comprehensive in the North of England was not that route. Anybody from a working class background was considered a potential socialist, and potential socialists, in the opinion of the man from the embassy, always constituted an unacceptable risk.

'Time for your medicine Mr Weston.' The entrance of the nurse with his sleeping draught broke into his thoughts. He swallowed the contents of the glass without protest although since the shooting, sleep rarely brought peace. In his nightmares the tall man came back to haunt him.

The air hostess placing the meal in front of O'Donaghue paid little attention to her passenger. The man was polite but distant, obviously not wishing to attract attention, and the well proportioned, if not handsome face had no feature which caused him to stand out from the crowd. For the other members of the group it took little imagination to picture him, biros pushed into his breast pocket, standing in front of a class of teenagers and revealing the secrets of Physics and Chemistry.

The decision to come had been made by himself alone. Since he had achieved absolute control he never consulted. To have sent somebody else would have entailed the appointment of yet another link in the chain, another potential informer, and he was determined to avoid that at all costs. From the beginning, he was aware that the Brits might combine with the FBI to make life difficult for him, but in a country where the quality press referred to the members of his movement as guerrillas, not terrorists, and where senior politicians were always careful not to get on the wrong side of citizens who supported them, he knew that short of being found in

30

possession of a smoking gun there was little they could do. There would be little welcome for him from the authorities in the Irish Republic, or the Free State as he contemptuously called it: the fact that they had executed IRA men during the Second World War would never be forgotten or forgiven. However, here again the policitians had their tightrope to walk. To be seen to be doing the Brits' dirty work for them was not on, and, as always, he expertly played the situation to his advantage.

'Enjoy your meal?' The middle-aged lady sitting beside him was bored and in search of conversation.

'Oh yes. Very nice.' Again the reply was polite but firmly indicated a lack of interest. Pressing the lever at his side he pushed back against the seat back easing it into a more comfortable position. He then closed his eyes forcing the woman to seek companionship from the passenger next the window.

The shock of discovering that his cover had been blown had caused a tightening at the pit of his stomach which, at first, almost caused him to become physically ill. For a few days after the incident in the bar he had been constantly on the look out for a tail following the group, and when nobody appeared he concluded he was being watched from within. Then followed an exhaustive examination of his every move since landing at Kennedy Airport. It took hours but in the end he was satisfied that nothing of value had been given away, his precautions had paid off. The only phone call he had made was to relatives of his father who lived in Chicago, and the thought of the FBI using up resources to check on the old couple he found amusing. Contact, when made had been arranged on the American side, and even he suspected nothing until the code word was used as they sat on the boat in the middle of the lake. If there had been somebody watching in Maryland it was probably the same man who had turned up in the bar. He was happy that his newly found American partner was more than capable of taking care of that little problem.

O'Donaghue's passion for secrecy, for never allowing anybody other than himself to know what he had in mind, had become an obsession. Too often he had watched the best laid plans lead to disaster because of a careless word or action and so he trusted nobody. It was only in the beginning that he had pushed himself to the fore because for a young ambitious volunteer it was the only way to come to the notice of the all-important Brigade staff. In a short time he had established himself as one of the top messengers. Moving from one area to another proved to be an ideal way of making an impression on the local leaders, the men whose support he later used when making his bid for control. The more that was asked of him the better he had liked it, never missing an opportunity to add to his prestige by displaying his expertise with explosives. By the time any potential rivals became aware of what was happening it was too late. He was the one with the contacts, the knowledge, and the power.

Once established, the next few years had been spent working hard to become a man with no footprints as far as the enemy was concerned. Passing on orders through three trusted lieutenants, none of whom had been ever allowed a glimpse of the full picture, he presented the image of a quiet respectable citizen who, having gone astray for a time as a youth, had now rejected all ideas that violence was a solution to political problems. Protected by the cloak of anonymity he felt free to wander the streets of the city and carry out his business without fear of being watched. The granting of a visa to enter the US had convinced him that the strategy had worked, but now he knew better.

How long had they known? That question had tortured him from the moment he rushed from the bar and made his way back to the hotel room. He was certain that nobody ever followed him on his travels around Belfast. An organisation with over twenty years in the business had ways of preventing that. Every effort was also made to prevent bugging. The sickly feeling again gripped his stomach when, after hours of thought, he reached the only possible conclusion. There was an informer: somebody very close to him, and somebody he would have to take care of on his return.

'Excuse me, sir. Would you please pass this across to the lady sitting next to the window?' He opened his eyes to see the hostess, now selling duty free, pushing a large carton of cigarettes in his direction. It was as he reached out that he noticed the headline on the newspaper folded on the lap of the man sitting across from him.

'Anything of interest?' He waited for the hostess to push her trolley further along the aisle before gesturing towards the paper.

'Oh yes. Some major developments in your part of the world. Sir John Paget has been moved from the Foreign Office to Northern Ireland.'

'Hardly a surprise.'

'Yes, I suppose it was to be expected.' The pleasant-faced maths teacher from the south had noticed the lack of enthusiasm in O'Donaghue's voice, but a keen interest in current affairs decided him to press on. 'Certainly, the rumour machine as they call it at Number Ten had been working overtime preparing the public for the move. We are supposed to believe that this is not a demotion for Sir John, but a clear sign that the PM is determined to come to grips with the problems of the area once and for all. Do you think he will make any difference?'

'At least it appears we are no longer considered to be a dustbin.'

'Oh. Do you mean Jim Prior's reference to the Northern Ireland Office as being the dustbin of British politics, when he was there?'

O'Donaghue did not respond, but instead adopted a look of indifference to discourage the man from continuing. Finally, the maths teacher, an expression of disappointment clouding his features, gave up and handed the newspaper to O'Donaghue. 'Here. Maybe you would like to have a look yourself.'

It was a copy of the previous day's *Daily Telegraph* and across its front page it carried the announcement of the long-predicted reshuffle in Her Majesty's Government. After glancing at the large photograph of Paget which dominated the front page, O'Donaghue turned to the editorial section where he read that, in the editor's opinion, the long suffering Province of Ulster had at last a chance of peace and prosperity. He could not help but smile inwardly at the predictable rhetoric as he handed the paper back to its owner. Still, the political heavyweight had finally arrived, and O'Donaghue determined to put the other parts of the operation, designed to frustrate whatever great plans the new Secretary had, into place as soon as possible.

On arrival at Shannon Airport he made a number of phone calls. For O'Donaghue, things had changed greatly. Not only was it impossible for him to return to teaching, but he was also certain that somebody close to him was reporting his every move to the enemy.

Within hours an underground network had transported him back to the Republican ghettos of Belfast.

3

Two years later

'Damn the man. Doesn't he ever stop talking?' Robert Mac Entee checked the time on his watch before looking again towards the embassy door where Cunningham and the ambassador were still deep in conversation. There was no sign of Cunningham making a move. Mac Entee toyed with the idea of asking the limousine driver to go and remind the foreign minister of the lateness of the hour but, on consideration, decided against it. There was already enough tension between them.

Mac Entee, Minister of Justice for the Republic of Ireland, had always harboured a thinly veiled contempt for academics who deserted their well-protected ivory towers in search of political glory. Shooting stars he called them, producing a bright light for a short time and then disappearing for all eternity. He had expected the same fate to befall the foreign minister and found it difficult to conceal his disappointment when it failed to happen.

Cunningham was different. From the beginning, he seemed to have a sixth sense to guide him through the minefields and pitfalls of public life which took most politicians a lifetime to develop. He knew when to speak out and, more importantly, when to remain silent. And as for the media, right from the start he appeared to have them eating out of his hand. The handsome figure with his bag full of degrees and beautiful wife by his side was just too good to resist, and not a day passed without a mention of the newest and most talented – in the opinion of too many – member of the government. In private, Mac Entee referred to him as 'the academic'. He intended it as a term of derision but to those who heard it it indicated fear. For years, the justice minister had worked patiently to establish himself as the heir apparent to the party leader, and now just when it appeared to be within his grasp he was in danger of losing it to an outsider, a blow-in.

'Sorry about the delay, but something has just come through from Belfast that could be very significant.' The police started to clear a path through the heavy London traffic as soon as the foreign minister's door was closed, and they were already making their way down Halkin Street towards Hyde Park Corner.

'It seems Paget has called a meeting of the executive for ten o'clock tonight.'

'Had we any prior notice of this?'

'No, nothing. No agenda was issued and as yet our sources have come up with zilch.' Cunningham looked flustered as he placed his briefcase on the floor beside him. 'I just hope they are not going to pull another Lloyd George on us.'

'What the hell has Lloyd George to do with anything?' Mac Entee could not hide his irritation at the academic's habit of introducing vague historical references into the conversation.

'I mean that I'm afraid that they are going to land us in it, by making some kind of proposal we will not like but will be unable to refuse. You remember the talks in the early twenties which led to the foundation of our little state? When the negotiations were deadlocked, and the Irish delegation refused to sign a treaty, the little Welsh Wizard produced two letters one of which had to be sent to Sir James Craig, prime minister of Northern Ireland, before ten o'clock that night. The first, he said contained news of an agreement, the second indicated that the talks had failed and nobody was left in any doubt but that this would result in terrible war within three days. After listening to a colourful description of the train steamed up at Euston to take the letter to a destroyer at Holyhead it is hardly surprising that the delegates caved in.'

'Surely man, you are not suggesting they are about to declare war on us? Ever since they sent Paget as secretary to Stormont you have been predicting something big – which has never happened.'

'Nothing has happened!' It was now the foreign minister's turn to become irritated. 'Within six months he pushed the Unionists into a power-sharing executive with the Nationalists, something they would never have even considered before he arrived. It takes no genius to work out that a lot of promises combined with a lot of heavyweight arm twisting was employed to bring that about. He has poured resources into security as if there was no tomorrow; it seems as if nobody can move north of the border these days without having their name come up on a computer. And there is no point in pretending that we are not worried about the increasing strength of the Royal Irish Regiment, the home-grown members of Her Majesty's forces.'

Cunningham paused as if attempting to add emphasis to what was to come. 'Now to get on to why you have been brought here. I have got a suspicion that they are going to push us to introduce internment without trial in an attempt to crush the IRA once and for all.'

'Christ, that's all I need.'

37

'Why else should Downing Street request the minister for justice to be present at what is supposed to be a routine, post-summit meeting? All the signs have been there: for the past few weeks the quality press has been quoting government sources here who want a last final major offensive against terrorism etcetera, etcetera. You know the line.'

'Downing Street requested my presence. Damn it, I thought I was here because our beloved leader anticipated some awkward questions on security, and had decided it would be better to have the flak directed towards me than himself.'

'You had better get your arguments ready. I can't help feeling that our big and powerful neighbour is about to act in her own interest again, and all we can do is make the best of it.'

Mac Entee did not reply but retreated into the solemn silence which always indicated that he was worried. He had come to hate the British capital, its large imperial buildings conspiring to make him feel small and insignificant. At least in Dublin or Belfast there was a feeling of being centre stage, a possibility of creating the illusion that the decisions made would at least have some influence on events. But here, the hopelessness became all too obvious. It was impossible to miss the lack of sincerity in the eyes of the Whitehall mandarins as they presented yet another set of proposals for the solution of the bloody Irish problem; their resentment at having to play a part in such an insignificant little side show only very thinly disguised. It was here that the true purpose of the exercise was laid bare, could not be pushed aside. There was no solution, no way that the warring tribes could ever be brought together, so the cosmetic exercise of pretence continued while both governments struggled to keep the lid on the cauldron of hate and suspicion. If it were ever to boil over it could prove to be very inconvenient.

'Well, this is it. We're here.' Cunningham pushed a document he was reading back into his briefcase and snapped it shut. The first limousine with the Taoiseach (the Irish prime minister) and his deputy had already passed through the security gates and was making its way up Downing Street. Looking over his driver's shoulder Mac Entee could make out the figures of the British prime minister and Sir John Paget as they moved from the door of Number Ten and stood waiting to greet their guests. As he prepared to leave the car Mac Entee was suddenly overcome by a feeling of depression, as if the large buildings were closing in on him.

The light mist that was falling kept the greetings to a minimum. Once they were inside they paused for a time to allow the photographers and the television crews to take pictures, and the two leaders answered the routine questions put by the journalists who turned up. There were not many there: after an EC summit the political editors had already more than enough to fill their columns, and Mac Entee took some comfort from the fact that if something significant was on the cards at least the bloodhounds of the press had not sniffed it out as yet.

Only a few of the prime minister's staff were curious enough to turn out and watch as they made their way into the cabinet room corridor and started up the staircase which was adorned with portraits of all past first ministers of the Crown. Mac Entee glanced towards Cunningham, and smiled slightly, as they came to the image of David Lloyd George who looked benignly down on all who passed by. It was when he entered the study at the top of the stairs that the depression, which had lifted slightly, fell on him again even deeper than before.

The presence of the two junior ministers from the Northern Ireland Office was only to be expected, but the tall stately figure of the foreign secretary standing on their left came as a shock. Touching Mac Entee on the arm to attract his attention Cunningham used his eyes to indicate the short, portly figure who was examining the watercolours which hung on the wall opposite. A few seconds had passed before Mac Entee recognised him: the chancellor of the exchequer looked older than his photographs. For whatever reason, Her Majesty's government were out in force.

'Taoiseach, perhaps you and your ministers would take up your seats on that side of the table.' The prime minister seemed restless and anxious to bring the small talk that usually preceded such meetings to an end as soon as possible. 'On our side we have a very important request to make. We wish to put the agreed agenda for today's meeting to one side as we have something of great importance to discuss with you and your ministers.'

'We are pulling out of Ireland.' Skeffington searched the face opposite for a reaction but the man had already taken too much to drink and seemed to have difficulty comprehending. 'The government in the south and the executive in the north have been informed and given a month to prepare for the public announcement.'

There was no reply, just the appearance of that idiotic grin that drunks employ when they imagine they are about to say something of great significance. He ground his teeth hard in an attempt to contain his anger. The meeting brought back enough unpleasant memories without this display of pathetic self pity. Skeffington's failure to put family before job two years earlier had proved to be the last straw for his wife, Emma. She had left him and now he only saw his boys on very rare occasions. Now there was nothing left but the job, and the job had brought him to this.

'So as we are to go, we must go quickly. Is that how it is?' When Weston finally replied he did not look towards Skeffington but concentrated his gaze on the empty glass on the table between them. 'We stay there for over eight hundred years and spend much of that time encouraging them to hate one another. Now we are so generous, we give them a whole month to settle their differences and then it's bye, bye.'

'Any longer and a leak is inevitable, giving all kinds of crackpot organisations on both sides time to move against us. At least this way we stand a chance.'

'Why now?' The sluggishness was disappearing from Weston's voice as he became more alert.

'There are quite a number of good reasons. One being that the great British public are becoming heartily sick of being continually embarrassed by the damned Irish question. Over the last few years it has become almost impossible for a government leader to go abroad without the danger of being heckled by an IRA rent-a-mob, and as for having every tinpot regime who wants to have a go, accusing us of having political prisoners – '

'And don't we?'

Skeffington ignored Weston's interruption. 'The generals are also putting the pressure on. What with the glowing after-effect of the Gulf war fading into history and a falling birth rate combining with the demands of industry, it is hard enough to get recruits without the thought of a tour of duty in Northern Ireland making things even less attractive. After Paget took over, resources were poured in to keep things relatively quiet and now, with a bit of luck, we feel we could pull it off without too much loss of face.'

41

'What about the Unionists? Those people have stood loyally by the Crown through thick and thin and, I might add, fought beside us against Hitler, as well as providing our ships with ports when their southern neighbours remained neutral.'

'Loyal to what?' Skeffington spat out the words. He knew he was being baited, made fun of, and yet was unable to resist the urge to justify what was about to happen. 'There were times when I considered them less loyal than the bloody Provos. How many times did they do everything in their power to frustrate the plans of the legitimate government by starting strikes or some such nonsense? Damn it, man, there were even times when they attacked the police and soldiers because they were not happy with the way things were going! Some of them think that because their grandfathers fought at the Battle of the Somme that that gives them a free meal ticket for ever. Well, over the last few years they have pushed too hard and now we will see how they will fare on their own.'

'Dropped just like that. No warning and only one month to prepare.'

'They had ample warning.' Skeffington hesitated, as if regretting what he had said, but then decided to continue. 'Their leaders were taken to London almost two years ago, and the government's plans were outlined to them in great detail. In plain words they were told that unless they were willing to co-operate, their petty little state would disappear from the face of the earth after our withdrawal.'

'So that's why they were prepared to share power with the Nationalists.' Weston's eyes showed genuine surprise. 'And I take it that this also explains all the interesting developments I have been reading about on the security front?'

'The idea was that if we kept things quiet it would give the new administration time to establish itself. This would make it much easier for it to survive after we left.'

'There will be no major resistance on the mainland?'

'Have you attended any Northern Ireland debates in the Commons recently?'

'No. My line of work has given me little opportunity.'

'If you had, you would have discovered that the first thing that happens is that the majority of MPs get up and leave the chamber. Usually the only ones in attendance are the secretary of state, his opposition counterpart, and the Irish themselves. The fare is predictable. The secretary makes optimistic noises about his future plans, with which his opposition shadow agrees as there are no votes to be won or lost, while our friends from across the water dig into their respective trenches and hurl accusations at each other in the time-honoured fashion. Indeed, the only time the troubles win universal attention is when they spill over the Irish Sea and a bomb goes off in London, or an unfortunate MP gets himself killed. Even then, despite the brave rhetoric, it only increases the puzzlement and makes us wonder even more as to what the hell we are doing there.'

'It won't work. You know that.' A slight sluggishness had returned to the voice. It was as if the alcohol was struggling to retain control. 'Any political settlement will be little more than a stopgap, and when it breaks down this time we will not be there to keep them apart. What we have seen up until now will look like a picnic.'

'Ours is not to reason why.'

The response almost caused Weston to fall off his chair, the words shooting through the pit of his stomach like an electric shock. Inwardly, he had really known what was going to happen after first getting word, but that did not prevent him from hoping, praying that it would not happen. Now it was certain: he was being dragged back, pulled again into the sinister world of deceit and lies he thought he had left for ever. He decided to make one last fight against the inevitable.

'Two years ago, after I was given the boot, pushed out to sink or swim on my own, I dived for cover in there.' He nodded his head slightly to indicate the glass on the table. 'It took me six months to climb out, to convince myself that there was life after Her Majesty's Secret Service, that I still had something to live for. I hadn't touched a drop since, until last night that is. After I received your phone call I bought a bottle and ran for cover.'

'For God's sake, man, pull yourself together.' Skeffington's interruption was abrupt. The public schoolboy veneer disappeared, and his expression was now contorted with a mixture of anger and contempt. 'Who do you imagine it was who convinced the people around you that they should sit back and tolerate your little games while you found your true self? Why do you think that a second-rater like you should be set up as well as you are? You are a big boy now, big enough to know that nobody resigns and that if you do decide to kick, the loss of your cosy little Roman office will be the least of your worries.'

'Why me, for Christ's sake?'

'Because we want to reactivate the Penguin, and it seems that you may be the only one capable of pulling it off.'

Weston took in a deep breath and exhaled through rounded lips making a slight whistling noise. 'You really take the prize don't you? Pulling back one sucker to

44

bring another into play. How do you know he will re-surface? How do you know he's even alive?'

'He made himself known on only one occasion to the contact who replaced you, and that was to give details of O'Donaghue's trip to the States. Other than that, he failed to respond to any promptings and as we wanted to keep him in reserve for the big occasion we decided not to push it.'

'So he was your reliable source?' A wry smile appeared on Weston's face. 'After the way you exposed him the last time around I'm surprised he ever made contact of any kind again.'

'We provided a patsy on time. He had nothing to complain of.' Skeffington suddenly seemed defensive.

'Only after I almost had to hold a gun to your head.'

'All the more reason for him to trust you, dear boy.' The sarcasm in the voice was intended to cut deeply. 'Look, all the stops are about to be pulled out to see to it that nobody, but nobody, frustrates the noble plans of our political masters. In other words, everybody is expected to do his duty.'

'What if he decides not to play?'

'You're acting the boy scout again. You let him know in no uncertain terms that we tell everything, and I mean everything, to his friend O'Donaghue.' Skeffington removed a yellow plastic wallet from his inside pocket and placed it on the table beside the glass. 'It would be better if you went via Amsterdam to Dublin rather than going through London – less chance of you being spotted. Your flight leaves Rome tomorrow evening at five o'clock.'

Weston made no response but stared blankly again at the empty glass, as he had done at the beginning of the interview. It was not until Skeffington pulled the office door closed behind him that he reached out for the wallet and examined the tickets and other documentation inside.

4

Inspector John Gibbons leaned against the passenger door of his car as he watched the executive jet come to a halt on the tarmac of the military air base, just south of Dublin. His hand shook slightly as he struck a match to light his pipe. The thought of meeting Mac Entee again made him feel excited; the adrenalin was flowing for the first time in years and he was surprised at how good it felt. It was almost like old times.

'They have opened the door sir. Are you going over?' The sergeant, who was sitting in the driver's seat, had leaned over and wound down the window.

'No, it's OK. I'll wait for him here.' Gibbons moved away; he had no intention of satisfying his sergeant's curiosity. Besides, the minister would want everything to be as discreet as possible. The fewer people knowing about their meetings the better.

The talk at their first get together in years, which had taken place within days of Mac Entee's appointment to justice, had concentrated on the good old days, its real purpose never mentioned. The policeman was well aware of the politician's reputation. Word had it that he was not one to rely too heavily on the advice of his senior advisers. He always sought out a source in the ranks, somebody who would keep him informed of the feelings at grass root level, an interpreter for the double speak which civil servants so often used to confuse the issue. The seemingly casual meeting in the South Dublin bar had been but the initial contact; the next one would have more substance.

The Taoiseach was first to make his way down the short flight of steps, and after the obligatory conversation with the air crew got into the black Mercedes which would bring them back to the capital. Within minutes of his departure a fleet of official cars had cleared the tarmac of the Cabinet members and officials who made up the London delegation. Mac Entee's driver did not follow the others as they moved towards the main gate but instead turned and drove slowly towards the control tower.

'Good to see you again, Johnny. Glad you got my message.' A slight smile broke through the serious expression on the politician's face as he closed the car door behind him. 'I've used old contacts since my days in defence to get hold of the CO's office for a few minutes, so let's get in out of this bloody cold.'

Gibbons glanced towards Mac Entee as both men struggled to keep pace with the soldier whose job it was to guide them through the maze of buildings to their destination. Physically, the years and the pressure had taken their toll: the thinning hair, wrinkled face and bulging stomach all bore witness to that. But otherwise, it was as if time had stood still. Despite the outward display of *bonhomie* the eyes showed that the remoteness – that defensive armour which the detective always found impossible to penetrate – was still there. Nobody was allowed to get too close; his private thoughts would always be his own.

It had been the same during their footballing days. Gibbons was the hard man, the one who mixed it, the gladiator who did all the pushing and pulling to gain

48

possession. Mac Entee was the speed merchant, the weaver and space finder, who always stood waiting for the pass once possession was won. He was the type of player who others cursed for lack of commitment only to find his score tally to be greater than anybody else's at the final whistle. He had left the team after they had won their second All Ireland title. By then, it was obvious that the glory days were drawing to a close and when the opportunity to be a candidate came forward it seemed a chance too good to miss. There was no attempt made to present him as a baby kisser or back slapper, that was too much out of character. The party managers introduced him as the professional, the efficient technician who would get things done. It worked: the image combined with the fame saw him home with a large majority.

'Johnny, the Brits have landed us right in it this time.' The justice minister, who had settled himself comfortably behind the large desk in the spartanly decorated office, came straight to the point. 'In a month they will announce their intention to pull out. By the end of the year they will have withdrawn all military forces, other than the Royal Irish Regiment, and then we shall have an independent Northern Ireland. Another proud member of the Commonwealth of Nations. We were left in no doubt but that the Brits have just completed their last big push against the terrorists. But they are still prepared to make resources available to help with the transition provided we do nothing to screw up their plans. If we fail to play ball they will wash their hands of the whole mess and, if they stay at all, it will be in name only; a sort of third rate United Nations force. There will be a big cut in the amount they spend on keeping the peace; the generous grants of all kinds they make available will be pared back to nothing. In other words, the place will become ungovernable, and with it on our

49

doorstep need I spell out the consequences for us.'

'Christ! Can they get away with pulling out?'

'Of course they can. They will leave behind them one of the best equipped police forces in Europe, an army which is everything as good as anything we have, and anyway, as it has been official Irish government policy since the foundation of the state to get the British off the island, we are hardly in a position to object!'

'What are we doing to prepare for it?' Gibbons was still finding it impossible to comprehend the enormity of what he had just heard.

'In a few days, a delegation will fly out from Dublin to meet representatives of the northern executive some-where in Germany. The hope is that both sides can arrive at some agreement about working with each other before Her Majesty's Government drop their bombshell. If it works both announcements will be made at the same time.

'An agreement on security?'

'Security, trade, tourism, cruelty to animals, every damn thing we can think of.' Mac Entee leaned towards Gibbons. 'We can take it for granted that extremists on both sides will want to blow any such agreement out of the water. Therefore, as I see it, we have two main objectives. First, to keep it quiet for as long as possible, and with the help of the Official Secrets Act and our own little methods we should be able to do that for most of the time involved. Second, when it does finally leak out, we will have to make sure that any plans they have to disrupt the situation will come to nothing.'

'You expecting trouble from the UDA and the other Protestant psychos?'

'No, they have neither the know-how nor the local knowledge to be much of a problem on this side of the border. As always, it's our own dear Nationalist nutters, the Provisional IRA, that we have to be on the look out for.'

Mac Entee moved from side to side on the swivel chair, his eyes concentrating on the polished surface of the desk, as if he was considering his next move. 'Look, Johnny, right now I am walking on a tightrope, and if it were left to your worthy superiors, right from the commissioner down, they would have me do it blindfold. Since I took over the department a few months ago I am finding it almost impossible to squeeze any information from them. Christ, there are times when I'm sure if I asked one of them the time of day he wouldn't answer before consulting somebody else.'

'Hardly surprising when you consider that in the not too distant past doing the bidding of politicians landed a number of senior officers in queer street. Had to resign hadn't they?' Despite his misgivings about those above him, Gibbons was leaving his former team-mate in no doubt of his disapproval of direct political interference in police work.

'I don't care what the excuse is, I am still the political head of the department and entitled to have my legitimate questions answered.' Mac Entee allowed himself a rare show of anger before pausing long enough to regain his composure. 'Look, the only slight hope we have is that the power-sharing executive in Belfast will hold together. If it breaks down we are going to have a civil war on our hands. Not only will the IRA set up bases along the border, which politically we will not be able to touch, but the flood of refugees in this direction will make what happened in the early seventies look like a picnic. We don't have the resources to deal with that. The whole bloody country will fall apart. I'm sorry, Johnny. I can't allow you the luxury of high minded scruples. Besides from what I hear you are not exactly the most popular member of the forces as far as the powers-that-

51

be are concerned.'

'Probably not, and since you got your new job it seems my ratings have sunk so low that a minder has been appointed to look after me.'

'A minder?'

'Well, up until then it seems everybody was convinced that I was capable of pushing around the files which were forwarded to me without help from anybody. Then surprise, surprise, just a few weeks after we had that drink together a young sergeant was appointed to take some of the weight off my tired shoulders.'

'A spy. How the hell did they know about our meeting?'

'Ministerial drivers are said to talk a lot. Oh, and he would be horrified to hear himself described in such a way. Let's just say that he is an ambitious young officer, not unlike myself in the early days, who would find it to his advantage to report anything out of the ordinary to a higher authority.'

'Like this meeting for instance. What a curious way to use scarce resources.' A slight smile of amusement crossed Mac Entee's face. 'By the way, whatever did happen to that ambitious young inspector I used to know many years ago? I see you pulled out of your law degree course half way through the second year.'

'Somebody has been doing their homework.' Gibbons was beginning to feel uneasy but decided to continue. 'Let's just say I went in search of answers and found none, at least not the ones I expected to find. That, along with a wife who always insists on looking at things from the underdog's point of view, convinced me that there were many more shades of grey around than I once suspected.'

'I take it that those who mattered noticed the loss of zeal and put you out to grass.'

'Something like that.'

'You were a member of the Security Task Force?' The tone suddenly became serious again. The time for chit chat had passed.

'That was a number of years ago now.'

'Johnny, I want you to locate your old contacts again and find out what is going on. I know you can do it.' Again, Mac Entee leaned forward, as if to give extra weight to his words. 'Look Johnny, I need you to be my eyes and ears, to keep me in touch with what is really going on in the world.'

Gibbons did not reply but was surprised at how quickly he nodded assent. His motives were not clear, even to himself. Maybe it was because he enjoyed the idea of the discomfort he knew would be felt by those puffed-up officers when they finally learned what he was up to, or maybe he really wanted to get back to the centre of the action. Then there was always the chance that Mac Entee was right and that at last he had found something which was really worth doing.

Neither man spoke as they moved through the small outer office and out into the cold air. Once outside Mac Entee turned and looked curiously at the young sergeant who was now standing beside the car, before walking over to where his own driver was waiting for him.

The rows of empty seats and dormant television cameras were enough in themselves to indicate the lack of interest. The few reporters who did turn up at government buildings to interrogate the returning politicians did little more than put a few routine questions on EC agricultural policy. The meeting at Downing Street was not even mentioned.

Weston waited for the head of government

information to put a formal ending to the proceedings before slipping his notebook and pen back into his inside pocket. This time Skeffington had outdone himself. It was not until he checked the full contents of the plastic wallet at Rome airport that he discovered he was scheduled to attend a Press conference within an hour of his plane landing. The time spent in the bar drowning sorrows had not helped either. Now, the flight, a sore head and a frustrating taxi ride through the city's rush hour traffic made him long for nothing more than a hot bath and a good night's sleep.

Standing up, he stretched himself before reaching over to take his overcoat from the back of the seat beside him. The Taoiseach and his officials had already left and now the press room was empty except for a few reporters having off-the-record chats with two government ministers who had remained behind.

'Get everything you wanted, Philip?' The sound of the familiar voice caused him to turn around.

'Nora, and looking as beautiful as ever.' She had aged slightly but it suited. The hair-style had changed too, a little bit too short for his liking. Other than that, everything was as he remembered: the calm brown eyes, high cheekbones and stubby nose which, for him, added to her attractiveness. 'Do I now take it that you have abandoned the Civil Service to join us noble searchers after truth?' he asked.

'No, for my sins I am now with the Government Information Service. You know, a sort of nanny to look after innocent pressmen such as yourself.'

'Oh, the Ministry of Truth?'

'Well, let's just say we tell as much truth as your newspaper.'

'Oh dear, as bad as that is it?' He was surprised and relieved at how much at ease she seemed with him. It was almost as good as before that damned article had appeared. 'May I corrupt an upstanding government official by offering to buy her a drink?'

She consulted her watch but he knew it was only a formality. 'Well, maybe just one.'

As they crossed the street and walked towards a nearby hotel Weston felt the tiredness evaporate to be replaced by an almost boyish excitement. He liked the idea of being near her again.

'Who were the two VIPs who held on to satisfy the poor hacks' thirst for knowledge?'

'One was Cunningham, foreign affairs; the other Mac Entee, justice.'

'Any reason why I should be interested in what they had to say?'

'No, the two are contestants for the top job when the old man finally decides to call it a day, so I would say that what you were witnessing was each hanging on to make sure the other did not get one over him with you boys.'

A few drops of rain caused them to quicken their pace as they moved towards the brightly lit entrance. The lounge was almost empty and they chose an alcove furthest from the bar.

'You remembered.' She smiled as he placed the glass of dry white wine on the table.

'Could I ever forget?' He took a sip from his lager before putting it on the beer mat. 'Well, what did you think of your master's performance tonight? Seemed as evasive as ever.'

'He has little choice. After all, small nations can do little but pick up the crumbs which fall from the table of the mighty, no matter what the rhetoric.' A sharp bitterness replaced the lightheartedness as she replied.

'What's up? Where is the young firebrand who was

once convinced that all clergymen and politicians were rogues who did little more than exploit a false version of the past, and preached that what was really needed was a broom to sweep them away so that the next generation could reach the Promised Land?'

'Maybe she has grown up.'

'Oh-oh, do I detect that I sit with yet another recruit to the blame-the-Brits brigade?' Weston sensed that he was being drawn into an argument that was impossible to avoid. 'Look Nora, this damn little state has had its independence for over three quarters of a century. Now, surely it's about time it took responsibility for its own mess? As for your brethren in Northern Ireland, peoples all over the world who have different cultures and interests have managed to compromise and live together. Why should they be any different?'

'Maybe it's because you have still have to return to us the most important thing of all, something without which we will never come to terms with our problems.' Nora spoke quietly, pausing as if to consider her argument. 'Just after my mother died I visited the Holocaust Museum in Jerusalem. I remember our Jewish guide passing all those terrible photographs of gas chambers, starving people and concentration camps without showing any emotion. It was not until the very end, as he stood pointing towards a glass case containing ancient Hebrew scrolls which the Nazis had converted into lampshades and musical instruments, that he literally shook with anger. "That's what they tried to do to us," he said. "They tried to steal our soul." '

'And that is what you believe has happened? The cruel English have stolen the soul of the Irish nation and refuse to give it back.' Weston could have bitten his tongue. The response was too dismissive, too contemptuous, and now the anger on her face confirmed his worst fears.

'Can't you see? The imperial power has to convince itself that those it sets out to conquer are inferior beings. It's necessary to justify what they are doing. The problem is that in convincing themselves they often convince the subject peoples as well, and just because they withdraw in the political sense does not eradicate the terrible damage done. Did you ever hear of one Charles Knightly?'

'No, should I have?'

'No, I suppose not.' The voice went quiet again, but now there was an underlying hostility that was not there before. 'He was an English gentleman who journeyed around Ireland a little over a century ago. As he went along he used to write home to his wife, telling her about all the wonderful things he encountered as he travelled through this strange land of ours. The people he came across in the countryside he described as white chimpanzees. The fact that they were white he found very disturbing. It seemed that if their skin had been black they would have proved more acceptable.'

'That was over a hundred years ago. What's the significance?' There was resignation in Weston's voice.

'There are times when I believe that the way we are presented in Britain today is not very different from the way it was done in Knightly's time. More subtle perhaps, but every now and then a newspaper columnist, a sports reporter, or even a High Court judge makes a slip and the prejudice is exposed for all to see.' Nora took a sip from her glass and after putting it down again continued to cradle it between her two hands. 'You see, Philip, I can't help feeling the young girl you once knew who wanted to brush everything aside because it was different, was taken in. She believed the message that was churned out by the television images, radio programmes and newspapers which assailed her every day from the other side of the

Irish Sea. The only good Irish are the ones who agree with the Westminster line, all the others are either stupid or, even worse, self serving politicians. We want our self respect back, and the irony is that it seems that you bastards are the only ones who can give it to us.'

'Why such a complete change?'

'There were many things but I must admit that you yourself played a large part in the awakening of Nora Bonar.'

Weston remained silent. As the memory of the photograph flashed across his mind he knew that time had not healed the wound. If anything, it had festered into a hurt that right now made her seem a great distance from him. Lifting his glass from the table he took a drink as he struggled to find the words which would start the long journey back.

5

Jim Thornley knew that Blueface had something on his mind from the first minute he saw him that morning. Right from when he entered the drinking club the twitching had started, that constant, nervous movement which indicated the little man had something on his mind that he knew would be of significance to his protector. Still, he walked past his table without a hint of recognition and stood at the bar. It was up to the weaker partner to make the first move.

The unfortunate Blueface, with his short wiry body and thin sharp features was one of life's natural victims. Ever since he was a kid he was the obvious target for the bully seeking to impress or the gang in search of a scapegoat. The large birthmark which dominated his left cheek not only determined the name by which he was universally known, but was also to be the deformity which sealed his fate. Quickly, he learned that his one hope of survival was to shelter beneath the shadow of a strongman who, in return for unquestioning loyalty, would keep his tormentors at bay. He latched on to Thornley knowing that as soon as the word was out that he was within the orbit of the big humourless thug, he was safe, and free from the threat of the physical violence that he feared more than anything else.

But this morning he hesitated because his information

was mixed. It was something he knew Thornley would want to know, and yet he was also certain it would bring on one of his rages. When that happened, the big man was capable of lashing out at whoever happened to be nearest. At last Blueface lifted up the empty glass from the table and walked towards the bar.

'O'Donaghue's inside.'

'I know, I saw one of his guardian angels leaning against the wall as I came in.'

'You'll never guess who he has with him.'

'Hmm.' Thornley maintained his air of indifference, not even looking towards Blueface who had climbed on to the barstool next to him.

'It's O'Hagan. He's been there for about half an hour now.'

'That INLA bastard. Christ! Is there no end to it?' The response was whispered, almost inaudible, but the venom contained in the voice was enough to cause Blueface to veer away from the large burly figure in case he again became a victim of his vicious temper. Thornley had long looked upon the Irish National Liberation Army as little more than a bunch of indisciplined psychopaths hiding behind a fancy name, and his one meeting with O'Hagan two years earlier had done nothing but confirm his views. As a veteran of the movement he had expected to be treated with some sort of respect, but instead the little runt had poured scorn on every suggestion he made, even going as far as calling him a dinosaur. Now he considered O'Donaghue's meeting with him as a betrayal. It was not until Blueface suddenly deserted his stool that Thornley became conscious of the figure standing directly behind him.

'Well, fat boy, and how are things with you?' He recognised the voice immediately. It had not the sharpness of Belfast but the softer tones of the border areas. Glancing up he caught the loathsome face as it sneered at him from the large mirror behind the bar. The sudden surge of anger that welled up inside his large frame could only have one release and a breaking glass, dropped by a nervous barman, gave him the distraction he needed.

His right fish crashed into the younger man's jaw transforming the sneer into an expression of shock. The left gave even more satisfaction, hooking downwards with such force that it gave the sensation of dislodging the chin from the rest of the face. As his victim tumbled back against the tables Thornley, his earlier sluggish movements now giving way to ones of lightning speed, moved in for the kill. Before any recovery could be made he lashed out again, this time a kick which struck home just below the ribcage. Then, using both hands to grab hold of the expensive leather jacket, he lifted up the crumbled body and pushed it roughly against the wall.

'Well, clever boy. What's a little bastard like you doing here?' The disjointed nose, along with the signs of swelling that were already appearing on the bloodied face gave the victory a special sweetness. All the arrogance had gone, drained away by the completeness of the humiliation. The little runt would remember this one all right. Pulling back his fist Thornley prepared to strike again.

'He is here because I asked him to come.' O'Donaghue, who was standing outside the office doorway, spoke in an even voice that exuded authority.

'Since when are we dealing with INLA madmen?' Thornley's outburst betrayed both anger and bewilderment. There was no reply but on turning around the big man knew that he had crossed the boundary of acceptable behaviour. O'Donaghue's lips were pressed together as if he had to struggle to contain himself, and it was almost possible for Thornley to feel the stare from the passion-filled eyes burn into his brain. Survival, for all of them, depended upon complete and unquestioning submission.

As soon as Thornley released his grip O'Hagan slid out from against the wall and moved in behind the bar. Picking up a towel and using the large mirror for guidance, he wiped the blood from his face. He avoided eye contact as he zipped up his jacket and wiped the dust from his jeans. Then, without speaking, he hurriedly moved to the door and made his way outside. The silence was only broken when O'Donaghue turned and walked back into the office. The door was left open, an indication to Thornley that he was expected to follow.

The office was in reality a small, sparsely furnished box room. A large filing cabinet dominated the corner opposite the door while a small desk and three cheap plastic chairs occupied almost all the remaining floor space. O'Donaghue did not turn around as Thornley entered but remained looking out through the heavily barred window situated behind the desk. It proved an effective method of registering his disapproval.

'What the hell was I supposed to do?' There was desperation in the big man's voice. 'You know they are nutters, you can't trust them an inch.'

O'Donaghue turned slowly and looked directly into Thornley's eyes. 'What you did lacked discipline and I never want to see it happen again, understand? Now close the door and sit down.'

Having, with difficulty, fought back the urge to respond Thornley moved towards the chair nearest him. Harsh experience had taught him the futility of confronting a stronger enemy head-on, and he knew that in time an opportunity for revenge would present itself; it always had in the past. As he sat down he glanced disarmingly towards the face which was still glaring towards him from the other side of the desk. When it came to O'Donaghue, nothing less than public statements of loyalty would do. The victories would have to be savoured in private.

'We have news that the Brits are about to announce that they are pulling out.' The change to other business was abrupt and came without warning.

'There's a problem?' Thornley was wary: there was no sense of jubilation in the announcement.

'Oh there's a problem all right. They intend leaving the executive in charge. The intention is that our little Protestant state should remain intact. Now, as I am sure you will understand, we must do everything in our power to prevent that happening.

'Let them go and then we can take care of the Prods.'

'Don't be bloody-well stupid. When they pull out, they will leave their whole intelligence network intact and in the hands of the Prods. With the information they have gathered over the last few years they will pick us off like fish in a barrel.'

'Christ! What about Dublin? There's no way they can stand back and let that happen.'

'You poor innocent! Jimmy, did you ever hear of a gombeen man?' O'Donaghue looked towards Thornley, the expression of both pity and contempt on his face all too evident to his victim sitting on the chair. 'During the famine in the last century the man who went around from village to village selling scarce food at huge prices, the man who made a good profit out of the people's misery was known as the gombeen man. Dublin at the moment is dominated by modern versions of the gombeen man, people who have a vested interest in keeping their little realm just as it is and have no wish to see things change. Do you seriously believe that they, or their leader – the Great Gombeen Man himself – would lift their little finger to rescue us? They would be only too delighted to see us crushed.'

'What can we do? We can hardly ask them to stay after doing every bloody thing we could to drive them out.'

'That's precisely what we plan to do. When they leave they go on our terms, not on their own.' A seriousness and determination now came into O'Donaghue's voice. 'It's clear that Paget had two objectives when he took over as secretary of state. First, he wanted to set up an exceptionally strong security system which would be capable of keeping us in check for at least a couple of years after they had pulled out. Then, if the fighting did start again, the Brits could wash their hands, Pilate-like, and complain about the bloody Irish being at it as usual.'

'I still can't see what we can do. He has us bottled up in every direction, and every time you move you seem to have some security bastard on your tail or watching from a helicopter in the sky.'

'For a solution we must look at his second objective.' O'Donaghue's voice rose slightly; he did not appreciate the interruption. 'It's not enough to keep us quiet. He also has to convince the world, or to be more specific our European partners, that this little island of ours is at peace and that the departure of the imperial power will not have any adverse consequences. You see, the beauty of it is that without the agreement of those with the big economic muscle the deal is off. After all, who wants a potential Cuba or Lebanon on their doorstep? So, what we have to do is put on a display that will convince those people out there that if the Brits pull out all hell will break loose.'

'How in God's name are we going to pull that off?'

'To us who live here there seems to be a great division on this island but you must remember that to those looking in from outside, even the British, we seem as one. To them we are all Irish, north or south makes no difference, and that's why we can put on our performance anywhere at all.'

'You mean the Republic – you plan to hit Dublin.'

'Right into the heart of the land of the Great Gombeen Man himself.' O'Donaghue opened the drawer of his desk and removed a small black hardcovered notebook. 'Now, I want you to use one of your regular visits to Donegal as a cover to check out a few of the arms dumps we have up in the north-west. You're probably familiar with all the areas mentioned. Anyway, all you need to know is in here and you know the code. I don't need to tell you to guard it with your life.'

Thornley was feeling elated as he picked up the notebook and slipped it into his jacket pocket. Not only had the meeting gone much better than he expected but the secret information combined with the mission made him feel like an insider again. In some ways it was like the early days, but the memories were too bitter and the hatred too strong to allow them ever to return.

'Come on Blueface, we have a long journey ahead of us tomorrow.' He called out as he moved from the office door towards the exit and the lone figure rose from his corner table and followed him with all the obedience of a lapdog.

Captain Jimmy Johnson of the Green Jackets turned and looked back angrily at the young private unfolding the ration pack. The location of the observation post was exposed enough without some rookie blowing it completely by making unnecessary noise. When he was satisfied that his warning was heeded he pushed his self-loading rifle back into position and looked again through the night vision goggles towards the clearing in the distance.

This was his fifth tour of duty in this God-forsaken country and nothing seemed to change. Same fields, same rocks, same bloody rain that never seemed to stop. The first time he had listened. Listened to those learned officers who gave fancy lectures about the Irish, why they hated one another and why it was necessary for the British army to step in and keep the peace. But you soon learned that you were little more than the piggy in the middle, being spat at one minute by Nationalist schoolkids and having stones hurled at you by so-called Loyalists the next. It was the sight of the mangled, lifeless body of Dave Jackson, lying on a muddy Irish field after being blown up by a booby trap, that finally snuffed out the last remnants of idealism. The high hopes of adventure in such far away places as the Middle East or the Falklands that had encouraged both of them to join up a few years earlier were extinguished forever in an unending and unwinable local skirmish. Now there was no need to anguish over the rights and wrongs of it all. You just made sure you got the player before he got you.

Within hours of the battalion's arrival in Ulster he was sitting in a chopper studying the pale, frightened faces of the kids under his command. None, except for the two sergeants, was over twenty years of age. The flight over the drumlins of south Armagh was a short one, not more than five minutes, but it was enough to take them from the fortress at Crossmaglen into the heart of bandit country. Johnson welcomed the tightening at the pit of his stomach as he waited for his men to jump from the hovering Puma into the large field a few feet below. It signified that he was alert, ready for action, and as this was the most vulnerable part of the operation that was how he wanted to be.

They moved quickly through the wet grass and regrouped at a hedge about a hundred yards to the north. After pushing through the bushes one by one, the sharp thorns cutting at their hands, they came together again at the other side. The routine was soul destroying, all the time tempting the brain to turn to other things: food, ambition, women. But in a part of Her Majesty's realm where a British soldier must travel by air rather than use the roads, constant vigilance was the order of the day as the first mistake might prove to be the last. The falling darkness and constant mist made the movement across stone walls and through swollen streams even more difficult than usual, and the sighting of their target brought with it a general sense of relief.

A quick sweep of the outhouses revealed nothing and a computer check by the radio operator on the registration of the three cars parked outside proved negative. The pub itself, which served the surrounding rural community, was an old, two-storey building. There were two entrances: on the left a small porch which led to the lounge while on the right the less decorative doorway provided access to the bar. In the semi-darkness the light from a large neon sign, situated about half way between the two doors, gave an almost sinister look to the small tarmac covered carpark.

Having ordered MacIntyre to take his section and make a general search of the area, Johnson prepared to move in. Bradley, his most experienced sergeant would go through the lounge door while Johnson himself would push into the bar. On the signal both groups moved quickly, noise being kept to a minimum to maintain the element of surprise. Ten seconds later they were inside.

The two men sitting at the bar turned towards the soldiers as they spread out across the otherwise empty room, their initial surprise turning to expressions of studied indifference. Their hearts and minds could never be won. The barman, who had become accustomed to such visits, continued to wash glasses as if the soldiers who had just entered his premises did not exist.

'Nobody in here sir.' Bradley called out from the adjoining room.

'Right, Sergeant. Leave two of your men there and come on through.' As he spoke Johnson put his hand under his waterproof smock and removed the booklet containing the wanted pictures from his jacket pocket. He went through the motions of checking the faces of the three men against the photographs, but from the beginning knew it was a pointless exercise. The barman and the bigger of the two sitting at the bar were too old, probably in their sixties, and when the third man turned towards them he had noticed the withered arm which would have ruled him out as a 'player'. He had often wondered why the soldiers had chosen to give that harmless-sounding name to the ruthless young men who opposed them. It had probably made everything seem safer, more like a game, less threatening than terrorist or killer.

'Any sign of MacIntyre yet, Sergeant?'

'Nothing yet, sir.'

'Well I'm sure our friends here won't mind if we hang around until he returns.' Johnson sat down at the table nearest to him and started to flick absent-mindedly through the photographs again. It was a nervous glance from the barman that awakened his curiosity about the unusual state of the table to his left. There were a number of half-empty crisp bags scattered across it but no glasses. It was as if a group had left hurriedly, taking their drinks but leaving everything else behind. Then he noticed the cigarette placed on the edge of the ashtray, its smoke wafting slowly towards the ceiling. The bird could not have flown far, and the evening might yet produce results.

'Important message from HQ, sir.' MacIntyre had pushed into the bar without warning, causing some of the young soldiers to jump nervously.

'I'll take it outside, Sergeant.' Johnson shot a warning glance towards MacIntyre; nothing was to be said within earshot of the men at the bar. 'Sergeant Bradley take over until I get back.'

'We found a BMW in the clearing about a hundred yards away, sir. It's the one we're looking for.'

'Good. I know he's somewhere in the building. They must have slipped out of the bar just before we arrived. I want you to take your men around the back and prepare to move in.'

'We can't do that, sir. Our new orders are to observe and report back only. On no account are we to attempt to apprehend the targets.'

'Christ! What are they at? We got the bastards just where we want them.' Johnson turned towards the radio operator, the frustration clearly visible on his face. He would call in and argue his case, fight with those in charge. But it took only seconds to realise the futility of it all; he had failed so often before. Pushing the hand-piece back towards the operator he looked resignedly towards his sergeant. 'OK tell them we are moving out.'

It had taken some time to find an observation post that gave both a view of the pub and the clearing where the car was parked. The mist turned to rain which added to the dark mood as they considered the possibility of spending

69

days in such unattractive surroundings.

'Two men have just left the pub, sir, and they are moving across the road towards the wooded area.' Bradley took his eyes from the goggles which were trained on the building, a hint of elation in his voice that things should have started so quickly.

'The two customers?'

'No, sir, too young and their builds are wrong.'

Five minutes passed before Johnson picked up the two figures again as they entered the clearing and started towards the car. 'Coming in at nine o'clock, got them Sergeant?'

'Yes, sir.'

'Is it him?'

'I doubt it. One of them looks right but he's still too young.'

'Wait a minute.' Johnson again took the book of wanted photos from his pocket and placed it on a flat stone in front of him. Carefully using his left hand to screen the light from his torch so that it could not be observed from a distance, he moved hurriedly through the pages until he came across the one he wanted. 'Thought so, it's his younger brother. Right. Call HQ, give them the position and tell them there is a car about to pull out.'

The engine came to life with a soft purr at the first attempt, and the rain was clearly visible against the powerful beams of the headlights as the BMW slowly made its way along the grass-covered laneway. On reaching the road it turned east and increased speed as it moved away. The bright red tail-lights had hardly disappeared when the outline of a Ford Sierra came into the view of the watchers. This time there was no powerful beam, only sidelights to guide the driver as he followed his target into the darkness.

70

'The glory boys. We do the donkey work and they move in for the kill.' There was bitterness in Bradley's voice.

'Such is life, Sergeant. Now get the men ready to move out.' It was to be a night pick-up and Johnson detested night pick-ups. The one consolation was that the first patrol was almost over and he was one day nearer what he hoped would be his last tour of duty in this frustrating bloody country.

6

Nora Bonar struggled with the uncertainty of her feelings as she looked towards Weston sitting on the opposite side of the breakfast table. Last night she had felt a love that was all forgiving, but now, with the return of daylight, the dark stubble gave his features a cruel glare, which reawakened the old sense of betrayal with all its ferocity. It brought with it an overpowering urge to hurt, to wound deeply.

'A bit of a come down, isn't it? From the great heights of Washington DC to the relative backwater of Rome and finally to end up where you started, back in Dublin. Somebody must have blotted their copy-book very badly.'

'These things happen in the best of families.' He was playing it cool, failing to rise to the bait.

'Still, any hopes you had of becoming editor of *The Times* must be fading fast into the distance.' The knife was turned again.

'Nora, for God's sake! Are you ever going to forget that bloody photograph?'

'Photograph! What photograph?'

'Oh, come on, you know exactly what I mean.'

Of course she knew what he meant, how could she ever forget? The old man had been effectively stripped of every shred of human dignity as he stood staring idiot-

72

like into the camera lens. What he had intended to be a beaming smile only served to expose the large ugly gaps in the line of badly decaying teeth. His clothes were baggy, too big for his frail body, and the cloud-covered bogland and mountains in the background seemed only to add to his humiliation. How could he have done such a thing to an old man who trusted him? How could he have done such a thing to her father?

'He hardly spoke to me after that, it was as if I had sent the damn picture to your precious magazine.'

'Look, I said I was sorry, for Christ's sake. What more can I do? Anyway, are you sure that it is a deep concern for your father that brings about all this grief?' Wounded, he decided to strike back. 'Or might it have something to do with the glimpse it gave some of your nice new friends into that oh-so-private world of yours? Is that what's wrong Nora? Were you ashamed of your father, of where you come from? Were you afraid that those wonderful intellectuals, whose acceptance you craved so much, might discover that you were nothing more than one of those Gaelic speaking natives from the western seaboard that they sought to preserve in the same way as they would an Amazonian tribe? Maybe it is not only the English who are guilty of feeling superior?'

'You bastard! He liked you, brought you everywhere, showed you everything, and in return you stabbed him in the back.' Jumping from her chair she ran into the bedroom violently banging the door behind her.

The truth in his accusations made them all the more painful. It had been so easy to move between the two worlds as long as they remained apart. After the photograph appeared in the magazine supplement of the Sunday newspaper she had had to endure the condescending looks in the office, at parties, and on one occasion, during an interval at the Concert Hall, a comment made within earshot caused her to break down and leave in tears. At home it was worse, much worse. The once adoring father ignored her, while the greatest efforts on the part of her mother could not restore the unspoken trust that once existed between them. From being accepted and comfortable in two cultures she became an outcast in both of them as the world became a much darker place.

'Nora, Nora, I'm coming in.' His voice again. That sound when used in soft measured tones became hypnotic, impossible to resist. She rembered with amusement how she had once looked with contempt at women who tolerated any humiliation, unfaithfulness, desertation, even physical violence, and still clung to the man responsible. Now she was the victim and for some unknown reason it was impossible to break away. While he was abroad she had gone out with others but it had never worked. He was always there, dominating her thoughts, strangling at birth any affection she might have felt for a potential rival.

'We are going to have to stop fighting like this,' he said. 'It's ruining your complexion. Listen, I was thinking, why don't we spend the weekend in Donegal? It would be like old times again.'

By now he was in the room and as she felt his strong arms move around her waist, the last remnants of resistance seemed to melt away.

'I don't know. I haven't been back there since my mother died. The place is deserted and . . .' The protests were only half hearted and even before he pulled her towards him and kissed her on the lips it was clear that she would submit yet again.

Jim Thornley groped blindly in the darkness until he

74

finally found the alarm clock and put an end to its deafening clamour. After switching on the reading lamp beside his bed he lay back on the pillow before rubbing the sleep from his eyes. The humour was good, the meeting with O'Donaghue had gone well, but it was the memory of the fear on O'Hagan's face as he lay stretched on the floor that gave the greatest satisfaction, and was responsible for the inner feeling of well-being.

The big man had learned early the importance of fear. When he was four years old he had sat on the top step of the staircase in a small two storey terraced house, and stared at his father, lying blood-covered on the floor below. Some time had passed before one of the neighbours noticed and rushed up to carry him back into the bedroom he shared with his baby sister. It was the Prods who had got his dad – left him for dead. You learned to fear the Prods; not because they were of a different religion – you knew little and cared less about that – but because they were of the other tribe, the enemy. You feared them because there were more of them, because they surrounded the little Catholic enclave, which cowered beneath the shadow of the shipyards.

Every year, in July, when the drums beat and the bands marched to remind the Papists who was boss, who possessed the power, you looked towards the large towering cranes and you remembered. You remembered that it had been there that he worked with the black squad on the steel structures of the new ships that would one day sail the world. It had been there, as they prepared to celebrate the great Protestant victory at the Boyne in 1690, that the build-up of tribal frenzy among his father's usually tolerant workmates caused them to turn on him. The only hope had been to dive into the salty water and swim for the nearest bank. As he had struggled to reach safety they showered him with confetti, the iron and steel bolts coming from every side. He was already unconscious when his broken body was dragged from the Lough, and although ten years had passed before he was officially declared to have breathed his last, you knew that in reality he had died on that day. You feared, but you also hated and hungered for revenge.

As a boy Thornley watched and learned from those around him. A people surrounded by a powerful enemy had, in time, perfected methods which allowed the weak to strike back at the strong, to gain at least some satisfaction for the wrongs committed. The battle must never be fought in the open but confined to the shadows where the attacks took place whenever the opportunity presented itself, and came from the least likely angle. Because it was unwise to boast of victories won it was necessary to learn how to savour them in solitude. He was only seventeen when the body of the first member of the black squad was found floating in the Lagan, his neck broken. In the years that followed two more were to meet with violent deaths, and others had narrow escapes. Nobody ever suspected.

'You better get up, Blueface is already waiting for you in the kitchen.' The woman who had entered the room threw a large yellow envelope on the bed as she walked towards the window. 'That came for you this morning.'

'Just another one of those damn fishing circulars.' He glanced at the large typed message on the outside of the envelope before tossing it from him again. 'How are things today?'

'The same.' She hesitated, as if overcome by a sudden pain, before pulling back the heavy curtains and allowing daylight to pour into the room. 'It's always the same.'

76

'It'll get better, you'll see. Just give it a chance.'

'Oh Jim, Jim. It's over two years now, and the hurt is as bad as ever. It will always be the same.'

'No it won't, you'll see.'

He watched as his sister slowly made her way from the room, unable to speak any more. The short steps, stooped shoulders and wrinkled skin would make it easy to mistake her for a woman twice her age. How he longed for the days when she would have chastised him for taking the Lord's name in vain or nagged him into going to Mass on Sundays. The sparkle had disappeared on the night of the shooting and now he despaired of ever finding a way to rekindle it.

His mood was changing, the good feelings giving way to depression. He could still see his nephew's crumpled body, clearly visible as it lay under the street light in the narrow alleyway which divided the housing estate. As he moved closer the shocked expression on the face of the lifeless corpse brought back terrible memories of his father's haunted features. But it had been the Prods who were responsible for his dad and in some strange way that made what had happened to him understandable. This, this was different.

'Oh God, Jim, he's gone! He's gone!' Leona had rushed across the living room and thrown her arms around him as he entered. 'My poor Bobby, my poor baby. Why, oh why did they have to kill him? He meant no harm, you know that.'

'I don't know, they told me nothing.' He was conscious of the tears welling up in his eyes as he spoke. 'The bastard told me nothing.'

A special unit from outside had been brought in to do the job. It was thought to be a better method than using locals. Youths had been picked up, blindfolded, and beaten when they failed to answer questions to their interrogators' satisfaction. Gradually the names of the drug-pushers emerged. Bobby's was top of the list, and as this was a second offence a warning was not considered sufficient. This time it had to be something stronger, something to instill fear in others. Things did not go according to plan: the kid had struggled and kicked as they stretched him out in preparation for his punishment. There was no way Bobby would have willingly allowed the bastards to pump bullets through his kneecaps. It was when he had pulled himself free that the gunman had panicked, and the fatal shot cut a gaping hole in his skull.

Thornley had little interest in the members of the unit. They were but the instruments. It was the driving force he was after, the inspirer, the motivator, the one who had given the order. When, years before, the great leader had arrived in the city, an ignorant country kid, it had been Thornley who had adopted him and taught him the ways of the urban jungle before they had a chance to destroy him. Thornley had been the one who brought him to the Brigade Commander, and who had stood outside the door while the newcomer was sworn in as a member of the Provisional IRA. Thornley had been good enough for him then, but later, when it suited, he had been moved to the sidelines, orders issued for the shooting of members of his family without him even being consulted. Again, Jim Thornley was determined to collect what he considered was owed to him by a powerful enemy. A small amount of the debt had already been paid; a number of the great man's most cherished projects mysteriously going wrong since the boy's death. But now O'Donaghue, with his great notions of a united Ireland and prosperity for all, would pay in full. Thornley would destroy him.

Leaning forward, he picked up the envelope for the

second time and, after removing the circular, checked the serial number on the top left hand corner. Then, after throwing it aside again, he stepped out onto the cold floor. It was time to make a move.

'That's it.' The youthful voice tried to sound confident, but as this was the sixth country lane-way they had stopped at he could not fully disguise the panic that was eating him up inside.

'Are you sure? It sounds to me like another one of your bloody blind guesses.' Eoin O'Hagan made no attempt to hide his impatience. 'Get out and check.'

The man opened the car door and slipped out on to the road. After a slight pause he moved silently into the narrow lane nearby and disappeared into the darkness.

'Give him a chance, Eoin.' It was the driver who tried to calm things down. 'When they carried out their reconnaissance it was broad daylight, and it's not so easy to find places like this, in the country and in the dark.'

'For Christ's sake! All they had to do was pick out a few simple landmarks.' There was venom in O'Hagan's reply. The near miss of the night before was still nagging, eating into his mind. To be pushed around by the big dinosaur in Belfast was bad enough, but to have finished the day by being picked up in the heart of his own country by a bunch of green Brits would have been unforgiveable, the ultimate humiliation. There had hardly been time to push their glasses behind the bar and move into the back kitchen before the patrol had come crashing through both doors. What in hell's name had Patrick been up to? Surely to God he had seen them coming a mile off? Over and over again he had run the sequence of events through his mind, but each time it had become more difficult to find an explanation for his younger brother's lapse. Had the Brits decided to search the building his whole unit would have been lifted. The very thought of it sent shivers down his spine.

'Should we have somebody stand on guard outside?'

'No, no need on this side of the border.' O'Hagan looked sharply behind him at the man who asked the question, then at the driver, looking for a gesture, an expression, which would disclose the true purpose behind the question. But it was too dark to tell. Nobody had complained – they wouldn't dare – but he knew there was talk. All the signs were there: the conversations which stopped when he came within earshot, the glances that passed between them when they thought he wasn't looking. If the accusation was that Patrick had fallen asleep at his post it would have been bad enough, but now he suspected that there was something more. He sensed that an O'Hagan had been tried and found guilty of cowardice in the face of the enemy and the thought of it made his blood boil. Just let them say it to his face, just let them try. When it came to Republicanism the O'Hagans had a pedigree second to none, even equal to that of the O'Donaghues.

'Where the hell is he? Is the bastard ever coming back?'

'Nothing yet.'

'Get out and find him.' As the second man slid from the car, leaving the back seat empty, O'Hagan's mind sought refuge from depression in the memories of his childhood, his early days with O'Donaghue.

From the beginning, O'Donaghue had possessed a magnetism which made others long to be part of his circle, one of his gang. All the younger lads would sit spellbound as he told stories of the courageous deeds of the volunteers, and the treachery of the crooked politicians of the Free State who had abandoned the Nationalists of the north to the British and their Unionist quislings.

O'Hagan's favourite story was the one that told of the escape of their granduncles, an O'Hagan and an O'Donaghue, from Dublin Castle during the Civil War which followed the signing of the Treaty in London. In his mind's eye he could easily return to August 1922 and picture the two men, sentenced to death by court martial for being in possession of explosives, as they leaned against the wall waiting for their turn to go before the firing squad. It was then that the man with the wheelbarrow appeared and started towards the main gate. On the word from O'Donaghue both men took off their jackets, picked up nearby shovels, and accompanied the workman through the main gate, making good their escape on a passing tram. The story was important, not only because of the adventure it contained, but because it placed the O'Hagans on a par with the O'Donaghues and firmly within Republican folklore.

It had taken a long time to adjust when, after his grandmother's death, O'Donaghue had left to live in Belfast. They were each to go their separate ways, O'Donaghue joining the Provisional IRA, O'Hagan establishing himself as one of the wilder members of the maverick, often despised INLA. But the hero-worship remained, and when the summons came all the differences between the organisations were set aside, the families were together again, and O'Hagan was determined to carry out the operation in a way that would make his granduncle proud.

'This is it, OK? Everything we expected, no lock on the gate or anything.' The relief on the youthful voice was evident. 'Do we move now?'

'No, we wait for another five minutes.' O'Hagan looked towards the driver. 'Right Jack, go over your part again.'

'Jesus! We must have gone through this a thousand times. How many more – ?'

'Again, OK?'

'OK, OK.' The driver recognised all the signs of O'Hagan's savage temper about to erupt and decided to give way. 'After helping you to move the trailer into position I come back to the car and move it to a location where it will not be visible from the roadway.'

'Did you check that out?' O'Hagan turned towards one of the men sitting at the back.

'Yeah. Just up the road there is an old farmhouse where nobody has lived for years. If he drives in behind it he can see everything and there is no chance of being spotted by anyone passing by.'

The driver continued. 'Once I am satisfied that this part of the operation has been successful I make my way to the phone box, situated at a crossroads about two miles from here, and make the call.' He spoke in a bored mechanical voice. 'When there is a response from the other end I ask, "Is that John Garner?" The reply will be, "No, it is not". So I apologise for ringing the wrong number and hang up.'

'You know the number to ring?' O'Hagan had already opened his door and was now standing on the deserted road.

'Yep.'

'Make sure you don't mess it up then.'

One of the other men had already made his way to the rear and unhooked the small trailer that was attached to the car. When all four had taken up position, one at each corner, they moved quickly off the road and down the narrow lane, sharing the burden of pulling the trailer as

82

they went.

7

John O'Reilly paid little attention to the silhouettes of the familiar landmarks as they bounced towards him out of the darkness. He had passed them all hundreds, thousands of times before. His one great regret in life was that during his long career on the railways he had only spent one year as a fireman on one of his beloved steam-powered monsters: they had life, and character. When he retired in six months time he would feel no loss, no pain, at having to abandon the diesel-engined soulless pieces of metal that had replaced them.

The fire, when it first appeared, was little more than a glow which could easily be mistaken for a powerful electric light in a farmyard. It was not until the train drew closer, and he put on glasses to reinforce his weakening eyesight, that he could make out the unmistakable form of the flames as they jumped into the night sky. About three miles ahead he estimated, just at the crossing. The lone figure standing on the embankment, waving a red light from side to side finally decided him; he quickly applied the brakes.

Pushing down the window of his cab he leaned out and looked back along the train. It was just possible to make out the two figures in the distance, moving quickly up along the line. One was holding the red lamp while the other concentrated the beam of his torch on the uneven ground in front of them. As they ran directly beneath his cab window the beam was redirected into his eyes, blinding him so effectively that it was not until the man with the lamp had climbed up the side of the engine that he realised he was wearing a balaclava and holding a revolver in his hand.

'Just do as you are told and nobody gets hurt. We have already taken care of your friend at the back.' It was the man behind the torch who spoke.

'Yeah sure. Anything you say.' O'Reilly was surprised at the absence of fear. His feelings were more of anger and frustration and he was silently cursing his luck as he moved to make room for his two uninvited passengers.

'Move the train slowly towards the fire.' It was the man with the torch again, and it soon became obvious that he was the one in command. As the powerful engine edged forward the train driver could make out two other balaclava-clad figures moving towards the flames. They lifted something and started to push the fire to one side. It became clear to O'Reilly that the flames had never been on the track at all but contained within a small trailer which now could easily be disposed of. Within seconds, the two-wheeled vehicle was pushed over the side of the railway embankment and the flames were snuffed out as it sank beneath the water of the river which ran parallel to the railway line.

'Everything cleared from the track?' The commander called out from the open cab window.

'Not a twig left. There's no way anybody could guess we were here.' It was the taller of the two men who responded. 'Did you see the wagons? Lovely big flat sides. It's as if they were made for the job.'

'OK, OK.' The commander was becoming impatient with the small talk. 'You've got a phone call to make, so you better get moving.'

'Did we lose much time?' It was the man with the lamp who spoke as he opened the cab door and prepared to move outside.

'Nothing we can't make up.' The commander's voice became more relaxed as he checked his watch. 'Wave the lamp as soon as you are in position, and remember to keep well hidden until we are north of Dundalk.'

O'Reilly was silently watching the tall man as he climbed over the crossing gate which was used by the local farmers as they went about their daily business. He could not but envy him his freedom as he disappeared up the narrow lane. He glanced back towards the commander who was now leaning out the window waiting for the signal from the lamp. The idea of trying to overpower him came to mind but was quickly dismissed. The initial anger had now evaporated and the fear, which had been slow in coming, was now all consuming. Fear for his wife and family, fear that he had downed his last drink, fear that he would not live to see his retirement.

'All right old man, I want all the speed you can give to make up for the time we've lost. No tricks. I'm not in the humour for heroics.'

The train driver made no reply as he gradually brought the large engine up to its maximum speed. Silently he was praying, praying with a sincerity he had not known since his childhood.

Patrick O'Hagan kept the BMW at a steady fifty miles an hour, resisting all temptations to put his foot down and see what it could really do. This was probably his last chance to come through, to prove to everybody, in particular his older brother, that there was no need to be ashamed of him, that he was a true O'Hagan. The phone call was half an hour late coming through and that had given him time to think, to worry that they had already dumped him because of what happened at the pub. Now he was determined to succeed; nothing would make him blow it.

The powerful headlights illuminated the road ahead. There was no attempt to hide from the listening posts and watch towers which monitor all movements in the border area. He was depending on routine to make him invisible. Records would show that on every Wednesday night at this time he travelled along the same road heading towards his girlfriend's house. In the beginning he had been stopped at road-blocks almost every night, more because of the activities of his brother than in any great hope of obtaining information. But soon they tired of the game and now he was usually waved through without any difficulty. It was almost certain that out in the distance a soldier was entering his registration number into a log and that this would be later punched on to a computer file for future reference. All was as usual; nothing happening to arouse suspicion. A few miles ahead, Sheila's parents' house lay at the bottom of a steep hill, a blind spot, and it was there that he intended making his move.

Now that the action had started, he was feeling much better. The memory of what happened that night outside the pub haunted him. He'd had time to warn them, to get them away safely, but at the first sight of the patrol he had frozen like a rabbit caught in headlights. Nobody had said anything – with Eoin around that was too dangerous – but the looks were enough to convey the contempt they felt for him. Even Eoin hadn't mentioned it, never questioned him about what had happened, and his big brother's loss of confidence hurt him most of all. It meant that tonight's operation was doubly important, and he was going to succeed at all costs.

He changed gears as he moved downhill. On reaching

the two-storey house where the distant watchers would have expected him to stop, he switched off all his lights. His objective was a turn-off about five hundred yards to the other side of the house and the bright moonlight enabled him to reach it without difficulty. He eased the car on to the side road without using the brakes: the brake lights would expose his position. A little pressure on the pedal and the BMW moved effortlessly up the steep hill ahead. After crossing the summit, which he felt protected him from prying eyes, his confidence began to grow. This was to be his night, he felt it in his bones.

On rounding a bend, about half an hour later, he found himself letting out an involuntary whoop of triumph. Stopping the car he quickly reached into the back seat for the binoculars which would help comfirm the success. The derailment had worked perfectly and in the distance, clearly visible in the moonlight, he could make out the engine and trucks lying neatly in a row along the line. Two men were still putting the finishing touches to the markings on the side of the train while the third stood guard over the crew. Taking the binoculars from his eyes he glanced towards the digital clock on the dashboard. A quarter of an hour to go before pick up. He was right on schedule.

'Night Wolf, are you receiving me? Night Wolf come in!'

The sudden crackle of the radio on the passenger seat startled him, and he was already conscious of the cold sweat of panic enveloping his body as he hurriedly threw the binoculars to one side. Radio silence was broken. There was something badly wrong. His panic increased when, reaching too quickly for the radio, he succeeded only in knocking it from the seat. It hit the floor with a thud and valuable seconds passed as he struggled to recover.

'Night Wolf to Night Watch. What the hell's wrong?'

'You've got a tail on you, you stupid bastard. He's almost on top of you. Put your foot down and get out o' there!' There were no signing off formalities and the radio went dead.

The engine came to life at the second attempt and he was already building up speed when he stared hard into the rear view mirror. The shadows cast by the large bushes which arched the roadway made it impossible to make out anything coming up behind him. It was the explosion of light from the flare, let off by the lookout to warn the hijackers of the approaching danger that first made visible the outline of the Ford Sierra. It was about three hundred yards away and closing fast.

His mind started to race, the instinct to survive taking over. All thoughts of his mission were put to one side. Anyway, the unit was safe; fear of booby traps would keep the Brits away at least until daylight, giving plenty of time to escape. The getaway might not be as smooth as was planned but that could not be helped. Now it was time for him to use his knowledge of the mountain roads to give the hunters moving in behind the slip. Tomorrow he would be safe in the Free State.

At the first crossroads he suddenly swerved to the left, switching on the full glare of the headlights as he pushed the accelerator hard to the floor. The gentle purr of the engine changed to an angry roar, as if the powerful car resented being pushed up the steep road which wound its way through the mountains. The pressure was causing him to make mistakes and more than once he almost spun off the road at one of the sharp bends which seemed to lie in ambush at irregular intervals. The driver in the car behind was a professional, making every slip-up count, and each time Patrick glanced in the mirror the following headlights were brighter.

It was as if an eternity had passed before the straight, where he planned to make his decisive move, stretched out before him. He deliberately slowed, allowing the Ford to come closer. The large tree about half-way along was the marker, the one he knew concealed the entrance to the unapproved road. His pursuers started to overtake just on cue. About five yards from the tree he jammed on the brakes and then made a sharp turn into the narrow entrance to his left, leaving the other driver with no choice but to overshoot. The rear right wheel of the BMW hit the bank, but he swiftly regained control and was soon moving at full speed again.

Patrick looked out at the road stretching in front of him. All he had to do now was keep on course for the next few miles and he would be safe, beyond their reach on the other side of the border. This was a road without a customs post or check-point. The Brits had once sealed it off with cement blocks and steel barriers but local farmers, frustrated at not having ready access to their land, forced it open again. The Ford headlights appeared again in his rear-view mirror but now they were farther away than ever.

It was the first violent jolt that brought back the memory of the ramps. They lined the road to slow down the traffic as it approached the military check-point that had been there in the days before the barrier. He heard the hard tarmac scrape violently against the underbelly of the car as the two came in contact. Nobody had bothered to remove them; they had posed no problem for tractors or farm machinery. It was when the BMW hit the third one that the steering wheel lurched from his hand and then everything went out of control. The thick hedge seemed to rush towards the windscreen.

He opened his eyes and shook his head in a vain

attempt to clear it. The car had crashed through the bushes and come to rest upside-down in a shallow ditch on the other side. A piercing pain was shooting through his left shoulder. It was impossible to reach out and release the seat-belt which was binding him tightly in an uncomfortable position. In the distance there was the sound of footsteps running towards the wreckage. The beam from the powerful torch moved searchingly around the interior before coming to rest on his face.

'Is he alive?'

'He's alive all right, sir.' The man nearest the car was forcing the door open.

'You're sure he's the same little bastard we picked out outside the pub on Monday night?'

'This is the one.' After the release of the seat-belt Patrick was pulled unceremoniously from the car. The pain in his shoulder throbbed agonisingly and he had to summon up all his will-power to avoid calling out.

'Right, cuff him and let's go.'

As he was pushed into the rear of the Ford none of his earlier confidence survived. The four men with him remained silent. He was allowed to think, to worry; they would leave his mind to do much of their work for them. They were English, the accents told him that. Christ! English, out of uniform, and working along the border; SAS. A cold shiver ran up his spine and his hands began to shake. Those bastards were capable of anything. Anything! By the time they drove through the security gates of the Interrogation Centre at Castlereagh all thoughts of resistance were expelled. He would tell them everything they wanted to know if only they would leave his arm alone. He could not tolerate any more pain.

The two detectives sitting at the other side of the table made no attempt to hide their displeasure. He told them about the meeting in the pub, the hijack, the plan to write on the side of the train, but still they were not satisfied. It was in desperation, after they had bullied threatened and shouted for hour after hour that he blurted out the date. The date he had heard Eoin mention on at least two occasions.

'Jesus H. Christ. So that's what they are up to.' It was the tall burly detective who spoke, the one who looked like a rugby player.

Weston used his index finger to flick the half-finished cigarette into the murky water of the lake. He smoked only when he was disturbed or nervous, and on this sharply cold Spring morning he was both. Disturbed, to his surprise, because he had again deceived Nora; and nervous because he was far from certain that the Penguin would show.

Looking across at the mountains which seemed to form a protective shield around the large pool of water did little to improve his humour. From the beginning he had hated the place, and the ancients who named Donegal as the fort of the foreigners seemed to have an understanding of the hostility he felt towards it. He could still remember the mist driving against the windscreen and the cloud covered mountains seeming to close in on them when they first drove along the winding roads which led to her father's house. The never-ending bog-lands and the rocks strewn across the fields added a sharpness and ugliness to the landscape which made him wonder how anybody could live there.

The inside of the small cottage where her parents had lived only served to reinforce his revulsion. He had developed a violent dislike for the smell of the turf which fuelled the large open fire, and the religious pictures which dominated the walls were symbols of what was for him a primitive and superstitious faith which would be forever outside his understanding. The weather had improved during the first stay, the bright summer sun adding beauty to the mountains and bringing a dark blue colour to the Atlantic as it crashed against the rocky coastline. But the dramatic change in mood came too late. First impressions had proved all-important.

It was those impressions that had determined the composition of the photograph, the photograph which had caused the rift between them. He had expected greater maturity from her, an acceptance of his picture as a work of art rather than some mere family snapshot. Her intense anger had caught him unawares, but what shocked even more was her ability to wound.

She had been getting too close, and that was never part of the plan. Somebody on the way up, whose objective was the very top, could not afford any emotional baggage to divert him from the single-mindedness necessary to reach his goal. When the opportunity to go to Washington presented itself he was elated, not only because of the promotion, but because there would now be an ocean between them. It was after the shooting that she started creeping into his mind again. The shattering of his world brought about a change of values: companionship and a sense of belonging seemed more important. Now he was deceiving her again, using her for cover, and as he stood watching the small waves lapping against the shore he feared that if she ever found out he would lose her for all time.

The sound of footsteps on the gravel path behind interrupted his thoughts. Without turning Weston knew it was the Penguin. The distinct rhythm of the footsteps would be recognisable anywhere. It was the cumbersome way in which the big humourless man lifted each foot from the ground as he walked that had decided his code name.

'You got my message.' Weston had now turned around and was looking directly into the emotionless, fish-like eyes.

'Yeah. You still got a nice line of brightly coloured envelopes for your circulars.' A slight grin appeared on the thin lips but there was no laughter in the face.

'Why come now? My information is that you only surfaced once since I was here last. Don't you trust anybody else or are you just getting over that near miss we had three years ago?'

'What makes you think I trust you?' The Penguin was never one for small talk and now the abruptness was an indication of his growing impatience. 'Look, I do what suits me and you do what suits you. In other words we use each other. Now could we get on with what we came here for.'

'Fine by me.' Weston again turned and looked out over the lake. 'As you are here I take it you have something worth telling.'

'O'Donaghue knows that you crowd are pulling out.' The big man paused, his eyes searching Weston for a reaction. 'He's planning something big, really big. Ever hear of a character called O'Hagan, Eoin O'Hagan?'

'Is that bastard still on the loose? He's one of those INLA nutters, isn't he?'

'That's him. O'Donaghue had him in for a talk a couple of days ago.'

'But that makes no sense. I thought he detested that pack of thugs.'

'He does, but now he needs them. Over the past few months he has secretly brought in people from all over the place, some of them leaders of outfits every bit as wild as O'Hagan's. He's moving away from the idea of a small disciplined force and dragging in anybody who is willing

94

to have a go.'

'Any ideas on what he is up to?'

'Simple. There's no way he wants the Brits to pull out leaving the Prods in charge. The only way he can keep you bastards here is by messing up the lovely peaceful picture Paget had painted of this island abroad. To do that he wants to pull a stroke, and it has to be a big one so that the shock waves will go around the world.'

'So what is he going to do?' The Penguin's only response was to shrug his shoulders.

'If there is so much activity, how come you managed to slip away?' This time Weston injected a hint of suspicion into his question.

'He sent me to check on the arms dumps in the area.'

'Can you give me anything on them?'

'Yeah. But for Christ's sake, if you are going to move on them maybe this time you will give me a bit of notice, a chance to cover my tracks or get the hell out of the area.'

'I'll see to it that there is no repeat of the last time.' There was a look of embarrassment on Weston's face as he opened a small notebook and prepared to make notes. After writing down all the details he took a neatly bound wad of twenty pound notes from his fisherman's jacket and handed it to the Penguin. There was an expression of indifference on the big man's face as he carelessly pushed the money into his pocket. It had been clear from the beginning that he was not motivated by the thirty pieces of silver, but the real reasons for his informing had never surfaced.

Weston watched as the Penguin slowly made his way back up the gravel path towards the bicycle which was propped against the stone wall at the roadside. He waited until the awkward figure had disappeared around the

95

corner before walking towards his car. As he switched on the radio the news of the train wreck was just coming through and, after listening to the reporter on the spot, he decided it was time for another cigarette.

8

The narrow twisty roads made speed impossible and by the time he arrived back at the cottage Nora had already left. His note lay crumpled on the floor and the wardrobe, which showed all the signs of having being hurriedly emptied, stood with its doors wide open. She had probably called a taxi from the phone box at the crossroads. He was too tired for anger and a feeling of weariness drained away his strength as he slumped into the large wicker chair beside the living room window.

The house was situated on top of a hill and from where he sat it was just possible to make out the roof of the pub where he had first made contact with the Penguin. He remembered feeling relieved that night when Nora's father had turned from him and become involved in a conversation in Gaelic with a local. The old man had spent the evening lecturing his guest on Irish folklore and in the end, it became impossible to feign interest. Looking around, he noticed the two men sitting on their own in the corner of the busy lounge. The smaller one, with a large birthmark on his left cheek, sat concentrating on the pint placed before him as if taking pleasure in the anticipation of what was to come. The bigger man was nervous, constantly on the alert, his eyes darting around as if trying to keep everybody in the room under observation.

'Saw you out taking photographs today.' It was the big man who had slipped from his corner and moved over beside Weston as he waited at the bar to order the next round of drinks. 'A very expensive looking camera you were using. Are you a professional?'

'I do some photography but my main area is journalism. I am doing some freelance work at the moment.' The young Englishman found himself feeling strangely flattered by the attention of this complete stranger. 'You have no interesting stories you would like to push my way?'

'Ah, you never know, we might be able to help one another.'

That first conversation ended as abruptly as it had started and Weston thought nothing more of it until a week later when, out with his camera along the shoreline, he saw the tall burly figure making its way towards him. The eyes were again restless making sure the meeting was not being observed.

'I have some information I want passed on to certain people and you just might be the man to do it.' There were to be no formalities, just straight down to business.

'Why me?'

'Don't mind about that. Let's just say you're in the right place at the right time.'

'Will I be able to print it?'

'In time, but first I want it passed on to somebody who can use it. Somebody with clout.'

'Why should I?'

'Look. I've been watching your sort long enough. You're young and you want to break into the big time in a hurry. To do that you need contacts in high places, right? Well, I'm giving you the key. The information I have will open doors and once inside it's up to you how you bargain.'

The big man's timing had been perfect. When Weston first came to Ireland a naive confidence in his own ability had assured him that within weeks he would have unearthed the scoop which would cause editors to climb over one another in their attempts to offer him assignments in all the trouble spots of the world. With the passing of time and after a harsh dose of reality the dream had turned sour, and with his money running out he was near the point where he would have to return home and start from the beginning again. Now, out of the blue, he was being offered a chance – an outside one but at least worth a shot.

He had disliked Skeffington from the first meeting. Having failed to establish any contacts in the north he had no choice but to pass the information through the Dublin embassy and the pompous attitude of the MI6 officer, who seemed to take pleasure in shooting holes in everything he had to offer, made it difficult to control his temper. What if Weston was a plant? Where did this man live in Belfast? What was he doing in Donegal? The longer the interview had continued the more Weston was made to feel like an errant schoolboy caught smoking behind the bicycle shed. In the end it had been a relief when he was escorted to the door of the building and allowed to leave.

The encounter at the embassy was to prove the final straw and without returning to Donegal he had abandoned his Irish venture and returned to London. It was soon after that Jarvis re-entered his life.

Chubby little Jarvis; he should have spotted him a mile off. They had known one another to speak to at Oxford but he would never have considered him a friend, which made the little man's apparent delight at their chance meeting all the more puzzling. After retiring to the bar and spending much of the evening recalling their student days there was an exchange of telephone numbers and a firm commitment to meet again soon. Afterwards, it took only a few enquiries to discover that Jarvis was one of the latest group of high flyers to be recruited to the Foreign Office; a man considered by many to be on his way to the very top. When, after deciding to cultivate what one day might prove to be a useful source Weston made contact again, he found he was pushing against an open door. Over the next few weeks invitations from his new found friend to many official social functions were gratefully accepted.

Jarvis, like all those destined for greatness in Her Majesty's Civil Service, was a member of a club. He had not yet graduated to the inner sanctum known as the Carlton but the imposing building was situated in a fashionable area and was a step in the right direction. It was on a Wednesday evening after dinner as they sat talking in the library that everything fell into place. Weston had recognised Sir James as soon as he entered the room: the distinguished grey hair and long Roman nose were unmistakeable. Sir James, although not well know to the general public, was recognised by those in the know as a real force in the corridors of power. A senior civil servant with the ear of the foreign secretary is always somebody to be reckoned with. But it was the man with him that convinced the young reporter that their business was with him.

'Philip, I'm sure you recognise Sir James and I believe you have already met Mr Skeffington.' Jarvis sounded nervous and he stumbled slightly as he moved to one side to make way for his senior colleagues.

'Ah, glad to meet you Mr Weston. I have been hearing good things about you.' The grey haired man's handshake was firm, confident.

'Delighted to meet you, Sir James.' Outwardly Weston succeded in maintaining a calm veneer but inwardly everything was in turmoil, his mind racing in a hundred different directions. This was a golden opportunity, the chance of a lifetime, but how to play it?

'The information you fed us in Dublin led to the discovery of a large arms dump.' It was Skeffington who answered his unasked question.

'Good. I'm pleased to hear that.' As he searched for a more adequate response Weston noticed Jarvis make a tactical retreat towards the main hall. He was to be left alone in the company of the two men who had now occupied the plush armchairs opposite him.

'I have little time, Mr Weston, so I will come straight to the point.' Sir James motioned Weston to be seated. 'A difficulty has developed, I'm afraid. Your man, a source we now know to have much valuable information, refuses to make contact with anybody other than your good self.'

'Why me?'

'Our friend is clever, very clever in a primitive sort of way. He dared not give information to an established agent because that would have risked exposure. We know a few of ours have been turned, and we have managed to turn a few ourselves. So he was on the lookout for somebody who would not be directly involved but would still have the means to make the necessary contacts.'

'Somebody like me.'

'Exactly. In a way you are his creation, he chose you to be the go-between.'

'How do you know he'll talk to me? Did he say so?'

'Not in so many words. He just refuses to respond when any of our agents attempt to make contact.' The civil servant suddenly looked angry. 'The last time, he beat up one of our men and left him unconscious as a means of proving to his comrades the purity of his Republicanism. He'll take no chances. He's determined to see to it that information will pass only through the channel he established himself.'

'What makes you think I'm capable of dealing with him?'

'Oh, we have had you under observation for some time now Mr Weston and, let's say, we are satisfied with the results.'

'Jarvis. So that was his little game?' Weston studied Sir James's face but the expression never altered.

'I'm sure you will give our proposal some serious consideration. We, of course, would supply all the necessary training and back up.' The civil servant placed a small card on the table in front of Weston before standing up. He then extended his hand towards him, the meeting over. 'You can contact Skeffington at this number should you decide to help out. Goodbye Mr Weston.'

Weston had had to resist the temptation to give his decision at once; to appear too eager he felt would be a mistake. He could not help but feel a great euphoria, a sense of having made the big breakthrough, as he watched the two immaculately dressed men make their way across the library and into the great hallway. From being the outsider, the apprentice struggling to get his foot on the first rung of the ladder, he had just made a contact which could caterpault him to the top, the very summit of his ambitions. He knew how the game was played and he would play it for all it was worth. The wielders of power, the establishment, expected every man to do his duty. Those who complied reaped the rewards; those who questioned, the troublemakers, were forever to be outcasts. The old boy network had the power to make or break and now the boy from the terraced house in Halifax determined to use it to really move up in the world.

A certain unease, the fear of having betrayed a trust, had surfaced on occasions but was quickly brushed aside by an all-powerful ambition which had burned within him since his schooldays. After the acceptance of his piece on the natives of Donegal by a leading Sunday newspaper, the laying to rest of such scruples seemed a small price to pay for the realisation of all he had ever hoped for. He was good, but no better than thousands of others, and to get there you needed that extra push, a patron with influence who would pave the way.

The doubts and uncertainties had reasserted themselves on the night he received the telephone call from the Penguin. As he listened to the panic-stricken voice whine at how the police had acted too quickly on the tip off, not giving the big Belfast man enough time to cover his tracks, he suddenly saw how similar their positions were. They were both pawns who moved about the board at the whim of their masters, expendable when their purpose was served. That night his masters had made their calculations and decided that the Penguin was to be rescued, not out of a sense of loyalty or due to past services but because he still had something to offer. As he sat holding the receiver in his hand Weston had wondered how long it would be before the same calculations would be made and a decision reached that the lowly journalist from Halifax had become surplus to requirements. In the beginning, he had hoped for acceptance, an invitation to join the club, but the superior manner always adopted by Skeffington when dealing with him soon shattered that illusion. By then it was too late. Too many tentacles bound him and there was no escape.

The sudden appearance of the Penguin at the brow of

the hill brought him abruptly back to the present. The Penguin was walking, pushing his bicycle, while to his left came the smaller, leaner figure of the man with the large birthmark on his face. A routine had now been established; the morning's physical exercise over, the big man joined his companion for a drink before they made their way home. Weston stood up and stretched. It was getting late and he would have to put his things together before returning to Dublin.

John Mac Entee glanced over his shoulder before rounding the bend which would hide him from the view of those standing at the entrance to the forest park. He noticed that the Special Branch men had already left their car and were deep in conversation with his driver. At last he was unobserved.

Looking forward again he took in a deep breath of fresh air. The wide sand-covered pathway stretching out ahead never failed to bring with it a sense of elation, a feeling of freedom. After two months as justice minister he had still failed to come to terms with the cocoon of security which surrounded his every move from the first day of his appointment. The thought of giving up office, of returning to the back benches was something that would never be contemplated, but the price was high.

Mac Entee was of the old school, a man of the people who thrived on the opium of personal contact, the pressing of the flesh. Not for him the world of television cameras, bright lights and make-up artists. That he left to the trendies such as the professor and the other bright boys who always succeeded for a time but in the end never failed to trip up on their own hair-brained ideas. For the present he was prepared to allow the restrictions to cramp his style in the knowledge that the reward for his exertions would be a move upwards, perhaps to the highest office of all, and there he would be able to come into his own again.

After much argument the security chiefs agreed to allow him one short walk a day alone, and after the train wreck a few days earlier there was even an attempt to curtail this. While in Dublin he drove with his escort to the Wicklow mountains and there, while they waited at a prearranged rendezvous, he strode through one of the pine forests which cover the countryside. It was not always the same route, a pattern could never be established, but after a time he became familiar with the area and this enabled him to pick the place he wanted to go. Today that had proved to be very useful.

Rubbing his gloved hands together was as much an outer expression of his feeling of satisfaction as it was an attempt to keep warm. This morning he felt a new sense of purpose, a rekindling of the idealism that had not fired him since his first term as a public representative almost twenty years earlier. It was not only because an arch rival had made a blunder, althought that in itself was reason for celebration, but because the issue involved brought a spring to his step. Until now his rivalry with Cunningham had been on a personal level; the old faithful Party member versus the brilliant young academic. It had been a beauty contest, and in such a contest he had no chance. Now the decision of the British to pull out of the north had changed everything. The backwoods men had emerged within the cabinet, the successors of those who pushed for the invasion of Northern Ireland in 1969. They were advocating all kinds of crazy measures to frustrate everything, their ultimate goal being some kind of mythical united Ireland. That they should appear was no surprise, that Cunningham should throw in his lot with them was. The

105

professor had finally shown his true colours, his total lack of judgement. He was wrong, the whole lot of them were wrong, and Mac Entee was determined to use all his energy, all his political skill, to defeat them.

'Good morning, Minister.' He was expecting Gibbons, but the detective's sudden appearance from behind a clump of bushes still startled him.

'Good morning John, glad you got my note.' Mac Entee looked nervously around him as if expecting to see somebody observing them from a distance. 'Sorry about the cloak and dagger stuff but the longer we can keep these meetings under wraps the more effective they can be.'

'It's not going to prove all that easy. My ever-watchful sergeant almost stumbled across your note.'

'Did he see it?'

'I don't think he spotted anything this time.'

'Good. Anything to report?'

'Nothing that we did not know already. I've been away from the scene a little bit longer than I thought. The old contacts are not as forthcoming as they once were, I'm afraid.'

'Not to worry, there's plenty of time yet.' The minister seemed strangely unconcerned. 'What do you make of the train wreck?'

'Seems obvious enough. O'Donaghue is out to shatter the illusion of a land flowing with milk and honey that Paget has worked to create so successfully over the past few years, and if the Provos can pull off a few more stunts like that no amount of slick public relations work will repair the damage.'

'Hmm, that touch of writing Fionn on the side of the wagons was a master-stroke. In my game you need to know something about publicity and I can tell you that no photographer or newspaper editor could miss that

106

one. There's one thing I will give our brethren in the violent tradition, and that is when it comes to manipulating the media they take some beating.' Mac Entee was now absorbed in the conversation, his earlier nervousness having disappeared. 'Any thoughts about the word Fionn itself?'

'Well, from my schooldays I remember being told that Fionn Mac Cumhaill was the leader of that brave band of warriors known as the Fianna whose job it was to protect our coasts from invading foreigners. It's hardly surprising that his name was used, knowing how O'Donaghue is said to consider himself to be something of an expert when it comes to ancient Irish legend.' Gibbons started to fill his pipe from a tobacco pouch he was holding in his hand. 'My all-knowing sergeant is convinced that it has something to do with a tradition that was prevalent in the part of the country he comes from. According to this, Fionn and his men never died but are hidden away in a secret location just waiting for the signal to rise up and drive the foreigners from our shores.'

'And the train wreck is the signal?'

'So it would seem.' After striking the match the detective-inspector took a number of strong puffs on his pipe to bring it to life. 'The strange thing is, of course, that if the theory is correct, the signal will start events which are more likely to keep the invader here than to drive him out.'

'Still, your sergeant may be much closer to the truth than he imagines.' Mac Entee glanced around nervously again, his voice reduced to almost a whisper. 'Since the wreck, we have been getting reports of activity from all over the country, north and south. I agree that one reason for the large letters was probably to attract publicity but it also seems to have set off a chain reaction which is leading to something much bigger.'

'Are we moving to stop it?'

'Stop what? We've no evidence. Christ, John, I don't have to tell you the type of political tightrope we're walking on. If we move in and arrest a large group of Republicans just before the British announce their withdrawal we will be accused of doing Her Majesty's Government's dirty work for them and then all hell could break loose. Look, a wrong move at this stage and the whole island could go up in smoke leaving us with a conflict which would make the civil war of the twenties seem like the teddy bears' picnic.'

'Have we any bloody plan at all?' Gibbons found himself shouting.

'For all it's worth, we feel that the best hope is to allow them to develop their operation until it reaches a point where we can move in and pick up the necessary evidence to secure convictions.' A shadow of despair darkened the politician's features. 'The problem is that by that time they will be in a position to resist, and if they do, there will be killing. Let's hope it never comes to that.'

'Damn it, that's what made me give up on this job. The ordinary poor bastard who threw a brick through a window or stole a few quid was bashed with the full force of the law but the fat cats, who could afford the big lawyers, or worse still, the thugs who could cloak themselves in the Republican flag did what they liked, and walked away scot free.' Gibbons could not control the mixture of frustration and desire for revenge which was welling up inside him. 'Let the bastards try and take us on. Let them come out into the open where we can finish them off once and for all.'

'That's it, let the blood flow and all will be cleansed. You know that has always been considered a solution in this stupid country.' Mac Entee was looking towards the inspector, a look of resignation on his face. 'Why, in God's name, have we always considered the man of action to be superior to all others? Every nutter who has ever fired a shot seems to have had a book, a poem and a play written about his great exploits and in the end what are we left with? Our two main political parties are the result of a family feud which was fought three quarters of a century ago. Up north, for as long as anybody can remember, we have had a civil war which erupts every so often with devastating consequences for the poor bastards who live there. And what happens every time one of us contemptuous compromisers comes close to finding a solution to the mess? Up pops one of our wonderful patriots and plants a bomb or fires a shot which undoes everything. Just once, just this once could we grow up and be adult enough to accept that we cannot have everything we want in this life, and come to an agreement where we can at least live together.'

Gibbons removed the pipe from his mouth and knocked it gently against a tree. It was the first time the mask had dropped, the human weakness exposed in the plea for understanding, and he could not avoid feeling a certain sympathy for the politician.

'What makes you so certain it's going to happen down here? Why not the other side of the border?

'All the pointers indicate here. First, because of the resources poured in since Paget's arrival the Provos are finding all movement difficult and their chances of mounting a major operation are next to nil. Second, there is the matter we have come to term the American connection. A couple of years ago the British informed us that one of their agents observed a meeting between O'Donaghue and a hard man named Vogel in a bar in Washington. The agent managed to retrieve a newspaper used by the men and on it the lab found the impression of two words which were obviously written on a piece of notepaper placed on it. One word was Cuchulainn, the other Fionn.'

'Boy O'Donaghue is into Irish legends in a big way these days. And the significance?'

'Well, if you again return to your school days you will remember that the stories about Fionn were always situated more to the south.'

'So, because the word Fionn appeared on the side of the train we are to take it that the action is planned for our side of the border.'

'It's a theory, and the best one available at the moment.' Mac Entee hesitated, as if pondering over his next sentence. 'If I am to operate effectively on this I need somebody on the inside now, a source that will keep me up to date on what is going on.'

'Don't look at me. I'm the one who has been exiled for lack of belief, remember.'

'Yes, but I may have found a way around that. At the last meeting I had with your masters the matter of this character called Vogel was on the agenda. It seems he is capable of doing anything, but his main claim to fame is an expertise with explosives. Now, at the moment there are two schools of thought: one that he will come to help out with whatever is planned. The majority, however, believe that he is already aware that the British are on to him and that the operation is blown.'

'And in your opinion?'

'Oh, in truth, I go along with the majority, but that did not prevent me from arguing strongly against them at the meeting.'

'Why, for Christ's sake?'

'Because it gave me the opportunity to get your foot in the door. I sat back and waited for the usual cry about lack of manpower and how there was not enough resources to follow up everything and then I mentioned my old friend John Gibbons who spent his day shuffling paper in a little office.'

'That's going to make me flavour of the month.'

'From what I hear your popularity rating was never very high anyway. The upshot of it is that in the next few days you will be appointed, along with your sergeant, to the task force, with special responsibility for keeping an eye on Vogel.'

'Hmm. Right.' There was no enthusiasm in the inspector's response.

'Time I was getting back, or there's a danger that somebody will come looking for me.'

Mac Entee turned and started back in the direction he had come. After slipping the pipe into his overcoat pocket Gibbons blew through his cupped hands in an attempt to bring life back into his numb fingers. Suddenly, he had become conscious of the cold.

9

There was an unnatural silence as the patrol pushed its way out of the thick undergrowth and moved cautiously across the clearing towards the village. Nothing could be heard except the chickens as they angrily scratched the ground in their relentless search for food. It was always the same; the pattern never varied. He knew it was the blue mist rising from the paddy-fields beyond the peasant huts that hypnotised him into relaxing, lowering his guard, and yet he was helpless to resist it. The gook would appear as if from nowhere, just materialise in the space in front of him. And the gun was another thing. It irritated him that he could never recognise the make. It was real though, deadly real. He squeezed the trigger on his own weapon knowing it would jam, as it had jammed all those other times, leaving him defenceless, waiting for the explosion that would end it all.

Vogel was already sitting up on the bunk before opening his eyes, his body enveloped in a cold, sticky sweat. During that first year after his return from Vietnam, the hate-contorted face of the Vietcong youth haunted him nightly. Now it returned only at times of stress or failure. It was no big deal, easily dismissed, and a small price to pay for the great adventure in South-East Asia which had changed his life, taught him the skills to become somebody. The army had not been over-particular in those days, at a time when every city had its anti-war protesters and the White House was occupied by a colourless politician who lacked any power to inspire. The recruiting officers had welcomed all comers. The rhetoric and fancy talk about saving the world for democracy sailed harmlessly over the lanky seventeen year old whose only ambition was to get away, to escape from the drab, grey poverty of the one room apartment which he shared with his mother and sister.

It was the rifle that changed everything, bestowing on its bearer a power he had never before imagined. When you moved into a village it became yours to do with as you liked. You took whatever you wanted, destroyed at will and took satisfaction in the fear which radiated from the faces of the cowering peasants. They clung together, watching your every move, praying you would not unleash the awesome firepower at your disposal. Their feelings, traditions, culture counted for nothing, because from the beginning you had always looked upon them as dinks, slopes, gooks or whatever was the current fashionable word to describe the inferior rice farmers. Taking human life, any human life, soon became easy, satisfying and pleasurable.

Vogel reached out and switched on the reading lamp on the small locker beside the bunk. The newspaper lay folded just as he had left it three days earlier. The photograph of the wrecked train, with FIONN painted across the wagons, felt as if it was burning into his brain, mocking his inexcusable incompetence. Reaching out his right hand he violently knocked it from the dusty surface, sending it flying across the room where it landed on the floor just beneath the window.

The original plan had been for him to look out for the code word in one of the Irish papers which he collected off Broadway on a weekly basis, but the Irishman was clever, had given him a bonus, provided him with extra time. There was no need to wait for word from Dublin, no need to make the journey to the newsagents, because there it was splashed in large white letters across page two of the *New York Times.* Operation Fionn was on. A phone call to the sarge confirmed that the money was in place and the preparations could begin. Then, with one stupid mistake, one amateurish slip, he had blown it all, moved back to square one.

It was the sarge who had arranged the first meeting with the Irishman in Washington; the sarge arranged most things. Vogel had met the squat Bostonian first in an army camp just outside Qui-Nhon. He had the habit of keeping an unlit cigar in his mouth which he propelled from one side to the other with his tongue as an outward sign of his inner restlessness. The small pig-like eyes were constantly on the move and you could picture the brain behind them on overdrive, always on the look out for an angle, another way to make a fast buck. The sarge was the Mr Fixit in Qui-Nhon city, the man who could cater for your every need provided, of course, the price was right.

In the chaos of war, where everything from women to troop carriers are commodities on the open market, the ruthlessness needed to corner the trade must be continued if the stranglehold is to be maintained. To stay on top, the sarge was prepared to pay top dollar to those who had the special skills he needed. They were men like himself who never allowed idealism or conscience to stand in the way of ambition, and it took him less than a week to recognise all the required attributes in the kid who had come in with the new batch of recruits. There were suspicions – nothing more – of the lanky youth's involvement in the blowing up of the supply dumps of rival firms, and when a number of over zealous officers met with convenient accidents the look of satisfaction on the pock-marked face was noticed, but never commented upon.

After his return Stateside, Vogel served as a cop on a SWAT team in California but the lousy pay and the restriction of having to operate within the law soon brought back memories of more prosperous times and his former boss. It did not take long to find the sarge in the narrow streets of the Irish sector of Boston. The location may have changed but the business was the same, and his special skills were more in demand than ever. Soon it was as if they had never been apart. The smell of fear from the little people who could not pay their protection money reminded him of the shivering Vietnamese peasants, and it was satisfying to discover that the feeling of power was as electrifying, as magic, as ever. The kid from the Bronx was on a high. He was the one picked to do all the big jobs; he was number one.

Moving from the bunk, his feet pressed briefly against the stiff body stretched out on the uncovered floor. The changed look on the lifeless face caused him to wince slightly; overnight it had turned a sickly white and now, under the artificial light of the reading lamp, it took on the form of a grotesque circus mask. Again a sickly feeling washed over him as he was forced to relive what had happened, forced to confront his own stupidity. Lifting up a wad of dollar bills which lay beside the newspaper, he angrily thrust them to within a few inches of the unseeing eyes.

'Just a couple a hundred dollars, you poor bum. You poor stupid bastard. Was it worth dying for?' Of course it was. To a junkie whose only ambition was to get enough to cover the next fix it must have seemed like a fortune, sufficient to satisfy the craving for weeks, as far into the future as the crazed mind could imagine. What had

115

possessed Vogel to leave it out in the open, in full view of anybody who came into the place? He shuddered at the memory of th drug-filled eyes lighting up as they honed in on the greenbacks. The knife then appeared from inside the ragged overcoat as if by magic.

'Look man, I want it and if I don't get it I cut you, understand? I want it *now,* man.' After that, he knew the hard work of the previous few days was blown, the trust was gone and he could never use the guy.

'All right, all right. Take it easy, man! I'll give it to you.' The show of fear had caused the junkie to relax and the ex-marine had weaved past the knife and into position before his victim was even aware of the danger. The cervical column snapped like a twig.

'Too greedy, too greedy man.' Vogel's first reaction was to cruelly mimic the dead man as he carelessly let his body slip to the floor. Then, depressed, he lay on the bunk and gradually fell into a restless sleep.

When, three hours later, the nightmare reawakened him he found it difficult to motivate himself, to start from the beginning again. Finally, dragging his gaze away from the horror on the dead man's face he reached over and directed the light from the reading lamp towards the photographs which were pinned to the back of the apartment door.

There were four of them, all in black and white and taken with a telephoto lens. The beam first rested on the print on the upper right-hand side but was instantly moved away. There was no point in spending time on the features of the lifeless corpse which was lying on the floor beside him. It delayed for some time on the second picture before moving more quickly over the other two. The men in each photograph had similar features. The long oval faces making it difficult to tell them apart without close examination, and their blank expressions conveyed an airy sense of hopelessness. The clothes they wore were ragged and dirty and one of them, the man in the second picture, was clutching the lapels of his worn jacket tightly under his chin in what appeared to be a vain attempt to keep out the biting cold. They were winos, druggies, drop-outs, member of the dregs of humanity who occupy the hidden world which is to be found in every major city on earth.

Abruptly, Vogel put the lamp back into its original position. The decision was made. After pulling on the heavy coat which lay on the bunk he effortlessly threw the limp body over his shoulders. Disposing of it would not be a problem. In that part of the city the struggle to survive left little time for delving into the lives of others, and those who did notice something in the dimly lit corridors knew better than to ask questions. When, at last, he had left his crumpled burden lying in a stinking alleyway, to be found later by garbage-men, he had time to give his full attention to finding a replacement.

The next morning was spent moving along the lines that formed at the soup kitchen outside the Grand Central Station. The failure of his man to appear brought back the sickly feeling. The bum didn't form a pattern: this indicated unreliability and was one of the reasons he rejected him in the first place. The search went on; more soup kitchens, drop-in shelters, anywhere he might be hanging out. Vogel knew the territory as he had grown up in the city, but the search was eating up time, deepening the depression. He knew he would find him, but when? The longer the search the shorter the time for preparation; and the shorter the preparation the greater the risks. It was only ten o'clock, but already a knot was forming in the pit of his stomach, and if something didn't happen soon he knew that the gook with the rifle would be visiting as soon as he put his head down.

117

10

Weston had first met Gibbons when an editor gave him an assignment to examine the role played by the Republic's security forces in the fight against terrorism. Policemen are by nature suspicious of journalists. He could still remember the feeling of apprehension which caused him to shiver slightly, after being deserted by the young Garda who had shown him to the inspector's office.

'So, I'm to act as your nursemaid am I? The ultimate humiliation.' There was a severe expression on the features of the large, round face which slowly emerged from behind the newspaper, but Weston took comfort in the laughter he could detect in the pale blue eyes. 'Still, I suppose it will make a change from the humdrum routine of this place. Don't bother sitting down we have some walking to do.'

Gibbons jumped from his chair and within minutes they had made their way through the maze of corridors which made up the city police station and were standing opposite an elegant eighteenth-century building. It was there, without warning, that Weston first encountered the Irishman's unorthodox view of the past and irreverent sense of humour which did little to endear him to his superiors.

'Now, Mr Reporter, answer me this. What, in your

opinion, is the biggest mistake you can make when it comes to history?'

'I would need some time to think about that one.'

'Yeah, I suppose you would. Well, I'll tell you what I think. To me, the biggest mistake you can make is to assume that whatever has happened in the past was inevitable, and therefore above question. In some ways, that sums up the problems which have bedeviled this bloody island for years.'

'Please explain.' Weston was relieved to find that, far from resenting his new role, the big man was beginning to revel in it.

'That building over there is the home of the Old Irish Parliament, said to be one of the most corrupt political institutions ever to exist on these islands. But that's beside the point as it's now the headquarters of a bank.' Gibbons removed his pipe from his mouth using the stem to point towards the main entrance. 'Now, inside there you will find a symbol of what might have been. Hidden away and neglected is a plaque containing the names of employees who died fighting against the Germans during the Great War of 1914. The strange thing is that many of the poor bastards who accepted the King's shilling did not consider themselves to be fighting for the British Empire, but for Irish freedom. You see, the British government had promised Home Rule after the conflict provided every man did his duty, but as always, things did not turn out as expected. Whatever the great mistakes of history, those boys ended up committing the unforgivable sin of ending up on the losing side, thus having their memories swiftly despatched into oblivion.'

Without giving time for comment the detective turned swiftly on his heel and started to walk rapidly towards O'Connell Bridge, forcing Weston to break into a trot in his attempt to keep up. The lesson in Irish history had nothing to do with his assignment, but as he weaved his way through the pedestrians crossing the bridge the young Englishman was already captivated by the style of the unusual policeman.

'The men who fought the Kaiser were never to return as heroes because another outfit, with a little help from their enemies, were successful in turning disastrous defeat into glorious victory.' By now they had made their way half way up the city's main street and the pipe was indicating a large building dominated by rows of ugly windows and fronted by four Grecian columns. 'Half-way through the war a group of renegades, deciding things were not moving half quickly enough for them, set up their headquarters in the GPO over there and took on the British Empire in an attempt to establish a republic.'

'How did they do?'

'They lost of course. The rebellion was crushed within a few days and not only that, because they messed up one of the few public holidays of the year, the crowds lined up to spit and throw things at them as they were marched off to prison. The wives and mothers of the boys who had marched off to fight for the freedom of small nations did their share of shouting too, I can tell you.'

'You said they won a victory.'

'Well, this is where you lot come in, the enemy.' A tone of exasperation entered the big man's voice. 'You know something? For a people who succeeded in putting together an empire on which the sun never set there were times when you made some stupid mistakes. Deciding to execute the leaders of this irrelevant little side-show must rank up there with the best of them.'

'The creation of martyrs, I presume?'

'Got it in one. The problem with this particular bunch is that they have had us by the throat ever since; they

120

dictate from beyond the grave. Gradually, the idea that there were alternatives to the 1916 Rising disappeared and the ideas preached by its leaders became as if it were Holy Writ – those who questioned its objectives in grave danger of being burned at the stake. There are times when you think the whole thing is forgotten and then somebody goes on hunger strike, or makes an attempt at change, and out from the woodwork emerges the keepers of the Holy Grail warning against betraying the men of 1916. The names on the plaque are long forgotten, while the boys who fought in the GPO have streets and railway stations named after them.'

'Was it Napoleon who said that history was nothing more than the propaganda of the victor?'

'Yeah, but still you can't help thinking and wondering.'

'Would you go in and buy me a few fags, Mr Gibbons?' The sharp, pleading voice broke the spell and Weston found himself feeling an irrational hostility towards the thin-faced tramp who now stood looking up into the detective's face.

'Joey, would you cop yourself on. Can't you see I'm busy entertaining an important journalist from London? I have no time to be dealing with the likes of you.'

'But Mr Gibbons, they're a right shower in there. You know they won't serve me.'

'Well, maybe there is something.' The laughter had returned to the eyes as Gibbons winked at Weston before removing a large Havana cigar from his breast pocket. After tearing the wrapper and biting the tip he handed it to the tiny figure beside him. 'There, smoke that.'

But now the contrast was too painfully obvious. The devilment and hunger for life which had dominated the big man's features, as he watched with amusement the startled reactions of passers by when they became aware

121

of the cigar smoking tramp, had disappeared. The ashen-coloured skin and deep, furrowed forehead of the man sitting across from him in the small suburban sitting room had come as a shock to Weston.

'So you were the MI6 man in the States?'

'Sorry. I probably should have told you years ago.' Weston was nervous; it had taken Gibbons some time to respond to the confession and now he feared the severance of a friendship he both needed and valued.

'No, officially it was all the better that I did not know.' Again the policeman's reaction was to take him by surprise. 'Anyway, I suspected from the beginning that you had links with MI5 or one of that lot.'

'You bastard. How did you know?' The relief allowed Weston to laugh for the first time since the meeting began.

'Call is a sixth sense if you like. So what's the big deal? For years now we have been fighting a common enemy and it's only logical that we should work together. If the political situation forces us to keep it quiet, so be it. You know one of the big jokes of history is that we were supposedly neutral during World War Two, when in fact we passed every bit of intelligence that fell into our hands on to you lot as quickly as we could.'

Weston noticed the veil of depression, which had lifted slightly while the detective delved into the past, return again.

'Things are bad?'

Gibbons reached out and took the poker from its stand by the fire. 'When I was a kid, one of the things which attracted me to this job were the stories an old granduncle used to tell about his days on the force. Would you believe that his greatest ambition was to nab a character called Mixer, a rogue who committed the major crime of going about night after night without a light on his bicycle? One night he was sure he had him. He knew the route the arch-criminal would follow, so he hid himself in a ditch at the foot of a hill and prepared to pounce. Mixer came all right. The only problem was that he had built up such a speed there was no way my uncle could stop him. "Have you got a light?" he called out in desperation. "No why, have you got a fag?" came the bold Mixer's reply.' A wry smile appeared on the big man's face. 'Christ, those were the days. Now it's Uzi sub-machine-guns and Provos.'

A silence descended on the small room, and Weston was unable to find any words which would console the Irishman. The detective continued to poke aimlessly at the burning coals for a time before looking up from the flames again.

'Ever hear of Portlaoise?'

'That's the prison south of Dublin where most of the terrorists are held, isn't it?'

'Yeah, that's the one. Well, it was there that I learned that the world I was to operate in was to be very different from the one described by my uncle. I had been on the job only for a couple of years when all of us stationed in the city had to do a tour of duty down there guarding the prisoners. We went down by bus and after a few hours on the job were ferried back again. A few hours were enough. You should have seen them, Philip, young men who are so convinced of the rightness of what they are doing that no amount of reasoned argument can penetrate the sense of injustice which spurs them on. They have iron discipline, no outsiders let in, and all of it fuelled with a bitterness you could cut with a knife. Jesus, it frightened me then; now, with a wife and family to look after, it scares the hell out of me.'

'Well, in a way they have won. We are pulling out, and maybe that will lead to some kind of peace.' Weston's words lacked conviction.

'Ah, you know that's not true. It was the old policy of divide and rule which is responsible for the present mess, but it's some time since the Brits themselves were the real problem on this island.'

Gibbons moved from the armchair and stood looking out through the window at the children playing in the fading light. 'The most important regiment in the north is the Royal Irish Regiment. Up until a few years ago most of its members belonged to the Ulster Defence Regiment: men and women who are drawn from a community who want to keep the link with Britain not because they have any great love for London, but because they consider rule from Dublin as a threat to their whole way of life, a fate worse than death. In other words, the soldiers who carry out most patrols, suffer most losses and see most active service are not English, Scottish or Welsh, but Protestant Irish. The problem is, Philip, that these people have considered themselves to be under siege from all sides for centuries, and their hatred and bitterness is every bit as impenetrable as that of the men in Portlaoise.'

'So when we pull out they go for each other and all hell breaks loose.'

'That in itself would be disastrous enough.' Gibbons was back in the armchair and leaning towards the fire as if trying to gain comfort from the flames. 'The explosion will not be confined to the north east. Because of the ties between the Catholics on both sides of the border we are bound to be dragged in. In a way, the British pulling out is similar to the Kremlin withdrawing from the Soviet Union and Eastern Europe. All types of racial conflicts erupted between groups of almost equal strength and they went on and on because there was no Big Brother available to come in and bash a few heads together.'

'Why don't *you* just move out?'

'Too many ties. It's not just Kate and the boys. All my relations and friends are also here. It would be too much like deserting a sinking ship.'

'Look mate, the best medicine for you now is to concentrate on your own little part in this unfolding drama.'

'Even that is not as simple as it seems. Until Vogel moves, if he ever moves, I have no defined role to play, and because of my known association with the minister, I'm not exactly greeted with open arms at the operation centre. Right now, all I do is sit around depending on my beloved sergeant to ferret out what information he can.'

'At least get ready, be prepared for him if he does show. You know about the date we picked up in Castlereagh?'

'The Ireland–England rugby match on the sixteenth? We've known about it for the last few days. You've got to hand it to them. When they decide to put on a show they know how to pick their day.'

'Precisely. The crowds crossing the border for the match provides the cover for the movement of men and supplies, and the action takes place in a capital city crowded with media people which guarantees maximum publicity. But what the hell are they up to?'

11

'Go!' Superintendent Davy Bowman shouted the order into the microphone before slipping it back into its holder. The lead car, its hazard lights flashing, skidded slightly before disappearing between the tall hedges that lined both sides of the narrow lane. The second driver had already brought the engine of his car to life and, after expertly using the gears to build up speed followed on, leaving a third team of Special Branch men to bring up the rear.

On rounding the second bend the house came into view, a long thatched building with a large green door in the centre and two small windows at either side. It appeared deserted, but the winding black smoke rising from a single chimney indicated otherwise. Two men, each armed with an Uzi sub-machine-gun, jumped from the lead car before it ground to a halt in the centre of the farmyard. They moved quickly, taking up positions on either side of the green door. The one on the left used his boot to kick the door open while the other gave cover. They then pushed rapidly inside. Without waiting for a result the men from the third car were already pushing towards the outbuildings which stood to the rear of the house.

Bowman sat observing the operation, his impassive expression revealing none of the expectation or relief which were dominating his emotions. He knew the source was good. The information had always proved reliable in the past, and he was hopeful of having a haul of weapons by nightfall which would justify his actions.

Right up until the last minute he had expected the word from headquarters calling the operation off. His detestation of the desk jockeys in Dublin, whose only purpose in life seemed to be to make his job more difficult, was never far from the surface. Had they pulled the plug on this one he would have seriously considered resigning. In his world of black and white there was no room for diplomatic niceties. The political or tactical reasons put forward for holding back always seemed phoney, an indication of a lack of guts.

His thoughts were interrupted when one of his men emerged from the house. He wound down the car window.

'Anything?'

'Only the old dame herself, sir. Johnson is staying with her until you have the chance to have a word. I took a quick look around the place but there was nothing.'

'Hmm. Well, we were not expecting to find anything inside anyway.' The superintendent moved from the car and started towards the house. 'Help the boys check the area out, and I want special attention paid to the hay-shed.'

It was dark inside the house. The centre of the large kitchen was dominated by an old-fashioned, wooden table surrounded by a set of matching chairs, and on the wall opposite a small red light illuminated a large picture of the Sacred Heart. To the left of it, in the dimness of the corner, Bowman could just make out a portrait of Padraic Pearse, the leader of the 1916 Rising. It was a home in which his teachings would be no more open to question than those of Christ.

'Not talking today, Mrs Meehan?' Bowman spoke without looking towards the old woman sitting on the armchair in front of the open fireplace.

'I don't talk to Free State traitors.' The bitterness, the naked hostility in the response was something he had anticipated but he still could not arm himself against it and it cut deeply. Old woman or not he would strike back in kind.

'When are you and your lot going to stop living in this land of make-believe of yours? The Republic that Pearse is supposed to have founded has never existed outside the minds of a few dreamers. It's about time you came back from cloud cuckoo land and lived in the real world like the rest of us.'

There was no response but when he noticed the glint of victory in the old eyes which looked up from the fireplace he cursed himself inwardly. She had baited him, led him into a trap, and in his uncontrolled outburst he had admitted his doubt, granted her a victory. To the old woman he was the agent of a government who, by accepting a divided island, had betrayed a sacred trust and therefore had no more legitimate authority than the hated Brits. They looked at one another for a time, the religious fanatic endowed with certainty and the ageing policeman who, having abandoned the faith as a young man, at times found it difficult to suppress the nagging doubts.

'Suit yourself. We'll just have to wait and see.' It was Bowman who broke the silence first. Pulling a chair towards one of the small windows he took out a pen and gave the appearance of examining the crossword clues in his newspaper. Now the impassive features were disguising a growing anxiety. If there was something to be found they should have discovered it by now. The constant ticking of the large clock above the mantelpiece started to grate on his nerves, ruin his concentration, and in the end he stood up and walked outside.

'Any luck?'

The man standing in the small pit by the hay-shed looked up as he approached. 'Nothing, sir. This is the place all right, but as you can see it's empty. It would appear as if our bird has flown. We can get the boys from forensic in to find out what was stored here, and it might make it possible to press some kind of charges.'

As Bowman bent down to examine the empty pit he remembered the old woman's eyes. They had mocked him, laughed at his stupidity. For the first time he analysed all the tip offs, all the information which had come to him from the source he valued so much. The telephone was always used; usually the call was placed to his home. There were a few little things, a small arms dump here and there, which had built up his confidence, caused him to lower his guard and had allayed his early suspicions. The big tip offs had come as well – some important Provos lifted – but now, as he anxiously raced through his memory, he could not recall one that was original, one that did anything other than confirm what he already knew.

Today's operation had been intended as a move that would get one over on the top brass in Dublin, and prove that he had one of the best grasses in the business. The realisation of what had happened brought with it an involuntary shudder. It was as if somebody had hit him unexpectedly from behind. Some bastard had set him up, led him on by the nose, and now made him look like a bloody fool

'Pick everything up. We're pulling out.'

'Sir.' Recognising the tone, the sergeant decided against asking any questions.

The old woman stood at the window nearest the fireplace and watched the cars slowly making their way from the farmyard. The glare of the wintery sun highlighted the contemptuous smile on her wrinkled face. After seeing the conovy disappear around the bend in the lane, she returned slowly to her comfortable armchair.

Vogel arrived early at the airport and approached the check-in desk as soon as it opened. After completing the formalities he retreated to a position which would allow him to examine his fellow travellers as they hauled their luggage towards the girl at the desk. Usually, the beginning of a job brought with it an adrenalin flow which awakened a sense of elation, a feeling of being at one with the world. This one was different, bringing with it negative vibes from the start. First, he had had to blow away the druggie, and now there was an uneasiness which came with not being in full control.

It was the envelope with the airline tickets that had set the alarm bells ringing. Who did this Irish guy think he was? Did he imagine he was dealing with some greenhorn amateur or something? Vogel always made his own arrangements: travel plans, hotel reservations, the time and place for the operation. Never be dependent on others was the golden rule which had guaranteed a success rate second to none. The target and destination was all the client supplied before sitting back to await results. The sarge had listened patiently at the other end of the phone, giving enough time for Vogel's initial anger to run its course before mounting a subtle counter attack. The time-scale would have to be taken into account; there wouldn't be enough time for Vogel to make the necessary reconnaissance to mount the operation. This wasn't New York or Boston where he knew his way around. He was moving into strange territory where, although the language was the same, his accent, his manners and even his way of doing things would make him stand out in the crowd. Besides, the Irishman had assured him that he would have his very best men on the job. In the end the sarge had convinced him. Given time, the sarge could convince Vogel that black was white.

The group was the problem. A lone passenger on a scheduled flight awakened little interest; you were just another businessman making your way to a destination like millions of others. But in a group – and the Irishman's plan depended on travelling with a group – the loner stood out, his isolation making him conspicuous. It was the fatal flaw which would be spotted by a sharp-eyed undercover man at an airport, causing him to dig deeper. It was vital that Vogel merged, become just another tourist looking forward to visiting the great religious shrines of Europe.

The majority of the pilgrims who made their way through the security check at the main entrance were elderly or middle-aged women, who all moved along in groups of two or more. There was little hope of breaking into any of those closely-knit circles at an early stage of the trip. The few men all trotted along obediently after dominant wives who never failed to produce tickets, passports, and all the necessary documents from large handbags as they were needed. Eventually, there would be a male alliance which would break free and probably hold meetings in bars *en route,* but for Vogel the revolution would be too late in coming. In the end, he decided on the priest.

The small, overweight chaplain had already made a number of attempts to strike up conversations with different members of what, for the next few weeks at least, was supposed to be his flock. The response was disappointing, the cleric receiving at best polite but firm rebuffs. Now, the broad smile having disappeared from his cherubic face, he stood pretending to study departure times on the airport monitor. Vogel left his seat and moved towards him.

'Your first trip to Europe, Father?'

'Oh no. I have visited there on a number of occasions.' The look of gratitude on the round face was enough to let Vogel know he had guessed correctly: the man would be his friend for life.

'Indeed, I have had a great devotion to Our Lady for many years now and I have visited Lourdes in France on a number of occasions as well as going to pray at a number of other important shrines.'

'My first time and I am looking forward to it.' Vogel decided to pick up information which could add conviction to his stance as a pilgrim. 'This place, Knock in Ireland, our first stop, not very important as shrines go is it?'

'No, it could not be considered one of the major places of pilgrimage although it must be remembered that it was visited by the Holy Father which must be of significance. As for miracles, there are those who claim that the greatest one associated with the place was worked by a former parish priest who succeeded in forcing an unwilling government to build an international airport within a few miles of the shrine.' The small man started to laugh uncontrollably at his own humour and it was some time before he could speak again. 'However, I must confess to having a reason other than our pilgrimage to Knock for looking forward to our visit to Ireland.'

'Oh yeah?'

'Yes, my name is O'Brien, an Irish name as I'm sure you're aware. My grandfather came from a small village in County Cork, that's in the south of the country, in about the middle of the last century. I have already been in touch with the parish priest in the area and made arrangements to visit during our stay.'

'That should be interesting. Does that mean that you will not be travelling with us to Dublin?'

'No, I'll have to give that one a miss.'

Vogel greeted the news with an inward sigh of relief. Already the priest had latched on to him in a way that made him feel uncomfortable. Giving him the slip in Dublin might have proved difficult, but now that problem was taken care of. By the time the two men had taken their seats aboard the Boeing 747 Vogel was finding it impossible to concentrate on anything the little man was saying. The lecture on the places they were to visit just seemed to go on and on. Still, Father O'Brien was fulfilling his role admirably. To other members of the group, and more importantly to outside observers, it would appear as if the two men were old friends making the pilgrimage together.

The plane was already high over the Atlantic when the FBI informed both the British and Irish authorities that Henry Vogel had boarded a chartered flight at Kennedy Airport and was bound for Knock in the west of Ireland.

Thornley was within a few yards of the drinking club before he noticed that the sentry, who usually supplemented the ever watchful security cameras when the commander in chief was present, had not taken up his usual position. He glanced at his watch to confirm the time. It was not like O'Donaghue to be late, but if he was already inside, why wasn't one of his guardian angels leaning against the graffiti-covered wall at the opposite side of the street? After a second's hesitation he quickened his pace and pushed through the door before the doubts beginning to crystallise in his mind could take hold.

Inside, the room was empty. Newly cleaned tables and chairs covered the floor as if consciously waiting for the customers who, a few hours later, would gradually filter in for their evening's entertainment. But now all was silent and the fading light of the late afternoon gave the place a sinister, almost ghostly, appearance. Thornley did not move towards the sound of voices coming from inside the office. He stood still with his back to the door as he allowed his dark emotionless eyes to scan his surroundings. Over the years he had become adept at spotting the suspicious omission, the tell-tale sign. Doubts were now returning to warn against the instinct which encouraged him to forge ahead regardless.

Had O'Donaghue sounded friendly on the phone, perhaps too friendly? Was his great leader's sudden change of heart genuine, or was it an act to lull him into a false sense of confidence? Did the rat know something? If he had come to hear his report on Donegal then where the hell were the bodyguards? Satisfied that he was not under observation from any of the darkened recesses, the big man moved forward cautiously, trying in vain to make out what was being said by the muffled voices coming from the office. He halted outside the door and was just about to place his ear against the wood when it was suddenly flung open. The shock of what was revealed brought with it momentary paralysis. Now he wished he had followed those cautionary instincts.

'Ah, Big Boy, what kept you? We have been waiting for ages.' O'Hagan, wearing the contemptuous smile that never failed to infuriate, sat leaning back on the office chair with both feet placed on the desk. Behind him, one on either side, stood two of his henchmen, each armed with a heavy wooden club. But it was the thin, cowering figure leaning against the filing cabinet that brought the lump to the pit of his stomach, the premonition of doom.

'You good for nothing little bastard. I might have known, I might have known that there was no trusting a two-time little goat like you.'

'You . . . you're the informer, not me.' Blueface moved in behind O'Hagan as he spoke, a mixture of defiance and fear lighting up the large round eyes.

The sudden outburst brought Thornley's massive limbs back to life, awakening the instinct for self preservation. Like a trapped animal forced into a corner his moves became automatic, as if the body was acting without instructions from the brain. He grabbed the handle of the wooden door, pulling it shut, and immediately taking himself out of view of those in the office.

A sharp click came from the toilets to his left. He moved forward and bent down quickly. The man rushed towards him, somersaulted over his large frame and flew into the chairs nearest the bar. This early success gave him confidence and he moved on to the dance floor where he could make better use of his physical strength. The first man to come running from the office was also to underestimate the skill of his awkward-looking opponent. His inept attempt at a flying tackle ended as Thornley's fist crashed with full force into the side of his face. But the attack had distracted him just enough. A large wooden club struck home just below the big man's forehead.

The blow was not enough to finish him off but he

staggered backwards, and even in the dim light the daze which had fallen over his eyes like shutters was all too visible to his assailants. Like wolves anticipating a kill they mounted a co-ordinated attack. He continued to lash out blindly until finally a heavy blow to the back of the neck knocked the large ape-like figure to the newly polished floor.

The warm sensation of the blood which was oozing from his badly bruised gums was the first thing Thornley felt on regaining consciousness; the piercing pain which seemed to split his head in two came later. He used his tongue to slowly examine the gaps left by missing or broken teeth. The boys who worked him over had done a thorough job. When he tried to move into a more comfortable position he found that the ropes binding him to the office chair left no room for manoeuvre. After collecting his thoughts as best he could he forced open his right eye. The left one was so swollen it was tightly shut.

'Ah, Big Boy is back in the land of the living.'

O'Hagan was standing at the other side of the desk taking sadistic pleasure in a close examination of the heavily bruised face. 'We were afraid we had lost you and that would be a pity. You see, we have had our suspicions about you for some time now, from the time O'Donaghue went to the States, in fact. So on this occasion we decided to set up a little trap, and we asked our loyal friend Blueface to keep an eye on it for us.'

Thornley had to move his head slightly before he could make out the weasle-like figure who was again by the filing cabinet. Blueface was not cowering any more but, now that his former protector was safely bound, had taken up a more confident stance.

'I followed you that morning, the morning you went to meet the English reporter. I had a bike you didn't know about. I saw you talking to him, giving him all the information. You didn't see me, not for one minute.'

'Poor old Blueface, and who's going to look after you now? Him?' There was bitterness in Thornley's voice as he looked back towards O'Hagan. 'You poor bloody fool.'

'Remember a place called Melia's that Blueface and you visited during your travels?' O'Hagan continued as if no interruption had taken place. 'Well, they had visitors this morning, the Gardai. You know, your friends the Free Staters. Unfortunately, the boys were not there to meet them which it seems, caused them great disappointment. According to the mother they expected to find guns of all kinds. You know, the type that you saw when you were there.'

'Oh yeah?'

'Yeah. Now I wonder who could have given them that information?' O'Hagan had gradually worked his way around the desk until he was now standing directly above Thornley. 'Any ideas?'

The blow to the side of the head with a closed fist came suddenly, catching everybody in the room by surprise. The chair swayed to one side and Thornley, unable to keep his balance, fell heavily to the cement floor. As he was being pulled back into position the rough handling increased the pain from his cracked ribs to such a level that he was almost forced to scream.

'We are going to have a long talk, Big Boy, and you are going to tell us everything. Everything, understand?' The glare of satisfaction in O'Hagan's eyes indicated the pleasure he was taking in revenge.

'You jumped up little bastard. Who the hell do you think you are?' The combination of venom and contempt in Thornley's voice caught his tormentor unawares and shocked him into silence. The big man would not cry out in pain. There was no way scum like O'Hagan would force him into doing that. Still, he would tell them everything, reveal the lot, not because he was afraid, but because he wanted to watch those smug expressions change to looks of disbelief and finally humiliation when they found out how the slob from the Falls, poor old Thornley, had fooled them so completely over the years. They would find out how so many of their great schemes had come to nothing because he had passed on information under their noses. He would tell them about the young English reporter he had recruited to carry his messages, and how he had so often set up unsuspecting volunteers to take the blame for his activities. They would learn of everything except his reasons. Those he would take to the grave with him.

The words came flowing out as if a great burden was being lifted gradually from his shoulders. There was no need any longer to move in the shadows, to lead a double life, to mask his hatred for the man he had long pretended to serve. The end, when it came, could only bring peace and relief from a troubled and sorrow-filled world.

12

By the time the coach came to a halt in the large car park beside the hotel, Vogel had come to realise just how significant the sarge's words were. This was a different world. For him, religion had been something that was always far removed – a means of making kids fall in line or a consolation prize for the old – and yet dominating the skyline before him was a modern basilica dedicated to a god he had long believed dead. The bareness of the countryside on the journey from the airport and the bleakness of the small village on a cold, overcast day reinforced his feeling of alienation, of being an outsider.

He already knew that his arrival had not gone unnoticed. Horan International Airport is an impressive name for a small place, and the young cop had had nowhere to hide after entering the cramped reception area. The delay caused by an injury to one of the passengers would have exercised the inventiveness of a much more experienced operator, but all that kid could think of was to hide behind a newspaper. Vogel wasn't worried. He had anticipated a shadow and now he planned to use it to his advantage. The assignment of a rookie to watch over him revealed something else: he was not high on the priority list.

Father O'Brien was the problem. By now, the

protective mantle the priest had insisted on throwing over him was almost suffocating. The little man insisted on following him everywhere, looking after his every need. As long as the conversation was one-way there was no problem other than the sheer boredom. It was when the cleric started to ask questions that he began to sense danger. There were times when he had to trawl deeply into the lessons he had learned from the Sisters of Mercy many years before in order to come up with plausible answers for the innocent questions. He had allowed himself to believe that the nuns' teaching had given him an adequate reservoir of gestures and symbols in order to pass as an earnest pilgrim, but the obvious puzzlement on the part of the priest at some of his answers caused Vogel to reconsider. The invitation only added to the difficulties.

'Doing anything special this evening?' The priest had clung to Vogel as they left the arrivals area and was sitting next to him on the air-conditioned coach.

'No, nothing in particular. But I would like to have a good sleep after the journey and all.'

'Well, I'm sure you'll be able to have a rest in the afternoon. I intend to have one myself. The reason I ask you about later is that a number of us intend to get together for mass in one of the hotel rooms. I will be the celebrant and I would be delighted if you could come along.'

The priest looked expectantly at his new-found friend, with the air of a man who had just bestowed a great gift and now awaited the wholesome expressions of gratitude worthy of the gesture. Vogel was trapped. To refuse would be unheard of, but to accept would risk almost certain exposure as a fraud. He had not attended mass since he was eight years old and his recollections of what happened there were vague, much too patchy to allow

140

him to put up a convincing performance as a member of a small group. When should he stand? When to kneel? What prayer to say? What if he should be asked to play a particular part in the ceremony? He could remember how to bless himself and to genuflect before the altar, but that was it; enough to remain inconspicuous in a large crowd, but nothing more. Soon the whispering would start, the murmurings about his strange ignorance of so basic a sacrament, and all that was needed was one curious outsider to pick it up and he was blown. The knot began to form at the pit of his stomach; he would have to learn, and learn fast.

Later the priest delayed him again. Most of the group had retired immediately after the meal but the cleric insisted on continuing the conversation until in the end Vogel had to excuse himself and go to his room. It was late afternoon before he finally made good his escape through the hotel lobby and out into the open air. As he moved across the car park he pulled up the hood of his heavy overcoat to give protection against the persistent mist which was falling from the overcast sky. The next few hours would be spent observing, listening, absorbing the knowledge necessary to be accepted as a genuine pilgrim to one of Christianity's holy places.

'Can I get you something, sir?' The old woman standing beside her stall looked promising. The bad weather had reduced business to a trickle and the wrinkled face revealed all the boredom that comes with a slow day. She was ready to talk, to pass away the time with a curious stranger. For over a quarter of an hour he listened patiently as she told of the miraculous appearance of Our Lady to the local children. The visit of the Holy Father, and the great deeds of the parish priest who finally put Knock on the world map. When he finally left, taking with him his purchases of rosary beads and a number of small holy pictures, many trivial pieces of information were filed away which at some stage might be usefully dropped into conversation. The learning process had begun but the most difficult part had yet to come.

He sat in the basilica for over half an hour watching, scrutinising all those who came to worship, before being attracted to the woman who knelt at the edge of the seat in front of him. Her stillness alone was enough to radiate intensity but it was the sharp-featured face illuminated for less than a second by the opening of a side door, which finally made up his mind. He was good on faces and this one he had encountered many times before. It betrayed all the characteristics of a bigot, a zealot, one who was not only secure in the belief that her truth was the only truth, but was determined to reach out and impose it on others. Without standing he pushed across quietly and took up position behind the tall, thin figure as she continued to pray earnestly. It was not until she reached down to pick up a large prayer book on the seat beside her that he decided to break into her concentration.

'Excuse me, I wonder if you could help? You see, I am considering becoming a Roman Catholic but there are a number of things I still do not understand.' The eagerness in the small, pig-like eyes as the woman turned towards him served only to confirm his judgement. All his queries were answered at length and with enthusiasm, at times going into more detail than was needed, and as Vogel made his way to the mass in the hotel room that evening he was convinced that, if requested, he would be perfectly capable of performing the ceremony himself.

'The Garda Special Branch today raided a farmhouse

situated about five miles from Letterkenny in County Donegal. As yet, no further details are available but it is understood that they were acting on a tip off that there were weapons hidden in the area.'

Weston froze, the boiling water he was pouring into his coffee cup suddenly splashing over the edge. He looked in disbelief towards the television set before finally placing the kettle on the polished surface of the small table. It was only a throwaway line, a couple of sentences to supplement a report by the security correspondent, and yet it was enough. Enough to tell him that this time they had hung the poor bastard out to dry, fed him to the wolves.

Encircling his cup tightly with grasping fingers he had to restrain himself from venting the sudden surge of anger welling up inside by flinging it violently towards the carefully groomed newsreader who had so indifferently moved on to the next item. Rising suddenly from his chair he half ran, half stumbled towards the alcove where the telephone was fastened to the wall. Lifting the receiver with one hand, his anxiety caused him to fumble as he struggled to dial the number Gibbons had given in case of emergencies. The ringing seemed endless, bringing the feelings of helplessness and frustration to exploding point by the time he heard the click at the other end of the line.

'Mullens here.'

'Is Gibbons there? I want to speak to Gibbons.'

'Who is this?'

'This is Weston, Philip Weston, and I want to damn well speak to him. Is he there?'

'No, he's not here. Can I help? What the hell's wrong?' On recognition the sergeant's voice lost its composure and became more concerned.

'What in Christ's name are you idiots up to!' Weston

was now shouting down the phone, all attempts at restraint abandoned. 'You've exposed the Penguin. That raid in Donegal will blow him wide open.'

'Cool down! Cool down! Who's the Penguin?' The sergeant's response brought a weakness to Weston's legs. Damn Gibbons! Damn his secrecy! Damn his distrust of everybody, even his own sergeant! And now when he was most needed he was missing.

Weston was about to bang down the receiver in disgust, his mind racing in search of ways to warn the big Belfast man, when the first thud seemed to vibrate across the room. The second one came rapidly, this time allowing him to locate its source. There was an assault being made on the front door of the apartment; somebody was trying to force their way in. The tingling sensation at the tips of his fingers signalled the onset of the paralysis that, if he did not quickly fight back, would stick him to the spot, make him incapable of action. The third charge almost forced through the security lock. Soon only a flimsy chain would block entry. With a supreme effort he pulled the receiver back towards his mouth and forced himself to call out.

'Mullens, Mullens, they are here to get me. For God's sake, send help.' Now it was like a nightmare, his whole body covered in a cold, clammy sweat, the slightest movement demanding extreme effort. He left the alcove and moved across the main room towards the door which led to a small outside balcony. The banging on the door and the frantic voice coming from the telephone receiver, now dangling close to the apartment floor, made it difficult to concentrate enough to pick out the correct key. At last he found it.

Once outside on the balcony he quickly closed the door again and relocked it. The short breathing space was used to reconnoitre his position. A large white Opel,

144

blocking the entrance to the residents' car park ruled out
escape in that direction. By now, a consciousness that the
men were already inside, wrecking every room in their
search for him, added urgency to his decision. He
needed cover, somewhere to hide almost immediately
after making his break from the apartment block. His
best option was to make for a small clump of trees which
sheltered the sports field next to the flats. He slid over the
side of the first floor balcony, holding on to the
ornamental iron railing. When he was at full stretch he
released his grasp allowing his body to slip to the ground
below bending his knees on landing to avoid taking the
full impact of the fall. As he rolled over and struggled to
get back on his feet the feeling of breathlessness caused
him to curse his drinking, his lack of fitness.

'He's here. He's outside.' The shout came from the
darkened interior of the Opel.

'Don't shoot! We want him alive.' The warning was
from the balcony; the locked door had already been
forced open.

Straining every muscle to obtain maximum speed
Weston pushed towards the narrow path, which was used
as a short cut to the football field. The tingling sensation,
which had disappeared briefly, was now making its
presence felt again and, despite all his precautions, the
fall reactivated his old knee injury. He hobbled on. When
he pushed through the narrow gap the bushes would
protect him from the car park lighting, and then there
would be a chance.

'Hold it!' Without warning a man stepped out at the far
end of the short path and even in the dim light it was
possible to make out the revolver aimed directly at
Weston's head. 'You're not going anywhere, Brit. We've
got a few questions we'd like you to answer.'

Remembering the order not to shoot, Weston

considered pushing forward, making a break for it. This time his body refused to respond, the tingling having taken full control. Within seconds another man had grasped him roughly by the shoulder and together his two captors frog-marched him back to the Opel. He was still struggling to regain his breath as they pushed him into the back seat. Two miles from the apartment block they transferred to another car, this time a BMW, and, after turning right at the airport roundabout, the driver gradually increased speed as they headed northwards.

All the lights were switched off on the Bedford truck as it slowly made its way up the deserted cul-de-sac. The driver ignored the bricked-up windows and doors of the red-brick terraced houses, his concentration directed towards the reflection in his side mirror of the dark figure just inside the corner of the street entrance. There would only be time for one signal, one wave of the hand, to indicate the approach of a police or army patrol; giving just two minutes to turn and move out.

'This is the one.' A military figure, a balaclava covering his face, had opened the cab door and was already sliding from his seat. As the truck came to a halt he jumped on to the footpath and walked briskly towards the nearest house, his eyes scrutinising the brickwork closely as he approached it. After a short examination he slowly began removing blocks from the doorway and carefully placed them to one side. Within a short time a large hole had appeared in the entrance.

Two men who had climbed silently from the rear of the truck carried a number of large circular tubes through the opening, up the narrow staircase and into a small back room. The front-seat passenger, after lifting two gas cylinders from the trailer followed on into the darkness.

The driver had time to turn the lorry around and place it ready for departure before one of the men reappeared.

'He says you are to take him up now. I'll take over and keep watch down here.'

'Ah, Christ, why can't you do it?' The man at the wheel, revolted at what was happening, had hoped to avoid taking part.

'Come on, John. You know what he's bloody like when he gets into one of his moods.' The voice, which never went above a whisper, was pleading.

Without answering, the driver left his seat and strode quickly to the rear of the truck. Pushing the rough canvas covering to one side he used his arms to hoist himself inside. After lowering the flap again he switched on a torch and hurriedly examined the stretched-out figure on the sandcovered floor below him. The bruised face almost looked clownish, both eyes surrounded by a dark colouring and the lips thick and swollen. The left jaw was badly disfigured, probably broken.

'What a bloody mess. You poor stupid bastard.' There was genuine sympathy in the exasperated voice. Slipping the torch back into his pocket he prepared to lift the broken body on to his shoulders. A muffled groan was the only indication of life to emerge from the crumpled figure as the driver again slid silently from the trailer and moved towards the newly opened doorway.

Once inside, he paused to take his bearings. To use the torch would be dangerous as the light might attract attention. As he moved up the narrow staircase, the great weight of the body made it difficult to balance and at one point he stumbled and almost fell through the railings onto the uncovered cement floor below. Beads of sweat were forming on his forehead and the strain on his shoulder muscles had become almost intolerable by the time he struggled across the small landing, falling into

147

the room at the other side.

'Drag him over there.' O'Hagan, his balaclava now removed, nodded to indicate the wall to his left. 'Then give Jimmy a hand at the window.'

The procedure with the back window was to be the same as the front door. Some time before a number of the blocks, used to protect the deserted houses from vandalism had been loosened, and now all that remained was to remove them. The first one was always the most difficult, the tips of fingers needed to coax it from its position, but after that the task became gradually easier until finally the opening was wide enough to serve its purpose. By then, all the necessary fittings had been added to the long cylinders and the mortar launchers were ready for action. The mortars themselves stood ready in the corner opposite the window. The equipment was old, dated, something that might arouse suspicion if enough of it was ever recovered. But as the purpose of the whole exercise was to cause confusion, to sow the seeds of doubt, that might prove to be a bonus.

'Right, move him over here.' O'Hagan indicated the floor just next to the launchers.

'Is there any need? The poor bastard's already been through the mangle.'

'Move him now.' The venom in the response made the driver regret his outburst. Punishment for dissent was often as swift as it was vicious. 'I want to make sure that no clever-arsed medical examiner can make out what happened. I want to keep them guessing.'

'Any word on the English guy he squealed to?' Now the driver appreciated his companion's attempt to divert O'Hagan's attention as he moved the body into position.

'The information was passed on hours ago. If they want him he will have been picked up by now.' O'Hagan pulled the balaclava back over his head before making a final check around the room. 'That's it, everything's in place. Now move.'

The driver was the first to make his way across the landing and run down the staircase towards the opening. Once out on the footpath he stood in readiness to start rebuilding the blocks as soon as the other two emerged. The work was carried out quickly. It only had to be good enough to avoid attracting attention in the dark. After stopping briefly to pick up the look out, the truck moved away from the city and out into the Antrim country-side.

The motionless figure lying on the dust-covered floor was oblivious to the small light bulb which lit up, indicating that the first mortar was about to go off. Neither was there any visible indication that he heard the explosion when, five seconds later, it exploded harmlessly a few yards away from an army post. The second bulb did its job in setting off the propulsion charge, but this time the bomb was flawed and instead of taking off in search of some distant target it blew up before leaving the tube. The explosion shattered the stillness of the deserted street and completely destroyed the small terraced house.

Normally there was but one punishment for informers: they were shot as a warning to others who might be tempted to betray the movement to the foreign invader. But to publicly expose somebody who was known to be so close to the leader could only do harm, and dent the image of infallibility which had been nurtured for so long. After consideration it was decided to use the elimination to raise questions, to invalidate the source. When the Brits discovered the body they might suspect the truth, but then they could never be sure. Was the Penguin's information reliable or was he playing a double game? The empty arms dump would deepen concern and a notice in a newspaper a few days later, mourning the death of a volunteer on active service, would do little to dispel nagging doubts.

Even in death, Jim Thornley would prove to be an awkward customer.

13

A heavy throbbing, which seemed to explode at the centre of his head before thumping against the back of his skull was the first thing Weston became aware of on his slow return to consciousness. It took some time before he could remember being pushed into the back of the BMW. The blow to the back of the head and the flashes of bright lights had quickly followed. Since then there had been nothing but darkness. Now, the constant swaying motion of the speeding car brought on nausea, making it difficult to regain any sense of composure.

'He's coming round. Should I put on a blindfold?' The sound of the broad Dublin accent was enough to arouse his curiosity, pull him one step further on the road to recovery. Opening his eyes slightly he could make out a large burly figure, silhouetted against the night sky, sitting across from him on the back seat.

'No, no need. We got him where we want him now.' The darkness made it impossible for Weston to make out the features on the face which had suddenly turned towards him from the front of the car. The voice this time had the sharper tones of a northerner. 'Welcome back to the world of the living again, Mr Weston. I'm sure you'd like to know that we are bringing you to meet an old acquaintance who would dearly like to meet you again.'

'Oh, that will be nice. Know him well, do I?' Weston was surprised at the lack of concern in his response. It wasn't the first time his voice had failed to reflect the growing anxiety inside, and he had come to look on it as some kind of subconscious means of defence.

'I wouldn't get too clever if I was you, Brit. Word has it that you have a few interesting questions to answer when we arrive.'

'Wouldn't know what they were I suppose?' He pressed on, hoping the veneer of indifference might goad the man into revealing something relevant. 'You see, in my job, I'm usually the one asking the questions.'

'Oh yeah. Any more fairy stories while you're at it? I think the best thing is for all of us to wait and hear the questions together. Right Dub?' The face turned towards the second man in the back seat.

'Yeah, that's a good idea.' The gruff response marked an end to the conversation with the man at the front turning to look out through the windscreen again.

Weston strained his eyes in an attempt to pick out landmarks but after the car turned off the main highway and started to make its way along narrow country roads the exercise became pointless. For most of the journey his view was blocked by high hedges which lined each side of the road, and even when a break came the moonless night allowed him to make out little more than the outline of a farmhouse or a hay-shed, with absolutely nothing to distinguish them from thousands of others which dotted the countryside. He gave up and started to concentrate on making himself more comfortable, a task not made any easier by the brutal way in which his hands were tied behind his back.

'This is it!' The suddenness with which the driver jammed on the brakes caught Weston unprepared; the unexpected jolt projected him forward so that his head came crashing against the headrest on the front seat. 'Now for Christ's sake get him out of here, quick. The boss will do his nut if any activity is spotted by a bloody patrol in this area.'

'OK. Jack, get him the hell out of there.' It was the front-seat passenger who barked the order, stepping out on to the road as he did so. The Dubliner leaned over Weston and pushed the rear door open as wide as he could. He then proceeded to bundle his prisoner in front of him out onto the nearby bank. There was no standing on ceremony. The leader held open the large iron gate until both men were through and then closed it again. The red tail lights of the car that brought them disappeared unnoticed into the darkness.

The Dubliner stood alongside Weston until the leader had time to catch up. Then both supported him under either arm as he stumbled across the uneven surface of the newly ploughed field. They moved towards a line of conifers sheltering the large farmhouse which could just be made out through the branches. To Weston, everything was a haze. The blow against the seat had started the throbbing again and this time it was accompanied by a sharp pain. It was as if somebody was pushing a needle through his forehead. By the time they reached the trees his inability to stay on his feet was sorely trying the patience of his captors.

Pushed through a narrow gap at the end of the row of trees he found himself in the corner of a farmyard. Once again, the Dubliner stood guard over him as the leader moved forward. The large lanky figure strode towards a hay-barn which was situated near a ditch farthest from the house, halting beside the large steel pillar which marked the end of the second section. He then used his heavy walking boots to stamp three times on the ground.

153

The sudden appearance of a hole in the hay-covered surface caught Weston by surprise, and it was not until he was standing over it that it was possible to make out the camouflaged trapdoor which had opened to reveal an entrance to an underground chamber.

'Now, you're going to have to climb down into the bunker. I'm going to have to guide you because the hands stay tied. Understand?' Without waiting for a reply the big man swung him around until they were facing each other. Then, after placing a hand on each shoulder, he moved him backwards until he was standing just above the entrance. The first two rungs of the ladder proved difficult but after that there were no problems until he reached the ground. The Dubliner followed him down; the leader taking up the rear, closing the trapdoor as he came.

'All right, switch on the lights again.' The voice came from the other side of the chamber, northern, but more cultured than the leader's. 'I'm sure our guest will have more than a passing interest in his surroundings.'

The sudden flash of light from the powerful bulb hanging at the centre of the room dazzled Weston, temporarily blinding him. He had to blink hard before he could make out the figure sitting on the timber bench which lined the opposite wall, and even then it proved impossible to bring the face into focus.

'Well, Mr Weston, are you impressed? Surprised?' The figure stretched out a hand to indicate the surroundings before standing up to walk towards the new arrivals.

'Interesting. But if I am to make notes you will have to untie my hands.' There was a tremble in his voice. Now even the false bravado was deserting him.

'Notebook?' The figure stopped, his face now hidden in the shadow. 'Oh yes, you are a reporter. Now, Mr Weston I think it's time we dispensed with that little fiction, don't you? We have had a talk with a friend of yours, a one Mr Thornley, or the Penguin, which is the name you might be most familiar with. He had very interesting things to tell us about your reporting, very interesting indeed.'

Now the figure began to walk again, away from the shadows and into the full glare of the artificial light. He was unshaven, two days of growth emphasising the already tired look on the pale handsome face. Recognition came to Weston suddenly, bringing with it a slight shudder. The last time he had seen that face was in a dimly lit bar in New York. He was in the presence of O'Donaghue.

Gibbons folded the newspaper roughly before slamming it angrily on the wooden seat next to him. His bad humour had made it impossible to concentrate on what he was reading. The consolation he had obtained by tearing strips off his know-all sergeant was short lived. No matter which way he looked at it, the buck stopped with him. He was responsible for the whole bloody mess. Still, Mullens should have known. Damn it, everybody knew Bowman was a madman, a lunatic capable of messing up the best laid plans without even trying. As soon as word had come through that the nutter wanted to make a raid he should have been consulted, and all the half-baked excuses about not knowing where he was were just not good enough. Christ! He should have been found.

'You were right, sir. We have got a file on our friend.' Mullens looked apprehensively towards Gibbons before lifting the newspaper and sitting down. 'His name is Hogan, Jack Hogan and he lives in Darndale. First came to our notice when he took part in actions against drug-pushers in the area a few years ago. You know the usual, the law cannot protect our kids from the merchants of doom so Sinn Fein and their friends the Provos move in to do the job.'

'How far will he go? Anything on him being prepared to use firearms?' As he spoke, Gibbons moved his attention from the players on the pitch who were only going through the motions for the press photographers, and looked towards the man leaning against the barrier at the far sideline.

'Nothing that can be proved.' The sergeant flicked over to the next page of his notebook. 'He is suspected of being involved in a knee-capping about three years ago and we are fairly certain that he took part in the assault of a couple of pushers. One of them was lucky to escape with his life. But, as usual, nobody is prepared to talk.'

Gibbons tapped his teeth with the stem of his unlit pipe. It was as much curiosity as professional interest that had brought him to the airport the evening before. His interest in athletes – their size, their weight, their potential speed – was not unlike a punter's fascination with thoroughbreds, and where better to view them than in the arrivals section?

He had decided against waiting on the ground floor. There was too great a chance of being spotted and forced to talk to one of his colleagues on official duty. Instead he had taken up position in a restaurant which overlooked everything. As he observed the comings and goings below his policeman's mind decided that the slightly balding man with the large, ungroomed moustache did not fit in; he was not part of the pattern. The businessmen, confident and in a hurry, emerged from behind the glass doors and strode towards the exits and their waiting cars. Others, less familiar with their surroundings, moved more slowly as their eyes searched anxiously for whoever had promised faithfully to be there to meet them.

The tide ebbed and flowed but the man with the moustache remained constant; never checking the departure times, never looking up in search of a friend or relative. It was not that he lacked curiosity. From time to time, his eyes appeared briefly just above the rim of a thick paperback, and they nervously swept the floor for a watcher, somebody whose interest his presence might have awakened. However he had never thought to look up.

When the English rugby party made their way from the customs clearance area Gibbons was finally convinced that he had hit on something significant. Not for a second did the man allow the excitement caused by the welcoming officials and the media activity to draw his attention away from his book. If ever there was a case of working too hard at being disinterested this was it. After the group had left the building he made a telephone call before departing himself. And now, here he was again mingling with the small crowd of reporters, photographers and hangers on who had gathered to watch the first training session of the visiting team.

'Shall I pick him up, sir?' The sergeant's voice broke into his thoughts.

'For what?'

'Well . . . acting suspiciously?'

'In what way? He may be just a rugby fan who wants to watch the opposition prepare for Saturday's match.'

'Ah, sir, a fanatical fan – from Darndale. It just won't wash.'

'And you'll stand up in court and say that before some clever dick of a solicitor will you, sergeant?'

Mullens didn't respond immediately. His eyes were

directed downwards to avoid the sarcasm in the inspector's tone. 'But what the hell is he up to?'

'Who knows?' Gibbons pushed his pipe firmly into the corner of his mouth before continuing. 'But think of the coup if they succeeded in pulling off something big during the match. News of it would be flashed around the world complete with television pictures within hours.'

'But hardly the type of publicity that even they would want, sir.'

'Maybe not.' Gibbons snapped open his lighter, allowing the flame to ignite the carefully prepared tobacco. 'Anyway, this Hogan is only small fry. What we need to know is the overall plan, who are the main string-pullers. I want you to follow him, sergeant, find out where he goes, where his orders are coming from.'

'On my way, sir.' Mullens did little to disguise his relief. He was fed up to the back teeth with his inspector's bad humour.

Gibbons again turned his attention to the players on the pitch. Usually, he enjoyed the buildup to big sporting occasions, the soaking up of the circus atmosphere allowing him to relive his own past glories. But today, nothing could relieve the guilt of being responsible for the death of the northerner and the disappearance of Weston. It kept gnawing relentlessly at his insides. Resigning himself to going back to the office he reached out for the newspaper, only to find that Mullens had taken it. It was after he stood up that he discovered that his pipe had gone out.

'You know who's over there Leona? Mrs Johnson. You remember Mrs Johnson who used to live next door to me?' There was concern mingled with sympathy on

Madge Green's face as she put the half pint of lager on the table in front of her friend. 'Would you like to come over and talk to her? I'm sure she'd like to meet you again.'

'Ah, no. I'd rather not Madge. Oh, but you go ahead, you know how it is. I'd rather be on my own for a while.' The voice was weak, full of resignation and as lifeless as the brown eyes that looked up imploringly from the pale, wrinkled face.

'Are you sure now? She'd be delighted to see you again.'

'No, I just want to be by myself for a while. Do you mind?'

'Of course not. Anyway, I'll be back in a few minutes.'

'Thanks. You're very good.' Leona Pierce now regretted having allowed Madge to coax her into coming out for a drink so soon after getting the news. The woman's intentions were good, they always were. Still, it was too soon, somehow it showed a lack of respect. She lifted the drink from the table but then, changing her mind, put it down again without allowing the glass to touch her lips.

'Oh God. Oh God. What am I going to do?' What should have been a cry, a scream, was, little more than a whisper causing not a ripple in the noisy din of the crowded pub. The loss of a son had brought with it an emptiness, an everlasting ache she found impossible to explain to those who had never experienced it. She thought of him every day, the tears constantly threatening to well up and spoil the paper-thin front she struggled to present to those around her. She had convinced herself that there was no greater pain, that there was no room left, but she was wrong. The death of Jimmy, her protector, her comforter, her brother, had doubled the agony until it was impossible to bear. Her trembling hand lifted the glass again; this time she swallowed down a gulp of the bitter liquid in the hope that it might draw a veil over the pain.

The small, insignificant woman, absorbed in her own thoughts, did not even merit a passing glance from the two men who were moving from the bar towards the table just a few feet from where she sat.

'See the paper this morning?' The taller of the two spoke while pulling a stool towards him. 'That should cause a nice piece of confusion for the Brits.'

'Yeah, but the big bastard didn't deserve it.' The response was laced with an intense hatred. 'A volunteer killed on active duty! Christ, when I think of some of the men who did go out and die, and now to think that that traitor is going to be numbered among them. It just makes me sick.'

'Cool it, for Christ's sake. He suffered for what he did, that I can tell you.' The tall man inhaled smoke from his cigarette and retained it in his lungs for a few seconds before releasing it back into the already polluted atmosphere. 'God, O'Hagan's a sadistic bastard. One of these days I'll do him, I swear I will. You know when I carried the poor bollocks up those bloody stairs he was broken in bits, hardly one bone in his body was still in one piece. I mean, I ask you, what's the point in that?'

'It wasn't half good enough for him.' More venom had crept into the dissenting voice. 'Remember how he lorded it over everybody here, strutting about as if he owned the place? You could hardly open your mouth without having him come down on top of you like a ton of bricks. Jimmy this and Jimmy that, and all the time the great man was legging it off to Donegal and spilling his guts to the Brits. The lowest form of life is an informer and he was the lowest of the low.'

'No, I'm glad things turned out as they did.' The tall man placed his glass on the table and leaned back on the chair. 'He's gone, so he can't do any more damage. There's still a sister with a couple of kids left behind and I don't see any point in having them branded as the relations of a traitor.'

'I'm not so sure about that, not so sure at all.' The second man, who sat with his back to Leona Pierce, picked up the glass in front of him and emptied it without pausing for breath.

Madge Green looked concerned as she moved back through the tables. The conversation with Mrs Johnson had lasted much longer than she had intended and she now felt guilty for having abandoned her old friend in the poor woman's greatest hour of need. On reaching the darkened corner her heart sank as her worst fears were confirmed. Leona had gone off on her own.

14

'Do you have to stop here? You're blocking the whole bloody street.' The middle-aged traffic warden was struggling to regain ground, to salvage at least some semblance of his badly dented authority.

'It's official business and I'm in a hurry.' Jim Darby, already putting the warrant card back into his pocket, walked away from the humiliated official without even a backward glance. Normally he had sympathy for those who had to do difficult jobs. Being a detective he knew all about the problems involved, but now he was having to make a conscious effort to suppress the smug smile which threatened to cross his youthful face. The man had gone too far, played the little Hitler once too often, and now the young policeman felt no guilt at the inner glow of satisfaction that came with watching the deflated expression on the chubby overweight features. The warden had clashed with a more powerful force and he wasn't liking it one little bit. Anyway, there wasn't any choice. Without back up, and with the tour bus within minutes of its destination, he had no option but to abandon his car and follow on foot. If he had delayed the action until later the resulting hooting of horns and angry cries from motorists, trapped in the rush hour traffic, would have attracted too much attention.

The casual strollers, brought out onto the footpaths of

Merrion Square by the bright Spring sunshine, provided cover for the young plain-clothes man as he slowly gained on his quarry. He preferred to work in the city where the pedestrians and window shoppers made it possible to merge into the background and become part of the scenery in a way that made it almost impossible for a target to spot his tail. The thought of his first move at the airport still made him cringe. The journey there had taken longer than expected which meant that the plane had already landed by the time he was pulling into the car park. The doors to the small arrival and departure lounge had hardly closed behind him when he knew he had blundered, landed himself right in it. There had been no time to check the place out, decide on how he would shadow the group after they left for the hotel. Once inside he had panicked, deciding to stay put instead of making a hasty retreat. The longer he stood there, leaning against a wall and pretending to read a newspaper, the more conscious he became of the absurdity of his position. His youth, his clothes, his very attitude distinguished him completely from the group of middle-aged and elderly pilgrims who alone occupied the building. He stuck out like a sore thumb. The delay caused by an injury to one of the passengers was the last straw, convincing him that if Vogel was only half alert his cover was already blown.

The assignment was not on the high-priority list. If it had been Gibbons would have found the necessary manpower and there was no way that a rookie, less than a year out of uniform, would be left carrying the can. Still, it was an opportunity, a chance to impress, and he was angry with himself for having got off to such a bad start.

After a while, Darby's youthful optimism overcame the initial depression, helped on by the behaviour of his

163

target. Picking him out from the crowd had presented no difficulty: the briefing in Dublin had been spot on. In the beginning, Darby was cautious, doing nothing to arouse suspicions more than he had already done. It was after it became obvious that the American's energies were fully occupied trying to blend into the crowd, not to appear like a fish out of water, that the detective allowed himself to lower his guard. Even if the crouched shoulders to disguise his height, or the grey tinted hairs to add age had proved sufficient to deceive the onlooker, the ignorance the man displayed at religious ceremonies would still have proved his undoing; standing when he should kneel, failing to genuflect in front of the altar and having little idea of what to do at Holy Communion all detracted from his credibility as a true pilgrim in search of the holy places. The universal uniformity of practice in the Roman Catholic Church leaves little space for the non-believer to hide. By the time the stay in Knock was over, Darby had decided to keep his reservations about his first day's performance from his superiors at headquarters. What they didn't know wouldn't worry them.

Now he was having to struggle to suppress the doubts again. It was the delay that was giving them the opportunity to re-emerge. Having already passed the narrow entrance to the Natural History Museum he was forced to pause and lean for a time against the railings that stand guard over Leinster Lawn because, due to the heavy traffic, the coach had still not reached its destination. What if the guy had been playing him along all the time? What if he had already used some excuse and slipped from the coach and disappeared into the urban maze? He allowed the train of thought to continue until the first member of the party stepped out onto the footpath and started towards the entrance to the National Gallery. Then, with a supreme act of willpower he brought his thoughts to heel, and took control again. By the time his target alighted and moved towards the rest of the group his confidence had returned. He was ready for action again.

Darby waited until everybody was inside before moving forward to push through the glass doors. Once inside the entrance hall he moved to one side and pretended to browse through the books on display as he waited for the guide to finish her talk on the artist Jack B. Yeats. He then followed as she led the way to where the paintings were on display. The exhibition was housed in a large room and by sitting on one of the benches in the centre of the floor, it was possible to keep everybody under observation. It was a quiet morning. There were only two visitors other than the Americans, which meant any attempt at a clandestine meeting could easily be picked up.

It was probably Darby's conviction that art could never interest him, that he was immune from its spell, which allowed him to become absorbed in 'The Liffey Swim'. It was only the noisy banging of the crutches on the polished floor as the injured American struggled to catch up with the rest of the group, that drew him away from examining the faces in the picture and made him suddenly aware that the room was almost empty. As he hurriedly made his way towards the exit he had little time to examine what was left behind. But even if he had, he would not have noticed that a small black package which had been taped under the bench nearest the door as he came in, was now gone.

The tall building looked strangely more welcoming at night-time. Bathed in the strong beams of the floodlights, the wire mesh, which protected the windows, somehow looked less forbidding and the ugly barrels which acted as a barrier against car bombs, became almost invisible in the darkness. Leona Pierce stood for a time, attracted by the beckoning glow which filled the doorway, but still finding it impossible to come to a decision, turned and walked away for the third time.

It was years since the vallium had awakened a sense of well being, an inexplicable feeling of happiness, and now all she could hope for was a numbness that at least deadened the pain for a time. Today they had hardly worked at all. She had swallowed the tablets as soon as she got home from the drinking club and it seemed as if her head had hardly touched the pillow when the cruel world, with all its burdens, came cascading in to take over her mind again. Her two youngest, Sean and Aine, were now the only reason for struggling on, for not ending it all. Yet the thought of them did not bring with it any hope or relief; it only added to the helplessness, the despair, that stalked her every moment. Who was going to look after them now that Jimmy was gone? Who was going to protect them in this hell of a city?

Ever since childhood, Leona had felt safely cocooned in her big brother's strength. He even broke with convention by holding his little sister's hand as he walked with her to school during her first year. She still had a vivid memory of those fierce eyes challenging the other boys to sneer, call him a sissy. None of them ever did.

Much later, when she defied her parents and went ahead and married John it was Jimmy who had come to her defence, supported her through the ordeal. The marriage went sour very quickly, but due to a stubbornness which would never allow her to admit a mistake, and the arrival of children, most of whom were conceived in an alcoholic haze, there was no road back.

For years, a sense of shame combined with a warped loyalty caused her to hide the beatings from her brother, often disguising a bruise or creating a plausible story to explain away a black eye. The expression on his face the night he finally discovered the truth was something that would remain with her for ever. He had entered the kitchen unexpectedly, finding her leaning against the sink in an attempt to prevent her badly bruised body from crumpling into a heap on the floor. She was sobbing uncontrollably, unable to answer the battery of questions which came shooting at her. She remembered watching the intial look of concern become horribly warped as it gradually changed to anger when he realised what had happened. It was the first time she had witnessed her brother in one of his all-consuming rages and the experience had been frightening.

There was to be no reconciliation with John. He returned about two weeks later, still limping from the beating inflicted on him by Jimmy but only as a lodger rather than head of the house. One year later, unable to stomach any more humiliation, he left for good and it was after that Jimmy moved in. In many ways it was like old times; life became more tolerable again. Tolerable, that is until her son, her eldest child, was brutally murdered.

Her sudden anger at the memory of what she had heard in the bar pierced like an arrow through the despair. How could that little runt, that little nobody, tell such lies about her brother? Jim Thornley an informer, a grass? Impossible! Her brother had hated the Brits with every bone in his body and never would he, never could he betray his own people. Now it was those very same people who were forcing her, leaving her with no choice but to go against everything she believed in; to act against nature itself.

It was on rounding the corner, when the large floodlit building came back into view, that the faces of Sean and Aine returned to haunt her. Surely they would be able to provide a new identity, set her and the kids up in England, or even Australia. They had done as much for others who had helped them; she had read about it in the paper. Away from Belfast, a new beginning. The sudden onrush of euphoria was enough to prompt the first vital steps towards the distant doorway. But the harp on the cap of the uniformed guard standing at the entrance momentarily brought back the enormity of what she was doing. To her the harp was always the symbol of injustice, the badge of the agents of the Crown who harassed and suppressed the Nationalist minority while allowing the Protestants, with their drums and orange sashes, to trumpet their superiority and dominance to the world. But by now her purpose had taken on a momentum which was impossible to halt. There was no turning back.

'And what can I do for you Mrs?' The desk sergeant, who at first looked tense, visibly relaxed when he realised that it was only a frail, middle-aged woman who had nervously walked through his station door.

'I want to talk to . . . I want to talk to somebody in charge.'

'Oh, and your name is?'

'I'm Leona Pierce.' She hesitated before adding, 'Jim Thornley was my brother.'

'Thornley. Is that the guy who blew himself up with the mortars?' The plain-clothes man looked up from the papers he had laid out on a table a few feet from the main desk.

'He didn't blow himself up.' The contempt in the man's voice made her angry again but by now there was no choice but to continue. 'He was killed, they murdered

168

him because they thought he was working for you.'

'I'll take it from here.' The tall, well-dressed man moved from the table, through the flap, and was standing beside her. 'Now love, don't take it to heart. We would be very interested in anything you have to tell us. Why don't you come along with me?'

'But my kids, they're all alone. Will you look after them?'

'Don't worry about a thing Leona. We'll take care of everything.'

Moving along the corridor towards the interview room she had time to reconsider her first impressions of the man walking alongside. He wasn't cruel and unkind as she had first thought. No, now he was gentle and considerate and prepared to do almost anything to reassure her. She would place her trust in him; he was the one to provide her and the kids with the escape route she so dearly prayed for. It was like being a child again, just as safe as when Jimmy held her hand on the way to school.

15

O'Donaghue stood in the semi-darkness watching silently as his men carried weapons through the tunnel, from the small chamber, before placing them against the wall beneath the trapdoor. The emotionless mask he wore over his features betrayed nothing, leaving only the nervous twitching of his index finger, which tapped ash from a cigarette he was smoking, to indicate the inner impatience. The fools had hit the Englishman too hard, so much so that now, after almost two days, he had still not fully recovered. He was still sinking in and out of consciousness between brief periods of coherence. If he didn't perk up soon this whole part of the operation would be for nothing.

O'Donaghue disliked periods of inaction; they gave too much time to think. To get to the top he was prepared to say, parrot-like, all those phrases he knew were expected of him; to laud the heroism of 1916 and urge on the fight for the Republic so treacherously betrayed by the quislings at the beginning of the century. In reality, he detested the Fenians who depended too much on the Americans, and had little time for the United Irishmen or the alien ideas they had borrowed from the French Revolution.

Ever since he was a boy his imagination was captured by an earlier, more exciting time. A time when the Gaelic chieftains of Ulster lived and died in a whirlpool of anarchy and bloodshed, a time when the ever-present danger made life worth living. The men of the northern province had fought long and hard to keep the deadening tentacles of central government from enslaving them, from snuffing out their spirit. From the beginning he had modelled himself on the greatest one of them all, the chieftain who had fought the last great battle in defence of the ancient world. He imagined himself using wild lieutenants, such as O'Hagan, in exactly the same way as the cunning old fox had used guerrillas such as Tyrrell and Ownie O'More. They were to be flattered, cajoled, harangued, but never trusted; never allowed the information which would enable them to strike back. How he longed to shout out what he knew to be the truth; that it was in Ulster that the final stand was made, that it was Ulster which had preserved the faith, that Ulster was all that was worth fighting for.

'Ah, back in the land of the living, Mr Weston.' The slight stirrings of the Englishman as he awakened from an uneasy sleep, was enough to attract O'Donaghue's attention. 'You've been away for some time. We were beginning to get worried.'

'Your concern is touching.' Weston's attempt at flippancy was hampered by the dryness he felt in his mouth.

'You know, as you were sleeping, I was thinking of how appropriate your name is. The last great attempt to halt English imperialistic ambitions in this province was led by a great chieftain called Hugh O'Neill. He held you lot out for nine years. Now the interesting thing is that he had an English secretary named Weston, a man who turned out to be a spy. Isn't that one of the strange coincidences that makes life interesting.'

'Look, I already told you, I am a journalist.'

171

'We had our suspicions about your friend Thornley for some time. The arms dump just helped to confirm it.' O'Donaghue ignored Weston's protestations. 'He also proved useful when it came to spreading the odd piece of misinformation. As for you, Mr Weston? Discovering you proved to be an unexpected, and welcome bonus.'

'Well, if you know everything, you know it's all over. We're pulling out.'

'Yes, a right pack of rats deserting the sinking ship.'

'Christ! Where does it end? I always thought that's what you bastards wanted.'

'Ah, Mr Weston.' O'Donaghue sighed in disappointment. It was as if he expected a deeper, more searching response. 'After being our uninvited guests for almost a thousand years it is hardly fair that you should be allowed to depart on your own terms.'

'Our own terms?'

'Look around you. In this little corner of the United Kingdom where you now sit – you are back across the border by the way – in the last quarter of the twentieth century a man was elected to the European Parliament who firmly believes that the Pope is the Anti-Christ and that the European Economic Community is little more than a Roman Catholic plot. South of the border you have Catholic laws written into the constitution and any attempt to remove them results in uproar. You want permission to walk away leaving us firmly stuck in the sixteenth century, Mr Weston. We are left with a formula for stagnation, with the gombeen man and his power hungry friends using all their energy to keep their bankrupt little state afloat in the south, while in the north the holy protestants will be ever vigilant in their efforts to root out any fiendish Popish plots to extend the rule of Rome over their territory.'

172

Weston's journalistic instincts now came to the fore, suppressing earlier fear. 'There are those who say that your real reason for preventing the hated Brits from pulling out is that you need us to justify your grubby little war. If the imperialistic forces were gone, how could you justify the killing of fellow Irishmen, no matter what their political beliefs?'

'We need you, all right, and the strange thing is that it is your restraint rather than your determination to stamp us out that makes it necessary to hold on to you. In a sense you guarantee our continued existence.'

'So all the calls for the Brits to pull out so that a united Ireland can be formed is just so much hot air?'

There was no warmth in the smile that brushed slowly across O'Donaghue's face. 'Your faith in rhetoric is touching, Mr Weston. The problem is that no matter how empires break up, or how nation states regulate their borders, the oppressed will always be with us. If they are given a choice is it not reasonable that they choose the oppressor who will exert least pressure?'

'I fail to see the point.'

'The point is, Mr Weston, that we the Nationalists, the Catholics, the Republicans, or whatever you care to call us, have been moulded together by oppression and discrimination in a way which makes us unique on this island. We have no real connection with the people in the south. Oh, I know we hear fine speeches from their politicians from time to time but the truth is that neither they nor their electorate, understand or care. They don't want to know.' By now, O'Donaghue had moved forward and sat on a small stool opposite Weston's bunk. 'Now, if the Brits leave in the morning what will happen? We will be left with a reactionary government determined to bring to heel that part of the community it has most reason to fear. Full force will be used against us and as always we will be used as convenient scapegoats for everything that goes wrong. This time there will be no pretence at keeping within the law because, unlike Her Majesty's Government, they will have no pretensions on the world stage and, therefore, will not be very sensitive to world opinion.'

'The British and Irish governments would never tolerate anything like that.'

'Don't play games. You're long enough in the business to know better than that. The Brits will look worried and say how terrible it is that the stupid Irish are at it again, but by then they will be out and they will stay out. The Republic as we have learned to our cost in the past, will protest and tolerate us on their soil until we become a threat. Then they will come down on us like a ton of bricks. We are in danger of becoming a displaced people, Mr Weston. Europe's answer to the Palestinians, and I for one am determined that it won't happen.'

'So the hated Brits are at least preferable to the native alternative.'

'Precisely. It's worth remembering that no matter how bad things are now, they are, in many ways, better than before Her Majesty's troops came onto the streets.'

'That's a matter of opinion.'

O'Donaghue was no longer listening, his attention turned towards the approaching Dubliner. The two men spoke briefly before O'Donaghue stood up and went to supervise the men who had started removing the arms from the bunker. The burly Dubliner then moved behind Weston and without speaking, roughly pulled his arms behind his back and proceeded to bind them with a coarse piece of rope. He operated quickly, obviously under pressure, and did not notice Weston hold his wrists slightly apart as he tightened the last knot.

174

Political power is based on contacts, inside information, knowing the right people. The well-positioned office with its large, polished desk and expensive decor is but a symbol. Without the essential ingredient it can seem like a gilded cage. In public the possessor of such power attracts attention as a bright light attracts moths. There are always those eager to share a table, impart useful gossip or ask advice. These hangers-on, little people, act as a barometer, an indication of where you stand in the pecking order, and it is when they no longer crave your company or sing your praises, that you know you are on the way out, finished.'

Mac Entee was on the way out and he knew it. There were several theories floated as to why the once golden-haired boy, the future leader of the party, now found himself in no-man's land. The theory favoured by the professional pundits, the one pushed from on high for public consumption, was that his performance at justice was not all that it might have been, that it was well below par in fact. There was also a certain amount of gossip about the suitability of his wife: too pushy, likely to tread on the wrong toes. But the insiders, of whom he was one, knew the real reason. The once Crown Prince had mistimed his push for the top job; he had allowed himself to be panicked and moved too soon. The quiet word about his undoubted leadership qualities to trusted reporters, the intimate lunches with influential columnists, had all misfired. The leader, who still considered himself to be in his prime, feared a conspiracy. Now it was sources close to the ultimate seat of power who spoke darkly to the same reporters and columnists about the character flaws, the personality defects, which made the man at present responsible for law and order totally unsuitable for high office. A new heir apparent was being groomed and presented to the masses for their consideration. The man for the future was Thomas Cunningham, Minister for Foreign Affairs. The hated academic.

The knock on the door caused him to look up. It was a trusted aide, one who knew how to keep his mouth shut that he had held back to admit Gibbons through the small side door before leading him through the long deserted corridors to the ministerial office, but still he could not help feeling nervous. What if the man let something slip? What if somebody in security saw what was happening and reported it? In the conspiratorial world in which he existed a wrong move could make an already bad situation hopeless. It was only as the door opened that he realised that part of his uneasiness was due to the expectations he had of the meeting. It was as if in some strange way he expected the policeman to throw him a lifeline, present him with a solution to all his problems.

'Come in John and sit down. That will be all, Martin, thanks.' The politician's anxiety became obvious even before the door had closed behind the aide. 'Anything for me?'

'Nothing much. I suppose you already know about the guy we spotted watching the English rugby team?'

'Oh yes, your superiors were in a very talkative mood at this morning's conference. They even went as far as telling me one or two things about him. What do you think of the idea that they plan to hit the team?'

'Could be, but not likely. If they were to kill or injure any of the players, or any of the fans, it would hardly be in keeping with the image they are trying to project. For freedom fighters to kill a group of innocent rugby supporters would take a lot of explaining.'

'If an attack on the team is not part of the plan, why waste resources watching them? It hardly makes

176

sense.'

'They may have something else in mind, Minister.' The use of the formal title was deliberate, an indication that the detective still felt uneasy at being dragged into the shadowy political world. 'If they intend making a big show all they need to do is attract the media's attention. This might be achieved by delaying the team coach on its way to the stadium, or even going as far as kidnapping the players for a few hours. Either way, they get the publicity they need and it will all add to the impression of anarchy we assume it is their objective to create.'

'I suppose it would.' Mac Entee reached out for a manilla file which was lying at the corner of his desk, and flicked it open before continuing. 'This Hogan character keeps interesting company I see.'

'That's why he hasn't been picked up. My sergeant discovered his interesting connections the first day he tailed him, so we decided to keep the surveillance going in the hope that it might lead us somewhere.'

'And?'

'Nothing so far. He follows the same routine faithfully every day. After following the team coach back to the hotel he moves off to report to his overlords.'

Mac Entee leaned across the desk, a new intensity lighting up his features. 'You're parroting John, spouting out the official line. Damn and blast it, I could have picked up anything you told me from my wonderful morning briefings. If I'm going to have a chance I've got to know what the hell is going on!'

Gibbons hesitated, considering his response. When he did finally speak his voice betrayed resignation. 'The truth is that you are being fed the official line because none of us have a clue as to what they are up to. Take Hogan for a start. The man's an amateur, picked out on his first day. Why have the Provos, twenty-five years in the same game, selected this boy to carry out what appears to be a very sensitive operation? There are two possible answers. One, their manpower is so over-stretched they had no choice; two, they wanted us to spot him. So, we can't afford to ignore him in case he is genuine while, on the other hand, if he is bogus we are being made right idiots of.'

'The important thing is not to get bogged down in the relative side-shows to be orchestrated by Hogan and your American explosives friend. The accumulation of all the intelligence that has come in over the last few days suggests that the Provos intend putting on a display that will capture the public imagination with a vengeance. They want the 1916 Rising to happen all over again. We know that a few of their top people have been carrying out reconnaissance all over the city, paying particular attention to the GPO, I might add. Arms movements are also reported from all over the place. When you think about it, the strain all this activity is putting on their organisation might indeed explain the use of half-wits like Hogan.'

'You mean they intend taking over a few key points in the city and then daring us to put them out?'

'That's about it, and of course we will have no choice but to react. No sovereign government can sit back and let that happen, and I need not point out that there is no way we can be seen to negotiate with the IRA.'

'The whole thing's crazy. They're making the same military mistake that was made in the original rebellion, getting themselves dug in with no route of escape.'

'It makes sense if you look at it from their point of view. They are desperate. They know that if the British pull out it is only a matter of time before they are crushed. Oh, I know that after the first few months things might change, we might even have a civil war to contend with. But by

178

then, these boys will be yesterday's men. Their little empires will have crumbled and a new generation of hard men will have grabbed the torch. It's a last desperate gamble to preserve their power.'

'The men, the equipment they'll lose, how in Christ's name are they going to replace all that? They'll have nothing left.'

'I'm getting sick of people attributing super-human powers to these thugs. Is it not just possible that they are about to make a mistake?' Mac Entee immediately regretted his outburst and loss of control.

'Why don't we just move in and arrest them, cut the whole thing off at the source.'

'I've already explained that it is not politically possible to move now and later be accused of doing the imperialist's work for them after the announcement of withdrawal. It's asking a lot to ask any government to pay that price, John.'

'And then of course there's the hidden agenda.'

'Hidden agenda?' The look of puzzlement on Mac Entee's face looked contrived.

'The one that allows this government to have its cake and eat it. If the shootout takes place, the whole myth that the Brits have worked so hard to build explodes, forcing them to stay, while at the same time you get a wonderful opportunity to give the Provos a bloody nose.'

'OK. OK, but don't play holier than thou with me John. The truth is that the vast majority of our citizens, and that includes you, benefits if the *status quo* is maintained. If the British insist on going we will have to make the best of it, but by Christ I have no qualms in making their leaving as difficult as possible. And as for our great patriots, over the last few years they have almost become a state within a state – and now is as good a time as any to bring them to heel.'

As Gibbons walked back towards the small side door the lack of progress on all fronts gave him a feeling of absolute failure. He felt resentful at having been pulled away from his small, safe office. The information becoming available was confusing an already complicated picture, and he was still no closer to discovering the ultimate purpose of all the manoeuvring.

16

The hollow thud from the automatic rifle as it fell against the wooden bunk was enough to waken Weston; they were changing the guard again. As he opened his eyes and looked towards the figure that had thrown himself across the grey blankets he was conscious of a sinking feeling at the pit of his stomach. It was the man he had christened Nervy, and Nervy was the weak link, the vulnerable point. It meant that if he was going to make a move, it had to be now. There was no more reasoning the problem away, no more excuses. He was progressively growing weaker and soon it would be too late.

Three men had been left on guard, each spending half hour intervals watching over him in the large chamber while the other two occupied the smaller room where the arms were stored. He had not been physically attacked but from the beginning he was conscious of the softening up process to which he was being subjected. All requests for food or water were ignored and the prisoner was only communicated with when necessary, and in the roughest manner possible. The light radiating from the powerful bulb hanging almost directly overhead was boring into his brain making it difficult to concentrate. When the time for interrogation finally arrived the combination of isolation and disorientation would have broken down all defences and left him like putty in their hands.

It was the involuntary twitch in the man's left eye that had prompted Weston to nickname him Nervy as a way of distinguishing him from his companions. The other two were good, never allowing their concentration to stray from their task while on duty. But the slightly built man with the oily black hair parted in the middle was very different. From the beginning it was obvious that Nervy was bored, disinterested, wishing that he was somewhere else. His attention span was much too limited to notice the slight movements which were gradually allowing Weston's hands to edge their way free from the hasty bindings of the Dubliner. The chance seemed even better when an attempt by the sentry to join in the conversation of the other two was met with a stinging response. The irritation had made the twitch more noticeable than ever.

Nervy pushed farther into the bunk and sat with his back against the cement wall. Using his left hand he pulled a cigarette packet from the breast pocket of his military-style jacket and flicked it open. The actions of placing the filter tip between his lips and lighting the match were routine, almost automatic, but just needed enough concentration to allow Weston to make the final vital tug on the rope which brought freedom to his wrists, without being noticed. The hours of sitting with his arms tied in an awkward position had sapped all the strength from the muscles of his upper arm, allowing his hands to fall apart with the loosening of the rope. Had it not been for the playing cards, discovery would have been inevitable. Nervy had taken the pack of cards from a side pocket and, after allowing the pack to slide into his right hand, tossed it carelessly on the bunk. Soon the game of patience was to prove all absorbing, the prisoner sitting a few feet away all but forgotten.

Slowly Weston allowed his aching arms to slide down

along the side of the chair. As the numbness faded it was as if every sinew was silently screaming in protest at having been left in such an unnatural position for so long. To recover fully they needed time, time he could not afford. It was as Nervy pushed the second cigarette between his lips that he decided to move. Now both hands were occupied; one grasping the small box, while the other, holding the match between thumb and finger, slowly guided it towards the waiting sandpaper. The eyes continued to concentrate on the neat row of cards spread across the bunk.

Nervy's concentration on the card game was broken only by Weston kicking against the chair which was necessary to release his left foot from the final piece of binding. The unexpected movement startled him, reminding Weston of a rabbit paralysed when caught in the glare of oncoming headlights. When he did finally recover he made the wrong move, diving towards the rifle. Falling across the bunk exposed him to attack and the heavy blow to the back of the neck, delivered by Weston's intertwined fingers proved decisive. The frail body slumped to the floor, knocking over the rifle as it fell.

As he listened for a reaction from the other room Weston considered moving Nervy's body to one side so that he might retrieve the weapon, but because of his weakened condition he decided against it. The conversation in the other room continued as before. Phase one was complete. He moved silently across the chamber towards the ladder which led up to the trapdoor. Climbing onto the second rung he reached up and quietly released the bolt which secured the steel covering from the inside. The door was stiff, forcing him to exert all his strength in an attempt to push it open. When it finally gave way it did so suddenly, making a loud creaking noise. He listened again; now the talking had stopped and the silence seemed deafening.

Pulling himself hurriedly through the narrow opening he pushed through the nearest hedge, oblivious to the briars and thorns which tore into his exposed hands and face. On the other side he was confronted by a deep ditch, its dark muddy water standing as a barrier between him and the firm ground just a few feet away.

'You move towards the road. I'll check around here.' At the sound of the voice from the other side of the hedge Weston froze, not daring to move a muscle for fear of exposing his position. Deep breaths were taken in and silently exhaled as he attempted to regain his composure. The clear, windless night allowed him to monitor the muffled footsteps of his pursuers and he allowed himself a slight feeling of triumph when they finally faded in the direction of the outhouses which surrounded the farmhouse. Now he slid silently into the water at the bottom of the ditch and moved towards the high bank opposite. After pausing again, like a wild animal sniffing for danger, he dragged himself up into a newly ploughed field.

As his eyes scanned the darkness it was the flickering light which periodically illuminated a part of the distant hedge which gave him a target, provided an irrational hope. There just might be somebody there who would provide an avenue of escape. He had few options. In his exhausted state a move towards the road was too dangerous and to venture out into the open countryside risked being hopelessly lost.

At first he attempted to cross the ploughed field but he soon found the uneven surface impossible to negotiate in the dark and it was necessary to retreat to the grassy strip which went around the perimeter of the field. The effort had already made him breathless, every stumble draining away vital reserves of energy. He adopted the technique which had served him so well during his cross-country running days at school; he set up short term objectives, a bush here or a tree there, which allowed him to reach his destination in stages while shielding his mind from the true distance to be covered.

At last he stood peering through the bushes which separated him from the flickering light. There was a fire burning on the other side. He could hear the crackling wood and above him the brightly coloured sparks were clearly visible as they shot into the night sky. He could make out voices when he was still some distance away but now, right up beside them, it was impossible to make out what was being said because of the strange accents. At least they were not northern.

This time he hesitated before pushing through the bushes, the scrapes and cuts he suffered at the hay-barn still fresh in his mind. He paced backwards at first, in the hope that the greater the speed the less chance there was of him suffering further wounds. The slight rustle in a nearby bush, which he mistakenly believed to be caused by one of his guards, finally spurred him to action. Charging forward he tripped over a strand of bullwire, extended about a foot from the ground, before tumbling onto the grassy surface on the other side of the hedge. He narrowly missed falling head first into the bright yellow flames.

'What the Christ have we here?' The smell of alcohol from the small ugly unshaven face staring down at him succeeded in reviving and sickening Weston at the same time. 'Where the hell have you dropped in from?'

He turned to one side in an attempt to escape the foul-smelling breath and noticed the figures moving slowly towards him. Their initial shock at his sudden appearance was now overcome by curiosity. Poorly dressed children led the way, closely followed by their shawl-covered mothers. Tinkers! The sudden rekindling of hope caused all feelings of exhaustion to evaporate.

'Help me! I'll make it worth your while.' Slowly, so as not to arouse suspicion, he indicated his desire to place a hand in a pocket beside his belt buckle. After the small man had nodded his assent he used two fingers to remove the plastic wallet containing his credit cards. 'With this, I can withdraw three hundred pounds. All you have to do is get me to a cash machine in Dundalk.'

'Get in there!' The reaction was instant. The small man was now standing using his index finger to indicate a small circular tent a few feet from the fire. Weston did not stand, but crawled on his hands and feet across the wet grass before rolling inside. Through the flap he received orders to stretch out against the back canvas. He had hardly time to get into position before two children, each clutching blankets, followed him through the entrance. It was the small wiry girl, her hair cut short, who covered him over while the boy spread his blankets out on the floor. The operation went smoothly, giving the impression that this was a strategy often used before, and within seconds the pair were lying, as if asleep, using him as a pillow.

He was more relaxed now, the sight of the women bringing some relief from the earlier tension. It was the heavy dark skirts and chequered shawls that confirmed that he had landed among the outcasts, the untouchables. The era when the tinkers because of their ability as tinsmiths were welcomed by the housewives of rural Ireland had long gone. Once they were needed to supply and repair essential household items but the advent of mass production had rendered their skills redundant, and now the proud nomadic people could expect only hostility and pressure to move on from the settled community. Like all despised and oppressed peoples they had come to mistrust all outsiders, to live on their wits. The battles of the other world were there to be exploited. Their loyalty was available only to the highest bidder and for now, that was Weston.

'Anybody see a man running across the field over there?' The voice struggled for breath after the run through the ploughed field.

'What the hell do you bastards want here?'

Weston shuddered. The menace contained in the small man's voice was enough to make the gunman edgy, unpredictable.

'Watch it, you old goat or you might be sorry.' There was a clicking sound, a gun was being cocked.

'Ah, that's it all right. Great heroes you IRA boys when you got a gun.'

'For Christ's sake Da, will you shut up?' Weston did not recognise the voice of sanity. He could only guess that it belonged to one of the young men he had caught a glimpse of standing by the caravan as he crept towards the tent.

'That's it son, tell your old man to have sense.' The gunman's voice was now growing in confidence, the running footsteps indicating back up. 'It's about bloody time you got here. Check the tent and the caravan.'

The second gunman brushed against the canvas as he set about his task. One of the flaps was pushed back. Weston felt sick with tension as he became conscious of the interior growing brighter. He considered pushing out through the back and making a run for it, but the stiffness in his legs and a nagging pain just above his eyes made any such move out of the question.

'Ma, there's somebody shining a light in my eyes!' It was the girl who called out. She then started to cry; the high pitched wailing of a frightened child in an enclosed space was ear piercing. Within seconds the volume was increased by the boy screaming in sympathy with his sister.

'Take it out on the childer would ya?' It was the angry voice of one of the women, who, from the shuffling sound, Weston guessed had forced her way past the searcher. 'There, there, Grainne, your mammy's here now.'

'Make the brats shut up you stupid bitch!' Uncertainty in the gunman's voice already indicated defeat. The frustration with the whole business was getting too much for him. The flap was thrown back in anger and heavy footsteps passed the back of the tent as he moved off in the direction of the caravan.

'Keep the crying going until he is well away.' There was no need for the woman's instruction. If anything the volume increased. Practice had brought the act to perfection.

17

Weston's fingers felt numb. The freezing cold of the night before had eaten right through to his bones, and now even the heating in the van going at full blast failed to expel the pain which was preventing sleep. Looking up through the half closed eyes he was just able to make out the outline of the two young men who sat on either side of him. Staring out into the darkness they paid no heed to the crumpled figure stretched on the floor beneath them.

'You English are ya?' It was the taller of the two, the one Weston had come to like, who finally broke the silence. He was the one who had brought food when Weston was forced to wait in the wooded area near the caravan, smuggled out a blanket to protect him from the chill of an overcast spring day, and finally guided him silently through the trees and on to the canvas covered floor of the van he hoped would carry him to safety.

'Yeah, I'm a newspaper reporter.'

'Well, Mr Reporter, I think you can get up off that hard floor now and sit over here beside me. They've not attacked so far so the chances are we're safe, at least for the present.'

After awkwardly turning himself around, Weston pushed back on to the narrow wooden bench which lined the side of the van. 'Some damn job this, come to do a report and end up getting into this mess.'

'Look mister, keep your lies to yourself. We're not interested.' This time it was the weasel-faced older brother, sitting opposite, who interrupted. 'You needn't have any worries about us landing you back with the Provos either. We've made a deal with ya and, no matter what you and your sort think of us, we keep our bargains.'

The hostile interjection brought an abrupt end to the conversation, leaving Weston to stare, with the others, out into the night. The narrowness of the road and its state of disrepair, indicated by the constant bumping movement, told him they were using one of the unapproved routes to cross back over the border into the Republic. He struggled to remain conscious but in time the combination of heat and tiredness caused him to slip into a sleepy drowsiness which allowed his mind to escape from the constant pressure it had known for almost twenty-four hours.

'A few weeks ago they came to our camp accusing us of stealing from the church.' It was impossible to estimate how much time had passed when the friendly voice resumed the conversation as if it had never been interrupted. 'The Provos I mean. Shot my younger brother in the leg they did, and by God that was the biggest mistake they ever made. A lot of broken bones and bloody noses that night, I can tell ya. That's why the boys coming after ya last night didn't hang around for long. Afraid of their bloody lives they were.'

'Shut up for Christ's sake! You don't have to tell him everything.' It was not until the driver glanced angrily backwards that Weston recognised the evil-smelling face which had stared down at him when he first stumbled into the camp. 'Don't lead him on mister if you know what's good for ya. The less we know about you, and you know about us, the better for everybody.'

190

Again there was silence but by now the need for sleep was gone and he remained alert. The road was smoother, and the frequent glare of passing headlights was enough to confirm that they had moved from the sideroads onto a more important highway. The passing traffic would have made him feel more secure had it not been for the angry, bulging eyes he had caught gazing towards him from the rear-view mirror. The little man was hostile, on the make, and needed to be watched. From the beginning he had tried to win over the men in the camp, obeying every instruction without question and taking every opportunity to make small talk. The only positive response had come from the tall one. The father and his eldest son remained aloof, always keeping their distance. They were not going to allow him to establish a bond, a camaraderie, which might later act as a barrier when it came to exploiting his potential to the full. What he would give to know what was going on in that little scheming head at that very minute.

'Now, mister, it will soon be time for you to use that fancy card of yours to pay us what you owe. After that I never want to set eyes on you again.' The little man threw a knowing glance towards his eldest son as he spoke. 'Eamon, come up here and keep a look out for one of them machines.'

By now, orange-coloured lighting was illuminating the road and in the distance Weston could make out the traffic lights. They were entering Dundalk from the northern side. The border town had proved a good place for picking up stories in the early days, and his many visits there had made him familiar with its landmarks. Local knowledge was to be his only advantage, an advantage he would have to use well.

The old man slowed down the van as it passed the church and moved into the wide main street. Both footpaths were deserted except for a few late night drinkers making their way home from the pubs. The weasel-faced youth failed to locate what he was looking for on the first run, and it was obvious that the little man's patience was close to breaking point as he did a u-turn and headed northwards again; the discovery of the cash dispenser coming just in time to prevent an explosion of his pent-up anger. As Weston stood in front of the brightly lit screen he was surrounded on every side, all possible avenues of escape cut off. His decision to punch in the wrong series of numbers was deliberate.

'What in Christ's name is happening?' The little man stared in alarm at the brightly coloured warning which suddenly started flashing from the monitor.

'He's done the bloody thing wrong. The bastard won't be able to get the money!' Weston felt a sudden jab of pain as Weasel-face drove a tightly closed flat fist into his left kidney.

'Hold it! Hold it! It gives me a few goes before it eats up the card. I'm just nervous, finding it difficult to remember the number.' The tension was building nicely and as he stood preparing to punch in the numbers for the third time discipline had disappeared. Now all three craned over his shoulders in an attempt to watch the machine's reaction to his final attempt. It worked, access was achieved and Weston could sense the sudden relaxation on the part of his guardians as the new display appeared before them. His move was made against the youngest son, the friendliest, the weakest link in the imprisoning wall. The sudden push with the right shoulder opened up a gap wide enough to break through, to start his run for freedom. His knowledge of the local geography had allowed him to plan the escape route in advance. Within seconds he hoped to disappear into a maze of side-streets.

'Eamon, you come back here and work this bloody machine. Let Sean do the runnin'!' Again he had guessed right. The father had no intention of abandoning the money machine before it had yielded up its riches, and now there was the added bonus of having the eldest son pulled out of the hunt. The one pursuer left would be half-hearted, unsure of himself, partly because the odds were now more even but mostly because he had come to have sympathy for his prey. Soon Weston felt confident enough to slip in behind a garden wall and survey the territory behind him. The youth had stopped running and was now walking slowly along the road, occasionally glancing from side to side as he moved. Finally, while standing at the centre of a crossroad, he made a gesture with his long arms which was interpreted as a sign of farewell by a pair of eyes he seemed to know were watching him. A minute later he turned and started to make his way back to the main street.

Twenty minutes passed before Weston reached the square. While moving along the side-streets, with their tidy terraced houses, he had felt safe, inconspicuous. Now, passing the large civic buildings was like emerging from under a cover, coming out into the open again. He stood for a time in the shadows at the side of the courthouse, listening, watching, imagining enemies behind every tree that lined the footpath. Minutes passed before he summoned up enough courage to leave his hiding place and cross the street. He quickened his pace as he moved past the water fountain and was constantly looking back over his shoulder on the way to the railway station.

The waiting was to prove the worst part of all. When the mind is not occupied in directing actions it has time to consider, to worry, to know that if they really wanted to stop him this was one place they could not possibly ignore. He crossed the bridge and took up a position at the wall on the other side. It gave a clear view of the station entrance and there was a clump of trees nearby to provide cover. An hour later all his reserves of heat had been used up and the freezing cold started to bite again, gnawing at the tips of his fingers and turning his toes into blocks of ice. He resisted the temptation to clap his hands or stamp his feet. The clamour might draw unwelcome attention, and he had to be contented with blowing hot air into cupped hands.

It was half past five when the headlights of the first car turned into the long car park. Soon it was followed by another and another, as the passengers arrived to catch the early morning train to the capital. He walked across the road and hesitated for a time at the large gate before deciding to make his final move. The distance between the entrance and the main building was a long one and the nervousness at the pit of his stomach caused him to stumble slightly as he took the first step along the path. Moving towards the Victorian building housing the ticket office and the entrance to the platforms, he felt his body instinctively tense, as if anticipating an attack to come from one of the many dark hiding places left by the weak overhead lighting. When he finally walked into the entrance hall he found it deserted except for a porter who clipped the tickets of the passengers as they moved towards the platforms.

'Single to Dublin.' He pushed all his remaining cash under the glass window towards the clerk on the other side. The man's sudden startled expression made him conscious of his physical appearance. He had not shaved for days, and for a panic-filled minute he feared that he would not be allowed to travel. When, after a slight hesitation the ticket, along with the change, was pushed in his direction the relief caused tears to well up in his eyes. He was exhausted, depressed, and on the point of collapse.

His unkempt appearance was enough to guarantee him a seat to himself, and soon the rhythm of the wheels beating against the tracks had lulled him into a deep semi-conscious sleep.

18

'Mr Sharkey. Did anybody see Mr Sharkey?'

Jim Darby cursed silently as he glanced towards the anxious courier who was searching the lobby of the Grade A hotel for her missing pilgrim. Sharkey was at it again. Ever since the grey-haired old man had sprained his ankle at Horan Airport he had caused delay after delay, destroying any chance the detective had of remaining inconspicuous. He had pleaded with Gibbons, begging him to provide him with more back up, but all had fallen on deaf ears. He was given Smith, good old Smith, to cover for him at night and that was it. Vogel would need to be blind and deaf not to have spotted him by now.

'I'll go and see where the guy is.' Darby recognised his target's voice. It was obvious from the beginning that the big guy was attracted to the courier and took every opportunity to ingratiate himself. After a short conversation with the clerk on duty he picked up the receiver of one of the telephones on the desk and, after speaking into it, turned towards the courier again. 'He needs some help with his things. I'll go and fetch him down.'

After putting down the phone the tall figure climbed the steps to where Darby was sitting and, without even glancing towards the detective, moved quickly down the wide corridor and pressed the button beside the lift doors. The remainder of the party, resigned to waiting yet again, moved slowly to occupy the large plush seats which were spread across the reception area, while the coach driver, flapping his arms in a gesture of despair, walked through the main doors and went to wait outside. Darby sat for a time watching the numbers light up above the now closed lift doors and then settled back to concentrate on his newspaper.

It was a sudden clanging of metal on the tiled floor, as if something had fallen, which set the alarm bells ringing inside the detective's head. He looked up to see Sharkey struggle to recover his crutch which was spread out on the floor. The old man was hobbling, not from the lift, but from the small souvenir shop which was situated to the left of the reception area.

'Oh, there you guys are. How long have you been waiting for goodness sake? Somebody should have told me.'

'But Mr Sharkey, we sent Mr Vogel to look for you a few minutes ago.' It took all the courier's professionalism to disguise her agitation. 'Where have you been?'

'Why ma'am, I've been in the shop for the past hour or so. Somebody shoulda told me.'

By now Darby's attention had turned elsewhere, his eyes fixed firmly on the numerals above the lift door. It had gone up to the very top. He had watched the light flash from one number to the next. Even if Vogel had got out and used the stairway he still would have had to come through the wide corridor. Oh Christ, the garage! He had forgotten the car park in the basement with its own exit to the street. The bastard had taken him for a ride. He had gone up all right, right to the top floor, but then all he had to do was press the button and come right back down again. Jesus!

Pushing the newspaper to one side the detective sprang from his seat, landing awkwardly on the second step which led to the lobby. Without waiting to regain his balance he rushed towards the large glass doors. The smartly uniformed doorman, who for a second seemed as if he was determined to restrain him, was easily evaded Once outside he halted at the top of the stone steps which led down onto the street. His eyes darted in every direction, focusing on the garage entrance just in time to see the bright blue Opel emerge into view. The driver was tall, too bulky to fit comfortably in the confined space of the interior, and even before it turned towards him he knew who it was. As their eyes met a contemptuous smile brushed across the American's face and brought the detective's fury to boiling point. It took all his reserves of willpower to restrain the urge to rush into the passing traffic and stuff the smug expression down the bastard's throat. What was the point? There was no evidence of any crime being committed, and any attempt to pick him up would only make things worse. Now there was nothing for it but to stand and watch his target float away in the stream of passing cars.

Darby beat the side of his leg impatiently with the newspaper as he stood on the footpath waiting for the chance to move across the street. By the time he reached his car it would be too late to do anything but call in, and he was not looking forward to his inspector's reaction. It was Gibbons who had refused to provide the men he needed, expected him to perform miracles, but it was the unfortunate rookie who always took it in the neck when something went wrong. It was an unjust, stupid, bloody world.

The tiredness was making it difficult to concentrate and

Nora Bonar had spent some time fumbling through her handbag before she finally discovered her flat keys. Nobody knew for certain where the leak which set off the panic had originated. The Irish view was that its source was London, probably some old imperialist determined to hold on to the first colony at all costs. Predictably the British version was somewhat different. Anyway, identifying the whistle blower soon went down the priority list as the day was spent manning the telephones in a desperate attempt at damage limitation.

'Deny, deny, deny.' The redness in the cheeks of the overweight head of government information indicated that he was agitated; banging on his desk with a closed fist confirmed it. 'The Irish Government knows nothing of a British plan to pull out of Northern Ireland and I want any story which indicates otherwise to be killed stone dead! Understand?'

Nora always liked it when there was a flap on, not only because she enjoyed being at the centre of things, no matter how insignificant the role, but because it usually meant that her boss was under pressure, being pushed through the meat grinder. How she detested the little puffed up political hack whose habit of lording it over morning meetings had always reminded her of a piece of newsreel film she had once watched, of Mussolini. When the pressure was on, as it was today, he was at his worst; bellowing, strutting, full of his own importance.

MacKenna was not a mover. Nobody believed that he had any influence over the actions of his lords and masters. But he had been around long enough to become an insider, one who could be told what was actually happening before being instructed on what line to take. In time his staff learned to detect the body language of deceit, the gestures which indicated a deliberate falsehood. The meeting was hardly five minutes old when they realised that they were again being sent forth to put expediency before truth, to lie for their government.

In the early days Nora had worried about the deliberate deception, the half truths which were churned out to protect the system and those who profited from it. Later, when she discovered that it was all a game, that neither side was really interested in the public's right to know, it became much easier, even enjoyable. The journalist, who had once seemed the fearless pursuer of truth, now became the instrument of his editor, allowed to report what would sell newspapers but not what might cause the whole structure to come tumbling down. In time you became cynical, wary of the seemingly innocent question so often the bait for a trap, conscious of the rules of give and take which helped to keep the gravy train on the tracks. From the time the telephones started to ring Nora had no difficulty in following her instruction to deny, deny, deny.

When the large red key ring with the letter N emblazoned on it finally became visible at the bottom of the bag she snatched hold of it firmly as if afraid it might suddenly disappear again. At first the battle had seemed hopeless. All the morning newspapers and news bulletins had given the story headline prominence, and it was not until after midday, when the British information services had added their muscle, that the counter attack started to have the desired effect. The early editions of the evening newspapers on both sides of the Irish Sea carried the denial and by nightfall it had left the front pages. The fact that it was not even considered worthy of mention on the nine o'clock television news was the final signal that everybody could at last go home. In a week's time, if the story proved to be true, those members of the public who remembered the denial would do little more than shrug their shoulders in resignation. After all what could you expect? For Nora Bonar it was just another day's work and now she looked forward to a hot bath and a good night's sleep.

The unexpected shove which propelled her forward into the darkness of the small living room came just after she had started to push the door open. The sharp edge of the small coffee table cut painfully into her legs as she fell over it, landing heavily on the carpeted floor. The suddenness, the tiredness, the painful thumping sensation which had started inside her head all combined to make her feel totally disorientated and vulnerable. Turning her head she found herself looking towards the outline of a man silhouetted in the open doorway. Before closing the door he reached out and switched on the main light.

'Surprised to see me?'

'Philip! What in God's name happened to you?' The hostility on the unshaven face and the bitterness in the voice unsettled her even further.

'Oh come now Nora, you know that I have spent the last few days in the company of your patriotic friends. They would have liked me to stay longer, but you know how it is?' He moved closer to where she lay, only stopping when he stood directly above her. 'No more time for playing games, my love. You see, it all fits together too neatly to be a coincidence. You were with me in Donegal when I made contact with Thornley and suddenly they find out about him and the Penguin is no more. Did you know that, Nora? Did you know that the poor old Penguin is no more?'

'Thornley? The Penguin? Who is Thornley, Philip? Please tell me.' She spoke in a quiet reasoned voice, as if trying to humour an insane man.

'And then there was the way they discovered my

201

apartment.' He ignored her questions. 'You see I had taken great care that very few people knew the location of where I stayed in Dublin, and you, my dear Nora, were one of them. I've given the matter much thought –having had plenty of time to think lately – and I can only conclude that you were the one who sent your Provo friends on a visit a couple of nights ago. A visit, I might add, which very nearly had fatal consequences for yours truly.'

'The Provos? Why should the Provos want you?'

'Oh come on, don't play the innocent with me.' The look of genuine puzzlement on the woman's face seemed to detract from his previous certainty. 'You know you saw me make contact with Thornley and I'm sure you couldn't wait to pass on the information. I mean who else could have done it? You're the only one who could have told them where to pick me up!'

'Oh God! Oh God!' Nora's weariness evaporated, her initial fear gradually changing to a burning anger, as she became aware of the substance of the accusations he was making. 'So you're one of them, one of the players in our deadly little game. One of the brave little boys who lets off the bombs, sets the booby traps, and pulls the trigger before riding off into the sunset leaving the parents, the wives, the kids to pick up the pieces. Don't you dare, don't you ever dare associate me with the stupid, meaningless, cancer that never stops eating into this God forsaken little dump of a country!'

By now Nora was on her feet again, moving towards him with clenched fists. The ferocity of her onslaught easily overcame his half hearted attempt at resistance and the blows to his chest eventually forced him back into the large armchair positioned to the left of the fireplace.

'You bastard! How could you? How could you?' The attack ceased only when the whirlwind of fury had run its course. Then, after allowing her head to rest against his shoulder her mood began to change. That feeling, that irrational affection she had felt for the Englishman since their first meeting, began to dominate, to take control again, and the desire to restrain it had gone. 'Oh God, surely you could not believe that I would ever betray you.'

'No. No! I'm sorry, love, I'm just confused.' He lay back on the chair, his eyes closed and hands falling towards the floor, making no attempt to return her embrace. It was some time before he spoke again.

'But if not you – who?'

19

'Philip wake up! Will you wake up for heaven's sake?' Hearing Nora's voice, Weston's instinctive reaction was to reach out and draw her towards him. The pushing away of his arm from her waist was good humoured but firm, and the realisation that she was already fully dressed caused him to open his eyes for the first time. 'Not now. Something important has happened. Will you listen?'

'What's up? Has the third world war broken out?'

'Cunningham has resigned. I've just heard it on the radio news.' The expression of bafflement which appeared on Weston's face soon turned her initial excitement to frustration. 'Cunningham is our foreign minister. Damn it, don't you know anything?'

'Enlighten me. I've had little time to catch up on the political scene since my return to your fair land.' Weston was now sitting up, fully awake. The resignation of a foreign minister was always of significance.

'Mr Thomas Cunningham was until yesterday one of the two most senior ministers in the government of the Irish Republic.' Nora placed a finger on her lips, an indication to Weston to remain silent, as she reached out to increase the volume on the small transistor radio she had earlier placed by the bedroom window.

'Here with me now is Mr Cunningham who last night,

in a surprise move, announced his resignation from the government.' The interviewer was finding it difficult to contain his excitement. This was a scoop, a guarantee of a huge audience, and he was going to milk it for all it was worth. 'Mr Cunningham, did you resign or were you sacked?'

'No, I was not sacked.' The question seemed to throw the politician off balance and there was a slight pause as he struggled to regain his composure. 'In actual fact I handed my resignation to the Taoiseach yesterday morning and he was reluctant to accept it. Indeed he asked me to reconsider my decision and it was not until I confirmed it at ten o'clock last night that he accepted my leaving as inevitable.'

'Then why go? Why leave at this stage in the life of the government?'

'Well, there comes a time in most people's lives when they want to try something new and, as you know, the life of a government minister is very demanding. It leaves very little time for family life and other interests.'

'Would you believe it? The old I-want-more-time-to-be-with-my-family routine.' Nora was shaking her head in disgust at the politician's response.

'Does that mean you intend leaving politics at the next election?'

'No, no. I shall continue to serve my constituents as I have always done and, as I am no longer a member of the cabinet, I shall have greater freedom to speak out on the things that interest me.'

'Northern Ireland, for example?'

'Among other things.'

'Mr Cunningham, as you probably know, there have been persistent rumours about differences of opinion between the Taoiseach and yourself on northern policy. Would you like to comment on that?'

205

'I am not aware of any differences. I have always remained faithful to party policy on Northern Ireland.'

'Would you care to outline for us what you consider to be the main points of that policy?'

'Our objective is to bring about a united Ireland. All the people on this island working together in harmony as a single state. The nature of that state, the governing structures, are something which are open to negotiation.'

'There is no way that you would accept that Northern Ireland and the Republic could achieve that harmony without political unification?'

'No. Northern Ireland is a failed political entity. There is no way I can see it finding solutions for its present problems as it is presently constituted.'

'Well, Mr Cunningham, I put it to you that no matter what you say there are marked differences between the policy you have just outlined and the one followed by the Taoiseach and his government over the past number of years. After all, representatives of the Dublin government have been in constant contact with their counterparts in the Northern Ireland Office, and there has been greater co-operation on security matters than ever before. Surely all of these actions could be said to prop up what you yourself have just called a failed political entity.'

'I can only repeat what I have already said on numerous occasions in the past, and that is because so many Nationalists are to be found within the area which is now Northern Ireland there is no way that it can succeed as a state. The only way for us to come to terms with the terrible problems facing this island is for everybody to come together under one political umbrella.'

'What about the British, Mr Cunningham? Should they leave?'

'Well, I believe they should eventually pull out, but not in a rapid, unplanned manner. Because of the events of history they have a responsibility to this country, and if they are to leave it must be a phased withdrawal giving us all plenty of time to come to terms with the new and potentially dangerous situation that would bring about.'

'I must still put it to you Mr Cunningham, that many of the people listening will be convinced that your real reasons for leaving the government have to do with differences between yourself and the Taoiseach on northern policy.'

'I can only restate –'

The interview was brought to an abrupt end as Nora leaned over and turned the radio off. 'He's said all he's going to say. From now on it will be only repetition.'

'What's he up to?' There was only curiosity on Weston's face. It betrayed none of the concern he felt at the sudden turn of events.

'Who knows? He's possibly firing a warning shot across the bows because government policy is moving in a direction he had his doubts about. This is a way of letting his cabinet colleagues know that he is prepared to fight against them from the back-benches.'

'Seems like the supreme sacrifice, giving up office on a matter of policy.' Now Weston looked doubtful.

'If it were one of the career men, the guys who entered the trade because they liked the life, I would have my doubts. With Cunningham it's different. Remember, he's one of those who escaped from academia and, therefore, is still likely to be tainted with such things as ideals and all that sort of baggage. Among my esteemed colleagues who work in his department – sorry, former department – word has it that he intends to practise what he preaches, and if things should go wrong the man would have no difficulty returning to the little room reserved for him in the ivory tower.'

'Is Northern Ireland thought to be that for which he is prepared to give his all?'

'Yes, without a doubt. If my informants are as reliable as I think they are the situation is very much like it came across in that interview. The dominant line at the moment is to take the situation as it is and make the best of it, while Cunningham, straight from the land of books and theory, insists on stirring the pot by reminding everybody about the official policy of unification which is accepted, in one form or other, by every major political party in the south. Bluntly, he wants a united Ireland ruled from Dublin and the Unionists can either like it or lump it.'

'If there is such a difference of opinion why wasn't he for the high jump long ago?'

'Oh, don't get me wrong. In some ways our Mr Cunningham may seem naive but when it comes to building up support among his fellow parliamentarians he is up there with the best of them. He was often observed in the Dáil bar lending a sympathetic ear to a member who was known to have problems, political or domestic, and should anybody be unlucky enough to fall ill they could always depend on a visit from their friendly minister.'

Nora stood up and walked to the end of the bed before turning back. 'Besides, it is always important to remember that deep down many of the parliamentary party are sympathetic to his view. They may not agree with the shooting or the bombing but in their more idealistic moments they do desire some form of unification. To them it feels like unfinished business they have waited a long time to complete.'

'So, better to have him inside spitting out rather than outside spitting in?'

'I would have worded it differently, but I think you have just hit the nail on the head.'

'Not a bid for the leadership, I suppose?' Despite his best efforts the alarm crept into Weston's voice, a change of direction by the Dublin Government was the last thing he needed.

'If it is, it's a strange time to move. As with your own system it is very difficult to remove a Taoiseach who is determined to hang in there, and all the signs are that the present occupant has no plans to move.'

'What would the chances be if the post were to become vacant?'

'The resignation wouldn't help. Being disloyal to the party is usually frowned upon. Still, he is very popular with the public and in the last analysis those electing the leader would go for the personality who would pull most votes in their direction. Yeah, on balance I think I would put my money on him.'

'But you don't think that was the motive.' Weston was now looking for reassurance.

'No.' Nora looked at her watch. 'God, look at the time. I'm off to make the breakfast.'

After she closed the door Weston slipped back between the sheets and closed his eyes. His mind was racing in so many directions he was finding it difficult to decide on his next move.

'For Christ's sake, get into the back before anybody spots that bloody uniform.' Gibbons issued the order from the passenger seat of his car. 'Is that the Opel directly up ahead of us?'

'Yes sir.' Garda Jimmy Keating, furious at the rebuke, was damned if he was going to volunteer any extra information. Typical of the Special Branch; think they're God Almighty. He was the one who had discovered the car, he was the one who had moved heaven and earth to get a match ticket that was probably useless because of the delay, and now he was supposed to sit here and take this crap.

'See anybody approach it?'

'No. When I discovered it, over an hour ago, it was parked in the same position as it is now. I immediately radioed for back up and, after putting my motorcycle out of sight, kept the vehicle under observation.' The young garda took some satisfaction in what he knew to be petty point scoring.

'Well spotted anyway.' The inspector's voice became more conciliatory.

'Sir, over at the monument.' Mullens was winding down the car window to get a clearer view.

'Is it him?'

'He answers the description Darby gave us this morning. Right height, and he's wearing dark clothes.'

The other two men followed the sergeant's directions and looked through the line of trees opposite towards the large obelisk in the Phoenix Park which commemorates all the great victories of the Duke of Wellington. The spacious, grass-covered area which surrounds the monument was almost derserted making it easy to spot the tall, darkly dressed figure standing at its base.

'It's him all right. Did you notice this fella up to anything while you were in hiding?' Gibbons directed his question towards the young garda in the back seat.

'I noticed him early on but I took him to be some kind of historian or something.'

'Why?'

210

'He walked around holding a piece of paper in his hand. It was as if he was making notes.'

'Really.' Gibbons was tapping the stem of his unlit pipe against his chin.

'Do we follow him, sir?' Mullens started to roll up the car window.

'No, this time I want to take him in. When he comes back to the car I want the two of you to pick him up.'

'What are we going to charge him with? He's done nothing.'

'Damn it man, don't go all technical on me. I'll think of something.' The inspector was in no humour to have his decisions questioned.

Keating was very conscious of the churning feeling at the pit of his stomach as he walked alongside Mullens towards the tall, powerful man who by now had reached his car. The uniform eliminated any chance of surprise, it also made him the most likely target if there was any attempt at resistance. He was on constant alert for any sudden movement, any sign of a concealed weapon as they quickened their pace. But when the plain-clothes man finally called out a warning, causing the long pale face to turn towards them, Keating found himself suddenly deflated by a deep sense of disappointment, a feeling of profound anticlimax. The eyes looking towards them were lifeless, almost fish-like, and the expression dominating the sallow features was one of absolute submission. The big man would offer no chance of adventure, no stories to tell his grandchildren; he would come quietly.

'This is Gibbons.' The inspector was speaking into the radio microphone as the handcuffed prisoner was pulled into the back of the unmarked car. 'We have arrested Vogel and are now taking him in.'

20

'Look at that idiot. Does he want to advertise to the whole bloody world that we are waiting?' The outburst came from Gibbons after he had glanced towards the roof of the GPO.

'Take it easy John, it's not your responsibility.' Weston shrugged uneasily as the two men stood waiting for the pedestrian lights to change. The inspector's mood had been foul since early morning and had he not vented his anger on the Special Branch man, who was clearly visible on the roof of the building, he would have found another target. 'Your job, your only responsibility, was Vogel, and now he's locked up.'

'Christ, Phil, that bastard was little more than a side-show, a diversion. The truth is that there are thousands of places in the city where they can hit and despite all our intelligence work, including the information you managed to pick up, we still don't have a clue as to what they are up to. All we can do is sit and wait.' The light changed to green and they joined the stream of brightly coloured fans crossing the street. 'Do you know the thing that gets to me, that really makes me sick? The only sport, the only event, that brings people from both traditions together, cheering for the same team, wanting the same thing, is an international rugby match and now the sick minded psychos have managed to exploit it, to turn it around for their own crooked purpose.'

Before there was time to respond, Gibbons strode between the large pillars and pushed through the doors into the main hallway of the GPO. The usual Saturday morning rush was added to by curious rugby supporters and, even though there were men posted to cover all strategic positions, it was obvious that the risk to innocent lives would make effective defence against sudden attack impossible. Gibbons made his way to one of the writing desks which lined the centre of the room and went through the motions of searching through the information leaflets. After a quick check through the phone booths Weston rejoined him.

'Things have started to move, sir.' Darby approached nervously, like a young schoolboy striving to regain favour with a popular teacher.

'What the hell are you doing here?' The inspector's response was abrupt, his eyes never leaving the leaflets.

'After what happened . . . .'

'After you lost Vogel.'

'I was reassigned to the security detail looking after this place. The brass seem to expect some action.'

'Well?' Gibbons turned towards him expectantly.

'Nothing here but there has been a bomb scare out at the Lansdown Road DART station. Trains are held up; they can't allow the supporters across the line to get to the pitch. It's chaos.'

Gibbons looked towards Weston but said nothing.

'I believe you have picked up Vogel, sir.' The young detective's growing confidence pushed him into more dangerous territory.

'The grapevine seems to be working overtime, doesn't it?'

'Get anything from him?'

Gibbons paused for a moment before deciding to relent. It wasn't easy being a rookie in the dog-house. 'From our Mr Vogel we got little more than name, rank and serial number. However, we have a good idea as to what he was up to. Darby, did you ever hear of Nelson's Pillar?'

'Yes sir, my dad mentions it from time to time. As a kid he used to pay a few pence for a ticket which allowed him to climb the spiral staircase to the top. There was a great view of the city from it.'

'That's the one. It was situated just a few yards up the street from where we are standing. It dominated the whole centre of the metropolis until one night in the sixties – bang! Up went Nelson and the Pillar too as the hit song at the time put it. A beautiful job, nobody injured, and just a few windows shattered. It caused a sensation, bringing with it world wide media coverage.'

'Who did it?'

'Nobody knows, the culprit was never caught. One theory is that an expert was brought in from the States to do the necessary and smuggled out again immediately after the mission was completed. I knew a woman in Mayo who was utterly convinced that a mysterious stranger who had stayed at her small hotel for a week before the event was the man himself. She claimed that he wrote to her from time to time. No address provided of course. Although, knowing how things are, I'm sure there are similar stories to be found all over the place.'

'Now you think Vogel is up to something similar?'

'Look at the evidence. We found our man in the Phoenix Park making a close examination of one of the great monuments left over from our imperial past; this time it appears it was to be the Duke of Wellington's turn for the high jump. I don't need to outline to you

214

gentlemen the nice little effect that would have when combined with whatever is to be the main course on today's menu.'

'You're certain?'

'Considering that the man's reputation rests, for the most part, upon his skill in handling explosives it seems the logical conclusion. Mind you, I have to admit that the good old southern boy wasn't in the mood for saying much.'

'Southern boy, are you sure?' There was no mistaking the alarm in Weston's voice.

'Well I've only heard it in the movies, but I think I'm right in saying that he uses that distinctive drawl.'

'Can I see him?'

'Sure.' The ominous expression on the Englishman's face was enough to send a shiver down the inspector's spine. He nervously pushed his unlit pipe back into his pocket as he followed Weston out of the building.

An imperceptible nervous smile brushed across Eoin O'Hagan's lips as he surveyed the small room. The waiting was beginning to get to him, make him edgy, eager to do something to break the monotony. He considered going over the plan one more time but on reflection decided against it. The men were tensed up, the adrenalin flowing, and like athletes ready for the off a wrong move could blunt their effectiveness.

The memory of his last piece of action, the elimination of Thornley still rankled, bringing with it the bad humour the others so feared. How he had looked forward to paying back the big Belfast man in full for his earlier humiliation. The contempt in which he had always held the ape-like moron made the defeat he had suffered at his hands all the more bitter, the contemplation of revenge all the sweeter. Yet, it had not happened. Thornley had refused to disintegrate and in place of the anticipated satisfaction there was nothing but a sickening frustration. Blow after blow from his aching fists had failed to wipe the contemptuous grin from the bloodied face. When the traitor decided to talk, to reveal all, it was obvious that he had not broken, that the physical pain had not influenced his decision. The man was gloating, taunting his tormentors, those who had always firmly believed in their superiority over him, with the fact that for years he had led them a merry dance. Even in death the big man had won his final battle.

After that the orders were to lie low, to disappear into the countryside and prepare for the big one. Their base was a small deserted house hidden in a clump of trees at the end of an overgrown lane. There, after meticulously planning every step of the operation O'Hagan had pushed his men to rehearse it time after time until the repetition, bad weather and boredom led to frayed tempers and many bitter arguments.

The day O'Higgins brought John's name into it was the worst. He was pushing them through the moves for the fifth time that morning when, in a fit of anger, the little toad had blurted it out. A coward and an informer he had called his brother. An O'Hagan an informer! The sudden draining of colour from his leader's face had been enough to alert the little man, to start him searching for the right words of contrition. It was a hopeless task; family honour had to be satisfied. O'Hagan's cat-like leap brought his knees surging into the small of his victim's back knocking the man face down onto the damp ground. The merciless kicking started immediately, only relenting to allow O'Higgins an attempt to struggle to his feet, the movement making the more vulnerable parts of the body accessible to the heavy

216

military boot. By the time the others had summoned up enough courage to pull their commander away, O'Higgins was lying on the wet muddy ground, blood flowing from a deep wound in his forehead. There was to be no more open dissention in the ranks.

Whatever his public actions, the disappointment with his younger brother was something he had to come to terms with inwardly. The recent failures, in no small way due to John not doing what he was supposed to do, had undermined his authority with his men and gave ammunition to vermin like O'Higgins to use against him. Worse still, the number of raids carried out since John's capture had reinforced the rumours which claimed the boy had talked, told them all he knew. That was not true, it couldn't be. An O'Hagan would never squeal; they would rather die first. Increasingly, he looked towards the operation as the action that would put everything right. This was the chance to re-establish his reputation, to prove to all the doubters that Eoin O'Hagan was as good as ever. A man to be feared and respected.

The sound of the Landrover entering the yard outside caused him to look out through the window. A sharp knock on the door preceded the entrance of the sentry to inform him that the scout had returned. A few minutes later the tall, slightly built man drew expectant glances from the men in the room as he moved through them before placing a newspaper on the table in front of O'Hagan.

'The phone call worked?' O'Hagan looked anxious.

'Like a dream. I watched the patrol pull out just before I came back, that leaves just two in the station.'

'Right, get something to eat. Pat, bring the van around.' As the scout turned to leave O'Hagan pulled the newspaper hurriedly towards him. Paying no attention to the main headlines he skipped through the pages until he came to the classified advertisement section. Using his index finger he searched through the columns, stopping only when he discovered what he wanted. For a time he stared at the newsprint, as if reading the same piece over and over again. Slight movements in the room indicated the growing restlessness of the men as they recognised the emergence of the warning signals. The eyes were growing brighter, the movements of the jaw indicating that he was grinding his teeth, and a slight quiver had just appeared at the corners of the lips. A volcano of anger was on the point of eruption and he was visibly struggling to contain it. Then, as suddenly as it appeared, the dangerous mood evaporated. The expression became calm and deter-mined again.

'OK. We go as planned. Everything ready to go?'

'Everything in position, chief.' It was the man he had ordered to get the van who responded.

One by one the men left the room through the narrow doorway and climbed into the large Nissan van parked outside. Before following, O'Hagan again glanced at the newspaper spread out in front of him. There was nobody left to notice the flash of anger which suddenly returned to his eyes.

'O'Donaghue, you bastard, nobody is going to deprive me of this.' There was a deep bitterness in the words he muttered under his breath. 'Not you, not anybody.'

John Shriver moved slightly in his chair before rubbing his hands together in an attempt to regain his composure. The big guy had said nothing about this, nothing about being picked up, nothing about spending hours in a stinking cell. Things were getting worse ever since the tell-tale signs had started to manifest themselves. The moisture was making the palms of his hands clammy and he was conscious of the beads of sweat forming on his forehead. Next would come the uncontrollable sneezing. He had one shot hidden in his ear when they picked him up. They never thought of looking in the ear. But now with its effects wearing off the feeling of panic and desperation, which he knew so well, was gradually taking control.

'That's not Vogel.' The guy with the English accent was on to him as soon as he walked into the room. One look and boom! The game was up. 'He's good. Looks a lot like him, but the eyes are wrong, not deep enough. I suppose there must be something about the eyes of somebody who attempts to kill you which burns into your brain.'

At first there was no sweat. He was on a high and the good cop, bad cop routine had seemed amusing. It was the Irish guy, the one built like a tank, who threatened to beat him up, hang him from the ceiling, and finally throw away the key of his cell. The Englishman played his part well, the sympathetic look in his large sheepish eyes as he stood observing his partner's tirade would have been enough to take in a less experienced victim. The customary cigarette was offered after the Irishman finally left the room and then came the concerned plea for information. Anything would do, any useful snippet which would allow this good Samaritan save the suspect from the terrible fate which would otherwise await him. At that stage everything had been fine. They had nothing on him and would finally have to let him go.

Once the shivering started the outlook changed dramatically. Soon the trembling would prove impossible to hide. Then the craving would take over, dominating his every thought, dictating his every action.

219

Once, while in a state of withdrawal he had caught sight of himself in a mirror and the trapped haunted look in the eyes which stared back would always return to torment him when the need was growing inside his system. The addiction demanded satisfaction; demanded the exorcism of the intolerable hunger growing within him. The hunger had dragged him from the small town in Alabama, where he first got some crack from a pusher in high school, to New York while still in his teens and now had ended him up being interviewed by cops in a country he had never even heard of six months before. By now the only certainty in his life was that a fix was needed, and needed quick.

'Just give me something to go on. Anything and I will be able to help you, get all the help you need.' There was still sympathy in the Englishman's voice but he was now poised expectantly on the other side of the table, waiting as a spider might wait for a fly to fall into its web.

'OK. What do you guys want to know?' When resistance ended it was complete, without conditions.

'Who are you?'

'Shriver. John Shriver. I'm from Alabama but I came –'

'How did you get here?'

'A couple of weeks ago I was approached by this guy who offered big money if I would play a part for him. I got five thousand dollars down and another five to come when the job was finished. He gave me clothes, airline tickets, cash. All I had to do was learn my lines.'

'You were to be Henry Vogel?'

'Yeah. Only nobody mentioned about being arrested and put through the third degree.'

'What did he look like?'

'He dressed like a bum, I can't tell you much about his face because he never shaved and he always wore an old hat. Every day he picked me up and we walked to this crummy little apartment hidden away in a block that should have been condemned years ago. Then we went over what I was to do and say when I got here. This went on for days until he was satisfied that I was line perfect.'

'What about the car at the hotel? Did you hire it or was it hired for you by somebody else?'

'You said you were going to help me, for Christ's sake.' Shriver was clasping his hands tightly together and a bead of sweat which had trickled from his forehead hung precariously on the tip of his nose.

'Soon John, soon. Now just answer the question.'

'Note under the door. My instructions were to just carry on as a member of the group and that a message would be passed on to me when it was time to break routine. The night before I moved an envelope was passed under the door of my hotel room giving me all the orders for the next day. It also contained the car keys and a map of the territory I was to cover.'

'How did you know it was genuine?'

'It was signed by some guy called Finn or Fonn or something. That was the code-word this guy said he would use. I was told to make it look as if I was trying to give the cop the slip while the real idea was to draw him out to that big tower in the park. Then I was to look as if I was taking measurements. Oh come on man, you know all of this already! Jesus man, I need help!'

'Soon John. Soon.'

'That dumb cop was supposed to stay with me. Why couldn't he have stayed with me? I had to hang around for hours before I was certain that you guys turned up.' Shriver leaned back on his chair, his face grossly contorted by his inner suffering. 'But you guys were not supposed to pick me up, that was not supposed to happen. That dumb cop was supposed to spend the day

221

folowing me around.'

'Who pushed the note under the door, John? Was it somebody on the pilgrimage?'

'Could be I guess. Look, how do I know? You promised man, Jesus, you promised.'

'OK. OK John. I'll get help for you now.' Weston stood up and quickly left the room.

21

Sergeant Mullens rapped softly on the small wooden door and, after receiving no response, quietly proceeded to push it open. Inside, the old-fashioned kitchen was deserted, the freshly washed cups sitting on the formica table the only indication that it had been occupied for some time. The voices he could hear in the distance continued without interruption, providing confirmation that his entrance had gone undetected. He moved swiftly past the table and chairs and out into the hallway from where the two men in the front room were clearly visible.

'Lucky for you it wasn't the boss, or somebody would be for the high jump. I thought one of you was supposed to be watching the rear.'

'Christ, Sarge, never do that again!' A heavily built man with a thick moustache and long sideburns turned from the window, a startled look on his face.

Mullens moved between the two men before peering through the fine net curtains out into the street. It was empty, the only movement coming from the smoke as it billowed from the chimneys of the row of small houses opposite. The street was short, bordered on one side by a railway embankment and on the other by a narrow bridge which carried a branch line out into the suburbs. A cement bollard placed under the bridge dictated that the only way a car could enter was along the road which ran between the embankment and the gable end of the last house in the row. A stranger would find it impossible to hide in this locality which was the reason it had been chosen.

'What are you doing here anyway, Sarge?' The second man sounded hostile.

'Oh, I just called in to see how things were moving.' Mullens was getting fed up with having to brazen it out. Right from the beginning it was known within the force that Gibbons had been imposed from without, an instrument of political interference, and because of that the word was that he should be frozen out. Mullens, as his Man Friday, was subjected to the same treatment by the more zealous members of the force. However, on this case Mullens was having none of it. He was the one who had tailed O'Shea from the rugby training ground in the first place; the one whose local knowledge enabled them to get the front room of the unoccupied house as an observation post, and there was no way anybody was going to push him to one side.

'All of them inside?'

'Yep, it's like the Annual General Meeting of the Dublin Provos in there.' The plain-clothes man with the moustache was now looking through the viewfinder of a tripod-mounted camera positioned a few inches from the net curtains. He adjusted the telephoto lens and aimed it towards the house at the end of the street before continuing. 'Your friend O'Shea went out for a while this morning and that was it.'

'Up to anything important, was he?'

'Nope. He returned after half an hour with the usual supplies, bread, milk and the newspaper.'

'Nothing more?'

'Not that we could see. We sent the photographs of his

comings and goings to the lab, so maybe they can spot something we missed.'

'Anything from inside the house?'

'Are you kidding? Anybody who tried to plant bugs or set up directional microphones in this spot would be prime candidates for the funny farm.'

'Stop the bloody nattering. There's something on the move.' The bitterness was still evident in the second man's voice as he reached out from his position to pick up the hand radio on the small coffee table in the centre of the room. 'This is Falcon One to all units, stand by. Falcon One to all units, stand by.'

The door of the end house remained open for some time before a tall, well-built man stepped out onto the footpath. He pulled the hood of his jacket up over his head before removing a pair or woollen gloves from one of his pockets. Then, after a slow, deliberate, survey of the street, he turned on his heel and walked rapidly towards the bridge. The police camera whirred furiously in an attempt to capture his every move.

'Falcon One to Falcon Two, Dub coming in your direction. Falcon One to Falcon Two, Dub coming in your direction. Do you read me?' By now the tall figure had passed under the bridge and disappeared from view.

'Falcon Two to Falcon One. I've got him. I'm on my way.' There was a mixture of excitement and relief in the disembodied voice which crackled back across the air waves. For a young detective the hours of boredom were over and at last he had something to do.

'Who the hell's Dub?' Mullens directed his question towards the more sympathetic man at the camera.

'It's our code name for Mulholland. Hold it, Sarge, there's somebody else coming.'

'Have we got a tail for all of them?'

'Yeah.' There was irritation in the voice as the detective attempted to focus on the second figure emerging from the house. 'Christ, I missed him. He slipped around the corner before I could get the bloody thing ready. Did you see who it was?'

'MacCreanor.' The second man lifted the radio towards his mouth again. 'Falcon One to Falcon Three, the Buzzard is on the move. Falcon One to Falcon Three, do you read me?'

For over half an hour Mullens stood and watched as one by one five other men emerged from the small terraced house, each with a code name and each with a shadow ready and waiting to report on his every movement. He decided against fishing for further information until the two watchers were satisfied that all the birds had flown.

'Any idea as to what they are up to?'

'Not an idea.' It was the man with the moustache who responded. 'But whatever it is they are stretching our resources to the limit.'

From where he stood in the ditch O'Hagan could make out the dark blue Ford Sierra as it drove past the police station and moved in along the footpath in front of the school building. The humour was good. Everything was falling into place on schedule. The one long street which made up most of the village was deserted. Reconnaissance had established that most of the shopping was done on Friday evenings, and now it appeared that all the inhabitants had decided to spend the cold spring morning indoors. His eyes moved from the car across the street to the two storey house they had taken over the night before. It looked serene and peaceful, betraying nothing of the drama he knew to be taking place inside.

The police station with its wire-mesh protection was situated on the outskirts of the village. Behind it was open countryside: large green fields which would mercilessly expose an attacker while he was still a great distance away. The assault would come from the opposite side, where the road was bordered by a thick hedge and a number of oak trees which provided excellent cover. Those who had doubted him, written him off, would soon be forced to eat their words. Three RUC men dead; an open attack on a police station. It would be the most talked-about operation in a decade. A glow of satisfaction visibly illuminated his face as he imagined the television images which would flash around the world confirming that Eoin O'Hagan was back, and back with a vengeance.

The policemen returning from patrol would feel elated, more than satisfied with a job well done. The information from the anonymous caller had been genuine. By now they would have uncovered the arms dump exactly where he had said it was. A bogus call would have been a mistake, have made them suspicious, wary of an ambush. The sacrifice of the three armalite rifles was worthwhile. It would instill the type of confidence which encourages carelessness, a carelessness which would grow as soon as the safe haven of the well-guarded police station came into view. They would pay little attention to the car parked outside the school and it was possible that they would not even hear the explosion.

The delay in opening the car door brought about a sudden change in mood. His sharp features suddenly grew darker. O'Higgins was dithering, being over-cautious. By the time he had the bomb primed the whole bloody British army would be down on them. The little coward was playing true to form. If O'Hagan had anybody else who knew anything about explosives he would have given the little bastard the boot years ago. Even when the stumpy, black-clad figure was at last standing on the roadway his actions were still irritating O'Hagan intensely. Closing the car door seemed to take an eternity. A cold sweat broke out on O'Hagan's forehead as he willed the man across the street towards the waiting two storey house. O'Higgins finally entered and O'Hagan experienced a sudden release of tension as the front door closed. He glanced back towards the van which was parked in a small clearing invisible to passing traffic. He could picture his men crouched inside as they nervously awaited the signal which would start them towards their combat positions. Satisfied, he leaned forward again against the bank. Now there was nothing for it but to await the appearance of the Landrover at the end of the street which would unknowingly trigger the operation.

It was only the slightest rustle in the hedge a few yards away, but it was enough to cause the hairs at the nape of his neck to bristle. The noise was wrong, out of place. Years of wandering as a boy in the woods caused him to dismiss out of hand any idea that it was caused by a bird or an animal. As he frantically scanned the area around him a sickly churning sensation began to erupt in the pit of his stomach. Every tree, every bush was scrutinised as he desperately searched for an explanation. It came again, louder, and this time there was no room for doubt.

'It's a set up! Get the hell out o'there!' Even before O'Hagan had finished shouting he was clambering up the bank and preparing for a quick sprint across the roadway. Once on the other side he dived blindly over a barbed wire fence, falling heavily on his back at the edge of a newly ploughed field. Short sharp bursts of automatic fire in the distance proved his instincts right. Somebody had sold them out. The field he was in slanted downwards and by creeping until he was below road level he hoped he might escape undetected. Fifty yards away there was a gap into the next field, a chance to get out of the direct line of fire.

O'Hagan was pushing through the narrow opening when he relaxed, became careless, and by standing up too soon to relieve his aching back presented the perfect target. The burst of fire seemed much closer this time and the explosion of pain which erupted in his left shoulder brought him near to passing out. Falling back against the hedge he turned and, using his good arm, fired wildly in the direction of his pursuers. The warmth of his blood as it pumped from the wound and seeped into the clothes under the combat jacket brought with it a panic which was reflected in the wildness of his shooting. At last, sensing that the shots would have sent those after him in search of cover, he propped the rifle against the bank and pulled a handkerchief from his trouser pocket. The halting of the bleeding, by pushing the piece of cloth under his shirt, helped to revive his confidence, although his first attempt at movement brought with it an uncontrollable shivering. It took a supreme act of will-power to pick up his weapon again and to stumble in the direction of the farmhouse. Like all good generals he had planned his retreat and, if he could just hold out, there was still a chance.

He was finding it difficult to breath by the time he leaned against the stone wall at the edge of the farmyard. There was no sign of the enemy in the field behind him but he knew they were there, cautiously stalking him as they would a wounded animal. His body heaved as it attempted to extract enough oxygen from the cool air, making it impossible to listen for the rustle of leaves or the breaking twig which would alert him to approaching danger. When he looked towards the farmyard his system received another jolt. It was empty, not a car in sight. It had been chosen because of the cars; the family owned two and there was always at least one of them parked in the yard. But not today, not today, damn it! As the anger subsided a hazy sleepiness began to close down his mind, the loss of blood taking its toll. His head had already slumped to one side and his knees were beginning to bend when a noise in the distance rekindled a last spark of alertness.

The car coming around the corner of the house was a Citroen, an automatic. At last his luck was changing. He waited until the woman brought the car to a halt outside the back door. Now, timing was all important. He wanted a hostage and to move too soon would give her an opportunity to escape. The pain and loss of blood was making calculations go haywire; his body was failing to respond quickly enough to the orders of the brain. By the time he had reached the hay-barn she was already standing outside the car preparing to lift out her shopping.

'Get back in! Get back in! You're coming with me!' Calling out made it even more difficult to breathe. The woman turned towards him, a look of shock and horror etched into her middle-aged face. An instinctive response, an act of desperation made her attempt to protect herself. The box of groceries came hurtling towards him. O'Hagan was caught by surprise. Stumbling, he fell heavily on the uneven cement surface. It gave her the break she needed and before he could recover, the farmhouse door was closed and bolted from the inside.

Through the open car door he could see that the keys

were still in the ignition and, abandoning the armalite where it lay, he struggled into the driver's seat. The engine sprang into life at the first attempt, but he struggled to lean over far enough to use his good arm to push the gear lever into the forward position. He moved slowly at first, guiding the car around the side of the house and into position at the top of the driveway. The controlled purring of the powerful engine seemed to bring to the surface a hidden source of energy, and he felt his confidence return as he pressed his foot against the accelerator.

As he sped past the ornamental lamp post marking the centre point on the driveway, the boiler-suited figure stepped from the cover of the large hedge. The man stood, legs apart, just inside the main gate. He took deliberate aim, as if taunting his intended victim. In a last desperate effort O'Hagan turned the wheel slightly, aiming the car directly at the gunman. The hail of bullets shattered the windscreen, and tore into O'Hagan's chest. He slumped forward onto the steering wheel. The car changed direction again, slammed into the large iron gatepost and exploded into flames.

Everything went dark.

22

'I've spent the last hour listening to the interview you had with that junkie this morning but there's nothing there. Not a bloody thing.' The agitation showed on Gibbons's face as he switched off the tape recorder and reached for his pipe which lay at the side of the desk.

'I've drawn a blank as well.' Weston closed the door of the small office before walking to the chair in the corner. 'I sat with him during the treatment but, as the experts predicted, all that happened was that he became more and more incoherent, rambling in every direction. Anything on Vogel?'

'Another bloody blank! Once I thought we had the bastard I lifted surveillance on the American group. Now I've had to send a man scurrying after them again.'

'Did he turn anything up?'

'One other member did leave the group after it arrived in Dublin. A priest of some kind or other. We're checking on him now.' Gibbons took a long puff from his newly lit pipe. 'My own feeling is that Vogel used the double as a way of distracting us while he slipped into the country by some other route. There is no advantage for him in having any direct connections with the pilgrimage.'

'What about reports from the other fronts?'

'We are being toyed with; it's a real cat and mouse game. The bomb scare at the rugby grounds turned out

232

to be a hoax, while, as far as Mullens can find out from his contacts, no pattern has yet emerged with the big cats we have under observation. Seems they all left the safe house and headed off in different directions, but as yet nothing of significance has been reported back. The car picked up by Shriver at the hotel was hired from a rental company and, you guessed it, nobody can give a description of the man who picked it up. The name given was false, of course.'

'One decoy on top of another.' Weston suddenly sat forward on his chair, his eyes becoming alert. 'Look, if Shriver was a decoy, somebody to lead us on a false trail, why shouldn't that be true of everybody and everything else? At the moment we seem to be following a whole series of trails which are leading absolutely nowhere.'

'It's possible.' Gibbons looked doubtful. 'But all our intelligence, every bit of information we have points to something big, something intended to have an impact worldwide.'

'For O'Donaghue it all seems wrong.' Weston now pulled his chair forward and leaned on the desk. 'He has always been cautious, everything planned to the last, resources used to the full. The idea of one big gamble, everything risked on one throw, is totally against the man's nature.'

'Normally, I would agree, but in this case he has no choice. His calculation is that if the Brits pull out he's finished, and therefore his only hope is to make a move that will prevent that withdrawal. To him the risk of losing a lot of men is worth it. At least, if he succeeds and they stay he can start to rebuild; while if he fails he's had a shot at it. Anyway, I don't see why you are so doubtful when, after all, he told you exactly what he planned to do.'

'Precisely. In a way he's spent his time signalling to

233

everybody what he intends doing. Was his conversation, my escape, all part of the deception?'

'You're becoming paranoid, man.'

'This man has studied guerrilla warfare. He knows that whenever a group like this breaks cover and comes out into the open against conventional forces they are on a hiding to nothing. Remember Vietnam and the Tet offensive. The Vietcong exposed themselves to the heavy armour and, although they could claim a victory on the propaganda front, as a force they were destroyed. Only the North Vietnamese were there to pick up the pieces when the war was over. The best O'Donaghue can hope for is that he will open the door for somebody else, and that just doesn't ring true.'

'There's no need to go to South-East Asia to pick up that lesson. The same thing happened to the old IRA here during the War of Independence when they came out and openly attacked the Customs House.' Gibbons pointed the stem of his pipe towards Weston, the expression on his face indicating his confidence that the next point would bring the argument to a close. 'You must still remember that it is enough for him to get the Brits to stay. Unlike Vietnam there is nobody in the wings who will want to continue the battle. We certainly don't. And because of that he will have all the time in the world to re-establish his position as king of the walk.'

'But what if he is successfully pointing us all in the wrong direction? We are so busy chasing around that we have no time to examine other possible moves which would keep his force intact.'

'Sir!' Mullens, in his excitement, had forgotten to knock on the door. 'Word has just come through that O'Hagan made an attack on an RUC station a couple of hours ago.'

'Well, for God's sake man, don't keep us in suspense.'

There was a look of triumph on the inspector's face as he glanced towards Weston.

'Intelligence proved to be spot on. The SAS was waiting and caught them flat footed. We don't know the full details yet but first reports have it that as many as six gunmen were killed.'

'And O'Hagan?'

'Nothing confirmed, but one version has it that he is among the dead. Oh, and something else, sir. We have also received a report on that priest who went south. It seems he's genuine.'

'Oh well, I suppose everything can't be perfect. OK, thanks Mullens. Keep us up to date if anything else comes in.' Gibbons looked back towards Weston as his sergeant closed the door. 'So now it's started for real.'

'He's only one and it's late in the day. Remember O'Hagan's a maverick, a real nutter.' Weston was far from conceding the argument. 'What are the rest of them up to? It's hardly reasonable to conclude that O'Hagan was ordered to move and everybody else told to stay at home.'

'You're clutching at straws, Philip, and to be honest you appear to be making the facts fit the theory instead of facing reality head-on.' There was a sympathetic smile on the inspector's face as he opened a drawer at the side of his desk. After removing a blue folder he pushed it towards Weston. 'Here's something to keep you occupied as we drive out to the rugby match. It's a transcript of an interview the RUC had with the Penguin's sister a couple of nights ago. The brother's death seems to have sent her over the edge because she does nothing but rant and rave about escaping to Australia, or that none of her family were informers etcetera. Anyway, the boys in the north could make nothing of it so they passed it on to us to see if we could have any better luck.'

Weston pushed open the flap of the folder and quickly examined the bundle of neatly typed sheets before following Gibbons out through the doorway.

'To your left you can see College Park which, along with all the fine buildings in the enclosure, belongs to the University of Dublin, or, as it is better known, Trinity College.' The courier looked over her shoulder as the coach turned to the right and moved up Kildare Street. 'Now, as we are almost there, perhaps I should tell you something about Leinster House, the building which houses Dáil Eireann. We shall be entering through what was once the courtyard and, as we move towards the main entrance, to your right will be the National Museum of Science and Art while on your left you will see the National Library as well as . . . .'

Externally Vogel looked calm and, if anything, slightly bored. Inside, his stomach muscles were beginning to tighten at the onset of the nervousness which always preceded action. That he welcomed. It sharpened his senses, heightened his alertness in readiness for any eventuality. But despite everything, he was still unable to shake off the uneasiness which had nagged at him since the beginning of the mission, and the nearer the completion came the more he regretted his impulsive acceptance of the sarge's offer. There was too much dependence on others, too much left to chance. He seemed to be forever moving over uncharted territory.

'It was on the lawn at the front of the building, Leinster Lawn, that the first balloon ascent took place on July nineteenth, 1783. A building of iron and glass was also erected there for the Great Industrial Exhibition in 1853 . . . .'

The last phone call to his contact had done little to bolster his confidence. Shriver had been picked up. For a perfectionist, somebody who prided himself on minute attention to detail, the memory of the wad of notes left lying on the cabinet rankled, ate into his pride. It was made worse by the certainty that the first bum had some control, would have at least held out for twenty-four hours. Shriver was weak. The addiction governed everything, and it was obvious from the beginning that he would crack at the first sign of pressure. The little rat had broken: a cop putting questions to the courier just before they pulled out was enough to tell him that. Now that they knew they had the wrong man the next move was to find out if anybody else had abandoned the group since it arrived in the country. He smirked involuntarily at the thought of the cops surrounding the house of the talkative priest's relations. A more unlikely fugitive from justice he found it hard to imagine.

'The greater portion of the building is made from limestone which was brought from an area known as Ardbraccan, County Meath. In the centre of the building you see four Corinthian columns . . . .'

Picturing the plight of the cherub-faced cleric was enough to move his thoughts in a more positive direction. Shriver knew nothing of value and it was almost certain that those who were out to get him were still searching in the dark. There was no need to panic, the target was in place, and there was still plenty of time.

The coach had by now parked outside the large iron gates and the courier struggled to fill in the time as she anxiously looked through the railings in the direction of the main doors. The politician who was to act as host was late. The delay made it more difficult to disguise his restlessness, and as he moved uneasily in the narrow seat

237

his mind raced in a thousand directions. What move would the cops make next? What had he told Shriver? Did he let anything slip when talking to the others? Never again would he leave himself so dependent, so isolated.

'Good afternoon. I am delighted to welcome you all to Dáil Eireann.' Vogel was so preoccupied with his thoughts that he failed to notice the entrance of the well-dressed figure who was now beaming towards his captive audience from the front of the coach. 'Just before we set out on our way you might be interested to know there are those who claim that this building served as a model for your own White House in Washington. I must admit to having my doubts about that, however. What is certain is that our parliament was dominated for many years by the American-born Eamon De Valera, and that in June 1963, just a few months before his death, John F. Kennedy addressed the house . . . .'

It was clear from the beginning that the politician had done his homework and was intent on making an impression on the hapless visitors. His presence made the movement through the main security gates a formality but his determination to dwell on the significance of every architectural feature meant that almost twenty minutes had passed before they reached the main doors. By the time Vogel was issued with his official visitor's badge at the desk in the main hallway, the tightening in his stomach had become physically painful. By now, the earlier optimism had given way to despair and he was only too well aware that if he did not get an opportunity to move soon he would have lost that vital edge which was so often the dividing line between success and failure.

It was as the party reached the end of the main hall, where each portrait and exhibit added to the delay, that the long-awaited chance presented itself.

'Ma'am, I'm sorry, I couldn't possibly climb those stairs.'

'Perhaps we could arrange to carry you, Mr Sharkey?' The courier's face lost none of its professional composure. It was the flash of anger that momentarily filled her eyes which told Vogel all he wanted to know. She had had it, reached the limit of her patience. She had tolerated his complaining and bad temper since the very first day, but this was it – the last straw. This time she had no intention of changing any item of the planned itinerary just to suit him and he could report her to whoever he wanted. A quick survey of his fellow travellers confirmed that the endless delays and incessant bickering had awakened the desired resentment in them as well. There would be no resistance to his next move from that quarter either.

'Na, na. That's no good either. Look, to hell with this. If it's all the same to you I'd just as soon stay here until it's all over.'

'Are you sure, Mr Sharkey? I'm sure we could arrange something.' There was no attempt to inject any feeling of sincerity into the offer.

'Just leave him here. He'll be OK.' There was a murmur of approval from all sides for the suggestion of the small woman in the flowery dress.

'Yeah. Yeah. I'll hold on. If somebody could just show me where the rest-room is.'

The politician appeared to consider alternative solutions to the problem but, on seeing the mood of the group, decided against making any suggestions. 'Just down to your right, Mr – Mr Sharkey. You can't miss it.'

Vogel turned and without making any reply, started to hobble towards the indicated door. His cane sank noiselessly into the plush carpet as he moved.

'Now, if you look to your right as we move towards the Dáil chamber I'm sure you will be interested in a photograph which is mounted on the outer wall. It shows Eamon De Valera, former President of Ireland, addressing in joint session both houses of the US Congress. That event took place in 1964. As I was saying . . . .'

The visit back on schedule, Vogel was already a forgotten man.

23

Vogel pushed through the door and suddenly quickened his pace as he made his way across the tiled floor. He chose the cubicle furthest from the entrance, where the things he wanted to discard were least likely to be discovered.

Once inside he slid out of his anorak and hung it on the hook at the back of the door. He then removed the jacket of his light summer suit before carefully turning it inside out. There was no lining but it was reversable, and he allowed himself a critical look over the dark navy colouring on the other side before placing it carefully on the toilet seat. After a quick examination of the buttons which were sewn to the interior, he removed the oversized trousers he was wearing. Underneath was another pair, the same colour as the turned out jacket.

A slight twitch of the eyes was the only indication of the shooting pain which followed the swift removal of the false moustache which had been in place since the beginning of the pilgrimage. As he squeezed the trousers tightly behind the bowl of the toilet he was glad he had decided to remove the plaster of paris earlier, it not only gave him more time now but allowed for the replacement of the crutch with the more manageable cane. Before putting the jacket back on, darker colouring now to the outside, he pulled a neck-tie from the pocket and, after stretching it to remove the creases, placed it around his neck.

It took longer then expected to remove the rubber stop from the end of the cane and it was with obvious relief that he watched the plastic package, which he had picked up in the art gallery some days before, slide from the metal tubing into his waiting hand. Normally he would have memorised the details and destroyed the evidence but this building was of a type that he was not used to, a maze of corridors and extensions, and he had decided to leave the final survey until he was on the spot. For the next few seconds his eyes absorbed the details before them and, when finally satisfied, he tore the page to shreds and threw them into the toilet bowl. He flushed the toilet before leaving the cubicle.

The wash-basin area was deserted, allowing him to dispose of the cane in the large waste bin below the hand dryer. He then used the mirror above the hand-basins to put a knot in his tie. The absence of onlookers also allowed him to use a blackening pencil to darken the grey areas of hair above each ear. This was the final piece of insurance, the professional touch which would eliminate any chance of recognition if he were to come in contact with his fellow pilgrims again. Standing back, he straightened his tie and took one final look at his handiwork. The result was satisfactory, almost perfect, giving a timely boost to his eroded confidence.

He knew that the uniform was slightly too bright, but still, it was good enough to pass anything but the closest examination. The harps secured to each lapel looked genuine and that was the important thing. For they were the badges, the symbols which would allow him to pass unnoticed to where his target was waiting. He had now converted himself into an usher; become one of the men who carry messages, help out with security, and guide visitors in the National Parliament to their destinations. As one of the team whose job it was to quietly oil the wheels which keep Dáil Eireann running smoothly, he would attract little attention as he moved along the deeply carpeted corridors. As a milkman or postman walking along an early morning street, the legitimacy of his business would be taken for granted. He had, for all practical purposes, become invisible.

After re-entering the main hall he strode with purpose towards the marble staircase. He did not mount the steps which led to the Dáil chamber but, turning right, moved into the labyrinth of passages which would eventually lead him to his destination.

'Where are you holding the Americans?' Gibbons had parked his car alongside the footpath. All the formalities at the security barriers would have taken too much time. By now his growing frustration almost led him to lash out physically at the young army officer who was staring blankly at the warrant card he had pushed towards him. Just when he needed action, initiative, everything was happening in bloody slow motion. Answers to simple questions seemed to take an eternity, and the longer he waited for a response the surer he was that this bunch of incompetents had blown it, failed to carry out the simplest order. 'Where the hell are they?'

'The gombeen man, the gombeen man! Damn it! *That's* what they're after.' The Englishman's words still cut through the inspector's mind like a knife. Gibbons had just turned off the main road and was making his way down one of the side streets leading to the rugby stadium when Weston's excited shouting almost made him crash against one of the parked cars on his left-hand side.

'What or who in Christ's name is the gombeen man?'

'Look, she mentions him at least three times.' Weston, his index finger implanted firmly on the typed sheet placed on his knee was finding it difficult to contain his excitement. 'The interrogator obviously did not think it significant because he did not know who she was talking about. But through all the mumbling and mixed talk she keeps coming back to it and trying to convince him that the gombeen man is the one O'Donaghue is trying to get. She's convinced of it.'

'I repeat, who the hell is the gombeen man?' By now Gibbons was becoming visibly angry at Weston's incoherence.

'The Taoiseach, don't you see? That's what O'Donaghue called him when he spoke about him in the bunker.' Weston bundled the sheets together before shoving them back into the folder. 'The bastards had us running in circles. Everything they have done up until now was planned to cause confusion, to pull us in a hundred different directions at once. We've been so stretched trying to follow every lead that there has been no time to look at the over-view, to examine the other possibilities. Everybody from O'Donaghue to Vogel has had us dancing to their tune.'

'Mullens, Mullens! Where in Christ's name are you?' Gibbons was no longer listening. In a sudden panic he had dispensed with all radio call-signs as he frantically attempted to make contact with his sergeant. Cars parked on both sides of the narrow street forced him to accelerate towards the nearest junction and do a u-turn before driving at speed back in the direction in which he had come.

'Sir.' Gibbons had already placed the siren beacon on top of the car when the breathless voice of his sergeant came over the radio.

'I want to know where the Taoiseach is and I want to know yesterday.'

'That won't be easy. You know what Special Branch are like on that kind of thing.'

'Just do it!'

'Sir.'

'If they get the Taoiseach that puts everything up the creek. It's perfect. There is no way that an agreement worked out in secret can be ratified by a government in the process of electing a new leader. Not only will it put the whole plan up in the air but they will probably get the added bonus of having Cunningham take over the top job.' Weston had thrown the folder onto the back seat and now peered out through the windscreen as if willing the unmarked car to move more quickly through the city traffic.

'Yeah, and it's probably told us what Fionn is about as well.' Gibbons continued to concentrate on the road ahead. 'It's no big military operation but a code name for a target they want to take out in Dublin. If Cuchulainn had been painted on the side of that train Vogel would probably be stalking the secretary of state right now.'

'I've got the information, sir.' The radio suddenly crackled to life.

'Go on.'

'It seems the Taoiseach likes to reserve Saturday afternoons for working in a small office reserved for him in the old section of Government Buildings. He's there today and is ready to move to his main office in the event of any major developments.'

'Oh Christ! That's where the Americans are.' Gibbons suddenly went pale. 'I saw it on the itinerary when I checked it after we found out the guy we thought was Vogel was a fraud. But I thought it was of no significance,

I thought Vogel had nothing to do with them, had only used them for his decoy.'

'For God's sake, do something man.' Weston spoke sharply in an attempt to lift Gibbons out of a state of semi-shock. 'Give some damn orders.'

'Listen Mullens, I want you to contact Dáil security and have them detain an American coach party which is probably on a visit right now. Tell them to check and make sure nobody has been allowed to stray from the group while they were there.'

'Understood sir.'

But nothing had happened. There was no need to ask, the puzzled expressions on the men standing guard told it all.

'Americans?' It was a uniformed policeman who broke the uneasy silence.

'Yes! Have you held them?'

'A party of Americans did pass through here about half an hour ago but we received no orders about holding them.'

'Anybody know where the Taoiseach's office in the Old Government Building is?' Weston looked around anxiously as he broke his silence for the first time since coming through the gates.

'I can take you there.' A small middle-aged usher emerged from the security box opposite.

'Right, come on.' Gibbons was already climbing the steps just inside the gate and heading towards the main door. There was no time left to plan; he was flying by the seat of his pants.

Vogel tensed on hearing the radio and, stepping back, he took a deep breath in an attempt to regain his composure. When there was no sound of movement from the corridor he relaxed again, realising that the combination of the commentator's voice and cheering crowds had drowned out the closing of the lift doors. Slowly he moved the side of his right hand along his left palm. It was an exercise he found reassuring. The hand was hard, rock hard, the type of hardness which is developed through hours of tedious, boring exercise. The type of hardness which converted his hands into lethal weapons which could be carried, without fear of detection, through any security system in the world. The one disadvantage was that, unlike using a gun, you could not kill at a distance. Physical contact had to be made with the victim.

Feeling fully under control again Vogel leaned out slightly and peered down the long line of doorways. A plain-clothes man sat next to one of them about fifteen feet from the lift entrance, the transistor radio on the floor next to his chair. The corridor was warm from the central heating, and he had removed his jacket, revealing a shoulder holster and revolver which stood out threateningly against the whiteness of a freshly laundered shirt.

Having decided on his move Vogel straightened the brown folder under his arm and stepped out into full view. The expression of surprise on the Special Branch man's face never turned to suspicion, Vogel's uniform having done its job.

'What's the score?' The American spoke quickly and indistinctly in an attempt to hide his accent.

'Nothing yet. It's only been going a few minutes.'

'I've a number of documents here for the Taoiseach.'

'Right. I'll take them and pass them inside.' The man misunderstood the look of disappointment on Vogel's face. 'Orders. Nothing personal.'

Vogel quickened his pace and was pushing the folder

into the detective's hands before he could stand up. The blow was struck before there was time to even open the flap. The side of his hand crashed home to the side of the neck, just below the ear. The body only made a slight thud as it slumped to the floor. Vogel made no attempt to examine him. Experience told him that the man, if not dead, would be out cold for hours.

He held his ear close to the door. Detecting no noise, he turned the handle and silently pushed it open. The venetian blind covering the only window was closed and the office was dominated by two large desks. On one there was an electric typewriter, while the well-polished surface of the second was empty except for two telephones. It was probably occupied by a secretary and a typist on normal working days. He went back outside and quickly pulled the limp body from the corridor across the carpeted surface, and laid it behind the secretary's chair. The detective's chair and the now silent transistor radio quickly followed. Vogel next moved towards the panelled door directly behind the secretary's desk and, after again checking for any sound from inside, slowly proceeded to turn the knob.

This room was much larger than the first and as the angle made by the slowly opening door widened, he could make out a long conference table surrounded by comfortably upholstered chairs. Between the large windows, allowing spring sunshine to bathe the room, hung multi-coloured modern paintings.

Vogel's heartbeat quickened as a lone figure, sitting at a large desk on the opposite side of the room, came into view. The man, his elbows propped on the dark brown surface, was resting his head in his hands as he concentrated on the papers which were laid out in front of him.

Vogel flexed the fingers of his left hand while slowly

releasing his grip on the door handle. The attack would depend on speed, the element of surprise. He would be already half-way across the floor before his victim was even aware of his presence, and by then it would be too late. A fully trained commando would have difficulty warding off such an attack; an elderly politician had no chance. Steadying himself he made a mental note to move on three. One . . . two . . . three.

Using his shoulder to push the door fully open he took his first step into the room. As he pushed his left foot hard against the ground to build up momentum the sudden reaction of the man at the desk alerted him to the impending danger. The old man had looked up too soon, disturbed by an unexpected noise from the outer office. The startled eyes rested only briefly on Vogel and then moved over Vogel's shoulder to concentrate on something behind him.

Vogel was already turning when the first shot exploded. The sharp piercing noise felt as if it was cutting his skull in two. There was no pain, just a heavy thump to the side of his body which caused him to turn around more quickly and lose sight of his target at the desk. He did not recognise any of the men who were looking towards him from the outer office. For a split second he imagined that the heavily built one with the revolver was the gook of his nightmares, but that soon passed. The last thing to register was the expression of horror on the wrinkled face of the small uniformed figure standing nearest the outside door.

The unbearable pain came with the seond explosion. Then darkness. Eternal darkness.

EPILOGUE

'And in conclusion it is essential that I emphasise yet again that there is no change in the policy of Her Majesty's Government towards Northern Ireland. The province shall remain part of the United Kingdom as long as the majority of the people living there wish it to be so. I am also confident that, after the implementation of the development plans I have just outlined, all of the people who live there, no matter to which side of the community they belong, can look forward to a brighter and more prosperous future.'

The sincere expression remained fixed until the face was replaced by a caption informing viewers that they had been watching a Prime Ministerial broadcast. MacKenna pressed the off switch on the large television set before turning to address the members of his staff who had gathered in the room. 'Well folks, it appears all is back to normal again, and I'm sure everybody is delighted to know that, as always, we were telling the truth all the time.'

'Did they ever intend pulling out?' One of the older men, sensing a willingness to talk on the part of the head of the government information service, decided to press for some information.

'Perhaps. All of this is off the record, of course.' MacKenna placed a cigar between his lips and lit it before continuing. This was one of those rare opportunities when he could show that he was in the know, a man who matters in the corridors of power, and he was going to milk it for all it was worth. 'Our friends in the US were said to be very nervous about a sudden withdrawal. After all, big problems in Ireland have been known to cause significant ripples in their own domestic political pond and who wants that? Anyway, according to reliable sources, Washington's man at the court of St James is said to have let it be known that his masters would feel happier if the *status quo* was maintained. More importantly, as time went by it became clear that our European partners were none too pleased with the idea of this little island of ours erupting into some kind of civil war, and in the process becoming a haven for every crackpot terrorist organisation in Europe. Echoes of Beirut and Yugoslavia, but this time happening within their own jurisdiction.'

'We didn't disabuse them of that idea?' The senior official pushed further.

'Well, there was a little prompting from our side after which they not only put on the diplomatic pressure but indicated their willingness to put their hands in their pockets to help bring about a solution. That formed the basis for the financial package the PM announced this evening.'

'All this resulting in the departure of our former foreign minister?'

'Let's just say that the idea of travelling to the capital cities of Europe in order to lobby his colleagues to have our beloved neighbours stay put on this island did not appeal to him.'

A sharp knock on the door was followed by the entrance of the young man who had been left on desk duty during the broadcast. 'Sir, I have a reporter on the line who wants a comment on information he claims has come from a reliable source.'

'OK, OK. What is it?' MacKenna roughly stubbed out the half smoked cigar into the ashtray. The abrupt manner of the kid who had replaced Nora Bonar never failed to irritate him.

'He said shots were heard coming from the office the Taoiseach uses in the Old Government Buildings on Saturday last.'

'What the Christ? Listen, I've been talking to the Taoiseach at least once every day for the past week and if something like that happened I think he might at least have mentioned it to me. Don't you?'

'So there's nothing in it?'

'Look son, would you tell him to take a double running jump for himself and, for God's sake, stop bothering me with such crackpot stories.'

'Yes sir!' The young man's exit almost met with disaster when he just avoided tripping over an empty chair.

'Now let's put our heads together and draft out a response for the Taoiseach to the Prime Minister's speech.' There was a slight smile of satisfaction on MacKenna's lips as he flicked open his lighter and prepared to grip a second cigar between his teeth.

Gibbons stood up and, after excusing himself, walked away from the table; after a heavy meal and a series of long speeches he needed some fresh air. The hum of conversation smothered the curse he let out on noticing Mac Entee make his way towards him through the crowd. Had he been aware of him earlier he would have taken evasive action.

'Ah John. Going for a walk. Mind if I join you?'

'If you like.' The response was even less enthusiastic than he had intended.

'Twenty years since we won the championship. Hard to believe, isn't it?'

'Yeah, I suppose it is. Although most of us have managed to get together every year since. It makes you more conscious of the passing of time.'

'I know. I know. I would have loved to attend but you know how it is in political life, not a minute to call your own.'

Yes, he knew how it was. Once a user always a user, and when it came to using people Mac Entee had no equal. He had used Gibbons in the same way as he had used his connection with the team, making contact when it suited and then disappearing until the next time. His appearance tonight was no accident. This was the twentieth anniversary of their victory and, in a county not overburdened with success, an occasion which was guaranteed to attract the attention of the local media. The presence of photographers and reporters was an opportunity too good to miss.

'Well, what have you been doing with yourself over the past few weeks?'

Gibbons recognised the technique at once. The minister was fishing. 'Oh, I have retreated back into my little office and busy myself going through the meaningless files they push through my door from time to time. It would also appear that I no longer require the assistance of a sergeant.'

'That, I take it, has something to do with my transfer to Foreign Affairs. There's no need to keep an eye on you any more.'

'Possibly, but then my betters do not consider it necessary to keep me informed about such matters.'

'Yes, I met them for the last time before leaving my old

office last Tuesday. They came to give me a final briefing on the Vogel affair. Took you all for a right little ride that gentleman, didn't he?' The minister paused, expecting a response. When none came he decided to continue. 'It seems he came disguised as Sharkey right from the beginning and had that fellow, Shriver, stand in for him. Considering that Shriver looked like a fish out of water right from the start I'm surprised nobody smelt a rat?'

'Smelling rats can be quite simple with the benefit of twenty, twenty hindsight vision.' The jibe cut deeply, forcing Gibbons to abandon his resolution to play it cool. 'We had no reason to believe that Vogel knew we were on to him. We assumed he thought he had killed Weston in Washington, and even if he hadn't there was no way he could have known about the fingerprint on the newspaper. No, like all thorough professionals he was covering every possible angle.'

'How soon do you think he was on to us?' The minister's tone was more conciliatory.

'It was only afterwards that Darby, the rookie we had following him, admitted that he blew it at the airport. So, within an hour of his flight arriving we may take it that Vogel had already decided to use his decoy to pull us in the wrong direction when it was time for him to strike.' The forceful way in which he was filling his pipe was the only visible sign of Gibbons's displeasure at the way the conversation was going. 'The fake accident was another nice touch to throw us off the scent. He refused to let the guide get medical help, telling her he could arrange it himself through some insurance scheme or other. We found the fake plaster and crutches in the hotel room.'

After a short pause the minister looked towards Gibbons. 'So there he was in a position to watch the man supposed to be watching him and at the same time pull the strings of the puppet that we all were following. I must admit that he had the ball at his feet.'

'He was also very clever.' Gibbons, now more settled, was pulling on his newly lit pipe. 'He formed a relationship with the priest so effectively that many of the passengers were convinced that they had known one another for years. He also succeeded in becoming so unpopular with the group that when he eventually wanted to be left alone they were only too happy to grant his request.'

'What about your former assistant. Heard anything from him?'

'No, Sergeant Mullens never even sent me a postcard.' Gibbons smiled slightly. The minister, having conceded the battle in one area, was now attacking on another front.

'Know where he is?'

'The last report said something about the States, but nobody knows for sure. I'm certain there's no great push to catch him as a trial could cause a certain amount of embarrassment all round.'

'Christ, that bastard led us a merry dance.' For only the second time Gibbons noticed the politician allowed his emotion to show. 'He kept them one step ahead all the time. Right from the beginning when he listened in to our conversation at the aerodrome until the American almost succeeded in assassinating the Taoiseach. He had access to everything: security procedures, the where-abouts of VIPs, the lot.'

'Yep, and he only had to expose his position by blocking my message to Dáil security. If Weston had not realised who the gombeen man was, Mullens might still be right in there at the centre. I still feel that I should have spotted something when he admitted to passing on the intelligence which brought the poor old Penguin to an end. Still, his excuse was so bloody plausible.' The two men turned and started back towards the hotel entrance. 'The only thing I cannot understand is why he told me where the Taoiseach was. After all, he could easily have led me astray.'

'According to the briefing I received afterwards there were two reasons for that. One, he wanted to keep his cover and, two, he was convinced the operation was complete by then. It seems as if the delay at the gate, when the tour party had to wait for the guide was the cock-up that saved the day. Mullens did contact Dáil security just after you arrived allowing a little extra time for Vogel to escape, but when he was told that you were already there he realised that the game was up and cleared out. I'd like to ring his neck!'

Gibbons looked for a time into the illuminated waters of the small artificial pond in the hotel grounds before making a reply.

'I never liked him, the little know-all, but still I can't help having a kind of sneaking respect for what he did. He believed in something and was prepared to sacrifice everything for it. Maybe, in the end, his only crime was to be taken in by all the empty rhetoric spouted from all sides about a united Ireland.'

'So nothing much changed after all the action.' Mac Entee changed the subject, deciding to evade the challenge contained in what Gibbons had said.

'Except for the extermination of O'Hagan and his mob. At least we achieved that.'

'Accepted, but then that was serving somebody else's purpose as well.' The look of puzzlement which appeared on the detective's face prompted the minister to continue. 'Are they keeping you in the dark? I thought you knew.'

'Knew what?'

'Our informants tell us that they were all ready for action. It was all to happen just as we expected. Then, on the morning all hell was to break loose, a code word appeared in the classified section of the newspapers calling the operation off.'

'Don't tell me. O'Hagan ignored the order and went ahead anyway.'

'You guessed it. The most interesting thing is that the same fate awaited any of their units who decided to go it alone. You see, we knew everything – time, places, the works. I would like to say that it was because of top-class intelligence work but nothing could be further from the truth. The fact is that we now know that all the information was fed to us from a very central source within the organisation itself.'

'O'Dongahue.' As the full realisation of what had happened began to dawn on Gibbons he began to feel sick. 'The bastard had us do his dirty work for him.'

'Yeah, the great chief decided to use government forces on both sides of the border to wipe out any rogue units which were not prepared to toe the line. It had the added attraction of confusing us even further.'

'So you're right. Nothing has changed.' A wry smile appeared on Gibbons's face, quickly followed by an expression of resignation. 'In a way it reminds me of that old joke that did the rounds about the time the present bout of troubles started. You know, the one about the pilot arriving at Belfast Airport who reminds his passengers to turn their watches back three hundred years. Ah, let's forget about the whole bloody mess and go back inside and enjoy ourselves.'

'Yeah, let's do that.' The minister smiled but his discomfort was abvious. The intimacy of the occasion was something he found difficult to come to terms with.

257

After the photo-call he would make his excuses and leave, the duties of state again providing an avenue of escape.

Nora Bonar stepped back behind a pillar before pulling her jacket collar tighter in an attempt to keep out the stiff breeze which was blowing in from the Adriatic. Her only previous visit to Venice had been at the height of the tourist season when thousands of people made the city vibrate with life. Now, in the early days of Spring with an almost deserted St Mark's Square, the discoloured decaying buildings took on an almost ghostly appearance.

She leant back against the pillar. 'I remember reading somewhere that this palace was once the heart of an empire which included Cyprus, Crete, the Dalmation coast and part of Italy. Now look at it. With all its power gone it's little more than a giant museum struggling to avoid sinking into the sea. Why can't we learn that most of our wars, most of the killings, are in defence of systems and ideas that will one day seem primitive and incomprehensible?'

Weston watched as a pained expression clouded her features. 'Maybe the systems and beliefs that we claim to defend are little more than a veneer, something to disguise the fear, hatred and greed that are so often the real motivators behind our actions.' Weston moved closer to where she was standing, having finally decided to pose the question he had been avoiding all week. 'Nora will you stay?'

'Why?' The bitterness in her voice discouraged him. He had expected it to be easier.

'Because a gentleman called Skeffington has informed me that, as my cover is now well and truly blown, I am

258

doomed to spend the rest of my life as a lowly journalist. Because a terrorist convinced me that, until now, I have been nothing but a savage, a true professional who gets nothing more from life but the absolute minimum.'

The words came out as he had rehearsed them but her face told him that they were not enough. He was conscious of her silently imploring him to speak of love, commitment, the need to be with her. In the end his final utterance was pathetically inadequate. 'Don't go back. Please stay!'

Nora moved from him again and walked into the square. She stood looking out to sea, her eyes seeming to search for something on the horizon.